CATH

WILD BOY

& THE

BLACK TERROR

WILD BOY

& THE
BLACK
TERROR

Rob LLOYD JONES

WALKER
BOOKS

THANKS

Huge thank you to everyone at Walker Books, especially Mara,
Gill, David and Victoria, as well as Deb at Candlewick Press,
and Owen Davey for his wonderful illustrations. Thanks
to special agent Clare Conville, and early readers and expert
advisors Jo Unwin and Fred Morris. And whopping great hugs
to Sally, Otis and Jago.

First published in Great Britain 2015 by Walker Books Ltd
87 Vauxhall Walk, London SE11 5HJ

2 4 6 8 10 9 7 5 3 1

Text © 2014 by Rob Lloyd Jones
Illustrations © 2014 by Owen Davey

This book has been typeset in Book Antiqua

Printed and bound in Great Britain by Clays Ltd, St Ives plc

British Library Cataloguing in Publication Data:
a catalogue record for this book is available from the British Library

ISBN 978-1-4063-5949-7

www.walker.co.uk

For Mum and Dad,
who always encouraged

PROLOGUE

MAYFAIR, MARCH 1842

Zero degrees and falling.

This was the winter that would never end. It was so cold that the air itself seemed on the verge of freezing solid. In elegant Mayfair, everyone shivered in scarves and shawls, minks and muffs and fox-fur mantles. Fogs of breath turned to crystals, glimmering in the cones of lamplight thrown onto the snow. Servants scraped ice from pavements, stamping their feet as much for warmth as to find a grip on the treacherous paths. A coachman snapped an icicle of snot from the end of his nose. A milkmaid kicked and cursed a frozen pail.

From the doorway of Lock & Co., London's most fashionable hat shop, the Servant watched them all. He tried to hide his mounting excitement, but his breath betrayed him, coming out in quick, frozen clouds. Tonight was the first test of his Master's power.

He tilted his hat, shadowing his eyes as they scanned the street for an appropriate target. In a way it seemed silly. All of these people would die soon enough, once his Master arrived. But after so much preparation, selecting a victim at random seemed unsatisfactory. Surely his Master would send him a sign?

And then, there he was: the perfect victim.

The man was short and squat, with a belly so large it hung to his knees. His cheeks were squashed together, as if an unseen force pressed against the flesh, upturning his nose into a snout and narrowing his eyes to dark slits in sweaty pouches. The man's fur coat looked like it had been stripped from a diseased dog, but overall his appearance was more like that of a hog.

This man did not belong in Mayfair. He had no business in its private clubs. He knew nothing of creaking leather armchairs, clinking crystal glasses or billiard rooms clouded with smoke from the finest imported tobaccos. Nor did he carry any parcels from the area's exclusive fashion boutiques. All he held was a small wire cage. And in the cage was a crow.

No, the hog man did not belong here.

And how he *loved* that.

He walked in a waddle, swaying with the motion of his pendulous gut. With each step, the crow scrabbled in its rusty prison. As he passed Lock & Co., the hog man thrust the cage at the Servant's face and gave a high-pitched giggle, and with it came a spray of spit. He had no idea that he had just sealed his own fate, or that it would be the worst possible fate of all.

The Servant followed.

He turned from the street and into an alley, flicking up the collar of his greatcoat. Frosty wind rattled the icicles that hung from a spluttering gaslight. And then the Servant walked in darkness as the alley turned, turned again and became a tunnel.

The smell of stale urine was so thick that he raised an arm to cover his nose. The rumble of carriages from the street was replaced by howls and growls, beery singing and the breaking of glass. A wooden sign hung over the end of the passage. Two words had dried in dribbles:

Rat's Castle

There were no rats and no castle. Rather, the passage led to a dilapidated coaching inn – a lamplit courtyard surrounded by crooked balconies, hanging gutters, windows without glass and roofs without tiles.

The Rat's Castle was a tumour in the heart of London's finest district, a den of thieves and every other class of criminal that preyed on the area: the cracksmen and magsmen, the footpads and garroters, the till-lifters, dog-snatchers and regular old housebreakers that prowled the streets of Mayfair when the lamps went out.

Around the courtyard, each room was dedicated to a different vice. In one, opium smoking; another, bare-knuckle boxing. In a corner room, the room to which the hog man waddled with his wire cage, there was crow-fighting. But the loudest cheers came from the inn's tavern. Inside, a dwarf danced on the bar, dressed in a costume of rat skins and old wigs. A poster on the door announced the play, the same show that had been performed all winter in penny theatres across the city:

The Savage Spectacle OF WILD BOY

BEING the Horrid HISTORY AND Horrific DEEDS OF the Boy Monster THAT TERRORIZED LONDON!

"Wild Boy."

The Servant spat the name as if it had dripped into his mouth from one of the inn's gutters. A few months ago, this city had been gripped by the fear of a circus freak called Wild Boy and an acrobat named Clarissa Everett. They were thought to be killers, savages. They still *were* by many people.

The Servant's lips curled into a sneer.

He would show them something to *really* fear.

But first a test and perhaps a little fun. He unhooked a lantern from the wall and made his preparations.

"Excuse me?" he called.

He raised the light, putting himself in silhouette – the top-hatted, well-tailored shape of an affluent gentleman. He tried to look like an easy target; lost and scared and ripe for robbing.

The hog man licked his lips. "Lost, are you, Mister—?"

"I am the Servant."

The hog man gave another childlike giggle. He came closer, feet crunching in the snow. "That so? Your Master hiding around here, is he?"

"He is not here. Not yet."

"On his way then?"

"You should not have put that bird in a cage."

The hog man's pig-slit eyes widened to black beads. He marched so close that flecks of his spit sizzled against the Servant's lamp. "Don't you tell me my business! Now, before I cut out your tongue, you're gonna tell me who this Master is of yours, and when he's getting here."

The Servant lowered the lamp. A twirl of dark smoke rose from the flame. "He is a demon, since you ask. And he will be here soon."

Another spray of spit, another giggle. "Haw-haw! Demon, he says! Sorry, mister, I don't believe in demons."

"You really should."

"Well, maybe I'll just—"

The words turned into a gasp so deep, the hog man's gut rose to his waist. He clawed at his limbs, as if suddenly under attack from stinging insects. His eyes stared wildly around him at invisible enemies that seemed to attack from the dark.

"No!" he shrieked. "Not that. Not them!"

The colour of his face changed from pink to ash grey, and then brilliant white; as white as the snow to which he fell with a *thump*. His fur coat opened to reveal his vast, wobbling stomach. Dark lines slid over white skin, like long black worms. They were his veins. They were turning black, slithering across his chest, up his neck and over his face.

The hog man stopped thrashing and lay still.

Finally the Servant allowed himself a small smile. He knew it was not appropriate to gloat. This was, after all, a mere test of his Master's power.

But how it had worked.

How *well* it had worked.

He picked up the cage and smiled at its feathered prisoner. The crow's beady eyes glinted, and the crow gave a loud, satisfied *caw*.

The Servant carried the bird back into the tunnel and to the street. Frosty wind swept along the pavement, but he did not shiver. He felt as if molten lava flowed through his veins.

He opened the cage and the crow took flight. It swooped down the street towards a turreted gate-house in the middle of a long red-brick wall.

St James's Palace. The Servant watched the building for a long moment. It looked like something from a fairy tale. Its golden gatehouse clock shone in the moonlight, and each crenellation was perfectly crowned with snow.

But the Servant knew that it was a house of secrets and lies. That palace was home to the Gentlemen – the secret organization of scientists and spies that protected Britain from her enemies. Yet here he was, surely the greatest enemy the Gentlemen would ever face, just yards from their stronghold. And they didn't have a clue.

They would, though, soon enough.

That was why the fire burned inside the Servant. That was why he smiled.

He thought again about the last monster that had terrorized this city. *The Wild Boy of London.* His grin widened, and with it came a laugh so loud that it seemed to carry the crow higher, over the palace and up towards the shivering stars.

Terror.

He would show them terror.

He would show them what terror truly meant.

PART 1

★ ★ ★

DON'T
Believe IN
DEMONS

· 1 ·

It was that dream again. The dream of the show. The only dream.

It was a dream that Wild Boy could smell. The reek of damp wood mingled with greasy smoke from the caravan's oil lamp and the turgid stench of the fairground field; that stew of rotting peels, churned-up mud and steaming dung.

The smell of fear.

Then came the sounds: whoops of tipsy laughter, shrieks from the circus tent, and the crows on the caravan roof cawing like they always cawed, like they were laughing. *Freak*, they said. *Dirty, filthy freak.*

Outside, showmen called to the crowd in voices rough as sandpaper.

"*Marvel*, ladies and gentlemen! Marvel at the sensation of the Two-Ton Man. He's so fat that only hogs can love him."

"*Stay away*, ladies and gentlemen! Stay away if you are of a delicate disposition. Or do you dare behold the horror of the Pig Faced Lady?"

"*Hear what they say*, ladies and gentlemen! Hear what they say about Wild Boy! He's half-monster, half-boy, but all freak. Poke him, punch him or kick him for a penny."

Wild Boy drew his knees to his chest and gripped them tight. Through a hole in the stage curtain he watched the showman – Augustus Finch – usher a small crowd into the caravan. The web of scars across Finch's face gleamed in the swaying glare of the ceiling lamp. Spit glistened on his lips.

"Gather round, ladies and gentlemen," Finch said. "Get in close to get a good gawp at the freak."

On the roof, the crows cawed louder. Wild Boy felt the pulse in his throat, his heart pounding at his ribs.

But there was something *else*. He had a feeling that something was wrong with this scene, that somehow he didn't belong here in the freak show.

He *was* a freak, wasn't he?

He leaned over the edge of the stage and considered his reflection in the yellow-brown contents of Finch's chamber-pot. All he could see of his face were his huge eyes, bright and green and gleaming like emeralds. Everything else – his cheeks, his chin, his nose and neck – was hidden by thick brown hair. It was the same hair that covered every inch of his body, other than the palms of his hands and the scratched-up soles of his feet. The hair that had caused his parents to abandon him as a baby on a workhouse doorstep. The hair that made him a monster, locked up alone until the day he was sold to the freak show. *His* freak show.

No! He *didn't* belong here anymore. He'd escaped this place. He'd found something else. A friend, a purpose...

Unless *that* had been the dream?

The audience pressed closer, sweating, dribbling, dangerously drunk. Finch grinned, flourishing a hand. "Wild Boy! Wild Boy! The ugliest freak at the fair."

"No..." Wild Boy gasped.

"Freak," the crowd chanted.

"Please..."

"Freak," the crows mocked.

"NO!"

Wild Boy opened his eyes.

He lay flat in his bed, his chest heaving with gulping, gasping breaths. The hair on his face was soaked with sweat. The longer strands stuck to the pillow.

An image from the dream flashed through his mind. He scrambled from the bed and into the darkness beneath. He waited, curled up tight, for his heart to settle.

"That ain't me no more," he breathed – those same words he repeated every night. "That ain't me."

He slid from under the bed and rose into the silver moonlight. The bedroom window was open, and icy wind rustled the hair on his face. The cold felt good, waking him further from the dream. But not far enough.

At the washstand, he poured water over his face, soaking the hair on his cheeks and the pallid skin beneath. He could just see himself in the mirror: the hair sticking up at strange angles no matter how often he brushed it down, and his big green eyes twinkling beneath.

Once, he had shuddered at that reflection. He knew now that he was more than the image in the mirror, but that didn't banish the memories. After four months, the freak show still seemed so close.

He was haunted by that caravan.

It didn't help that this room was so similar – a cramped attic space with a greasy garret window and slatted walls that creaked in the wind. It smelled the same too, the musty air tinged with damp. But really, Wild Boy's new home was as far from a freak show as he could imagine.

He pushed the window wider and climbed outside.

It was viciously cold but the night was clear. The full moon hung like a silver shilling over a jumble of rooftops that framed the four courtyards of St James's Palace – snow-dusted attics, lead gutters and twisted chimney stacks. Ice glinted on every surface, as if the roofs had been sprinkled with diamonds.

Brushing hair from his eyes, Wild Boy looked down to the palace's largest courtyard, a square of cobbles surrounded by arched brick colonnades. Flagpoles jutted from the arches, hanging icicle flags. A lonely lamp stood in the centre of the courtyard. A single crow perched on top, ragged and hunched.

"Bloomin' crows," Wild Boy muttered.

He pulled his coat tighter around his hairy chest, comforted by its embrace. He'd worn this coat – a red military tunic with gold buckles – for the whole time he'd lived on the freak show. He hated thinking about those days, but couldn't bear the thought of wearing anything else. This coat was part of him as much as all the hair. And he *never* wore shoes. They weren't exactly comfortable with all the hair on his feet.

The crow flapped away as a carriage rattled through the courtyard gatehouse. A golden symbol gleamed on its door: a large letter *G*.

The cabin doors opened and two men emerged, dressed identically in frock coats, tight white breeches and shiny beaver-pelt top hats.

"The Gentlemen," Wild Boy said.

Those men were members of the secret society that had been protecting him since he fled the freak show. He stepped back from the edge of the roof. The Gentlemen were a *very* secret society. They wouldn't be pleased to catch him spying.

A hand grabbed his shoulder.

Wild Boy whirled around, but all he saw were snow and moonlit footprints.

Excitement shone in his emerald eyes. Impossible as it seemed, someone had leapt over him and landed without a sound on the edge of the roof. Only one person could do that, and that was why Wild Boy grinned.

Clarissa.

He rose and stepped forward. A faint fog of breath drifted over his shoulder. She was following him, having fun.

Not for long.

He kicked back a heel, catching her in the shin. There was a startled cry and then a punch that found only frosty air as Wild Boy dropped to the snow. He rolled back, crashing into Clarissa's legs so she tumbled over him and onto the roof.

He sprang up but again she was gone.

"Up here, thickhead."

Clarissa Everett stood high on a chimney stack. She was half a silhouette, her long black coat lost to the night. But her rust-coloured hair shone almost golden in the moonlight, and strawberry freckles flared across her pale face.

"I won," she said.

"Won? You're shaking with fear."

"Ain't shaking. I'm shivering."

"Ha! I don't shiver."

"Cos of all your hair."

"No, cos I'm tougher than you."

"I'll shave you in your sleep. Then we'll see if you shiver."

"Shave me and I'll break your arms."

"Break my arms and I'll break your face."

"What with? Your arms will be broken, remember?"

Clarissa bit her lip, considering how the violence could be accomplished. "I'll do it with my feet," she decided.

Delighted with her own cunning, she leaped from the chimney and somersaulted in the air. She cartwheeled along the narrow ledge, as carefree as if in a summer meadow.

She was showing off, and Wild Boy loved it. He remembered the first time he saw Clarissa perform at the fairground. She'd danced effortlessly along the high wire, dazzling the circus crowd in her red and gold sequins. It was strange to think that they'd been enemies back then – until they were framed for murder. Everyone had turned against them: the showmen, the police, even Clarissa's mother. Their quest to catch the real killer had led them to the Gentlemen. Since then, they'd barely been apart.

Clarissa landed beside Wild Boy. Her hair hung wild around her face. "You had that dream again, didn't you?"

"Just a dream," Wild Boy said.

He almost laughed. *Just a dream.*

"You ever think about it?" he asked. "What happened at the fairground, with the killer, and then your mum?"

Clarissa looked away. Her frozen breaths quickened and her hands curled into fists. Then she sprang back and continued to flip around the rooftop obstacle course. But now the movements were fiercer, the landings harder. Her boots sank deeper into the snow. "Let's do something fun," she said. "Something dangerous."

Wild Boy knew he shouldn't think about the past. They'd been through so much. They were branded monsters, hunted for a reward. Most of London still thought they *were* monsters, at large somewhere in the city. But they were safe here, under the protection of the Gentlemen. Now they could have a little fun.

A smile rose across his face as he watched the Gentlemen in the courtyard. They were unloading a wooden crate from their carriage. Judging from the tremble in their arms, whatever was inside was either very heavy or very dangerous.

"They're up to something secret," he said.

Clarissa landed beside him. Now she was grinning too. "Definitely looks secret. Sort of thing they don't want to get seen."

"Or spied on."

"Well then," Clarissa said, dusting snow from her hands, "they shouldn't have been so bloomin' obvious about it. Let's go!"

• 2 •

The floorboards creaked under Wild Boy's feet, sounding like a moaning ghost.

Clarissa glanced back and scowled. "Can't you be a tiny bit sneaky? This is a spying mission."

"I *am* being sneaky. See, I'm on tiptoes."

"I've heard sneakier railway trains."

"Shut your head. You're being loud an' all."

He was lying and they both knew it. Wild Boy was certain he'd traced her steps down the stairs. How did she move so silently, even in boots? It was as if she was floating.

He raised a foot, determined his next step would be silent. Just as he set it down, footsteps thundered along the corridor below.

Wild Boy and Clarissa pressed against the wall. The men from the courtyard marched past the stairs, carrying their wooden crate. A lantern rested on top, rocking light around the corridor below.

"Quick," Wild Boy whispered.

They leaped down the last few steps and ran along a hallway. The windows were leaded and frosted, letting in only murky moonlight. Woollen tapestries sagged from the weight of their own dust.

Wild Boy remembered how surprised he'd been the first time he saw the inside of the palace. Everything was so shabby. After the Gentlemen's last headquarters, the Tower of London, were partly destroyed by fire, Queen Victoria granted them this palace as a new base. They had kept only a few of the most trusted staff, and barely a handful of its dozens of rooms remained in a condition that anyone might call palatial. Stucco decorations on the ceilings were black from lamp smoke, and peeling paper revealed walls that glistened with damp.

"Come on," Clarissa said.

They ran faster, turning a corner in time to see a door slam and hear the *clunk-thunk* of a lock turning on the other side.

"Can you open this?" Wild Boy said.

"Course I can."

Clarissa pulled a slim leather pouch from her boot and flipped it open. Inside were several thin metal picks. She'd learned another skill at the circus, from her father. He'd been a star there too – *an escape artist.*

She studied the lock, selected two picks and slid them into the keyhole. A twist. A turn. The door creaked open.

No light shone through. The only sounds were their own heavy breathing and thumping hearts.

Wild Boy pushed the door wider, revealing a room that might once have been elegant but was now musty and dusty and falling apart. Suits of armour stood along a wall, splotched with rust and clothed with cobwebs. There was a grandfather clock, a grand piano and a fire that looked like it hadn't brought warmth or light to the room in decades.

Otherwise the room was empty.

The Gentlemen had vanished.

Wild Boy looked at Clarissa, and his smile grew wider. Just because there were no doors didn't mean there were *really* no doors.

"Your turn," Clarissa said.

He began a slow walk around the room. His heart settled and his breaths deepened, rustling the hair on his chin. His eyes began to move, taking in every inch of the wood-panelled walls, the faded carpet, the clock and the armoured knights.

A thrill ran through the hair on his back, like a crackle of electricity. It was that feeling he got when he stopped looking and started *seeing*.

This was what *he* did best.

For most of his life, Wild Boy had been locked up alone, first in the workhouse and then the freak show, watching the world through gaps in curtains or cracks in caravan walls. He'd studied people, wishing he had their lives. He learned to read their stories from tiny details he spotted on their faces or clothes. Hardly anyone passed without some scar or stain or tear or tick that revealed who they were or where they were going. His eyes homed in on each clue, and his mind instinctively processed its meaning. Magic happened in his head.

Clarissa leaned against one of the wall panels, pretending to look bored. "Get on with it then," she said.

Wild Boy moved faster around the room. He pressed a palm against one panel, leaned in and smelled another. He stepped up to one of the suits of armour, ran a hairy knuckle over its metal arm and then peered into its open visor.

"You found it yet?" Clarissa said.

"Eh?"

"The secret door. You found one yet?"

"Oh. No."

"What? You're meant to be a great detective!"

"No, I mean I didn't find *one*. Found four."

He didn't want to show off, but he couldn't help it. Back at the fairground he'd kept his detective skills a secret, in case they made him even more of a freak. Now they made him proud.

"The first hidden door is easy," he said. "That wall panel there opens. See the carpet? It's worn down where people have climbed through. And there are small scratches on the panel next to it, where it slides open."

"I don't see any scratches."

"They're *very* small."

"So how does it open?"

Wild Boy rushed to one of the suits of armour. "See this feller? Why's his face mask thing up when all the others got theirs down?"

He rose to tiptoes and slid the visor down.

A hollow *thunk* came from inside one of the walls, then the rattle and jangle of a chain somewhere in the ceiling. The wooden panel slid sideways. A stale breeze rustled from the darkness beyond. The first secret door.

Clarissa's eyes lit up. Wild Boy knew she loved watching him use his skills as much as he enjoyed her acrobatics. But she would never admit it.

"All right," she said. "What clue shows a second door?"

"Something we can hear."

"I can't hear nothing."

"Exactly. This grandfather clock. Why ain't it ticking?"

"Ain't been wound."

"No. See these wax drops on the floor? They're about five hours old, I'd say. Someone's been here today, right by this clock. And look at the hands. Stopped exactly on midnight. Funny, that. The hour hand's all rusted, hasn't moved in months.

But the minute hand is nice and shiny."

He turned the minute hand a full circle, round and back to midnight.

Another *thunk*. Another jangle.

He stepped away as the clock scraped forward. Behind it was a narrow entrance to a tunnel.

"Brilliant!" Clarissa said. "I mean … what about the third door?"

"That's the fireplace. Turns in the middle. There's frost on the inside of the chimney, so it ain't been used, and soot marks in a half-circle on the carpet from where it swings."

"Well, that ain't a door then, that's a hatch."

"All right, so three and a half doors."

"Three and a *hatch*. Anyhow, which did the Gentlemen go down?"

"They took the fourth door. Another one of these wall panels opens. Can't see no scratch marks on it, so it probably swings. Only, I ain't sure how."

Wild Boy continued around the room, his big eyes searching for that last clue. He stopped at the grand piano, his eyes drawn to something on the keys. He wasn't certain what he'd seen yet; sometimes his instinct worked like that. He just knew that something was strange here. Brushing hair from around his eyes, he leaned closer.

There.

All of the piano keys were coated with dust, apart from one.

"So which other wall panel opens?" Clarissa said.

Wild Boy looked up and grinned. "The one you're leaning on."

He hit the piano key. There was a loud *dong*. The panel swung open and Clarissa tumbled through.

She jumped up on the other side, brushing dust from her coat. "I knew that," she said.

Tingling with excitement, Wild Boy followed her along a narrow passage, towards murmuring voices. Clarissa glanced back, her expression asking if it was safe to continue.

All that time Wild Boy had spent spying on people at fairgrounds had trained his ears as well as his eyes. He could distinguish the rattles of particular carriage wheels, the barks of different dogs, the smallest sprinkle of an accent in a distant voice. Right then he knew that the voices ahead were muffled by another door, at least half a foot thick. They were safe to continue.

The passage led to a windowless chamber.

"A laboratory," Clarissa said.

Chemicals fizzed in racks of test tubes. A rat cowered in a cage. On another table, a selection of headgear had been modified into weapons: a soldier's bearskin rigged with dynamite, a coal-scuttle bonnet concealing a brace of pistols, and a stovepipe hat fixed with tubes to release gas from its crown. They were lethal weapons, designed to kill. But Wild Boy couldn't help smiling. There was nothing he loved better than snooping and spying with Clarissa.

Light leaked into the laboratory around the frame of a larger, six-panelled door on the opposite wall. Wild Boy crouched by it and peered through a gap. Several Gentlemen were gathered around a table, studying the contents of the crate – a wooden box with a glass lens jutting from the side and metal plates rising from the top.

The men smoked cigars and sipped from crystal glasses. They seemed to be one group, but Wild Boy knew that wasn't quite the case. There were the two sides to the Gentlemen: military men and scientists. Outdoors, the military men wore black hats and the scientists wore grey, but even indoors it wasn't hard to tell which was which. Those who had been in the army – the Black Hats – were exceedingly proud of their bushy side-whiskers. Most of the Grey Hat scientists kept their whiskers trimmed in case of accidents during experiments, and their skin was pasty and pale from long days cooped up in laboratories.

None of the fifty or so Gentlemen lived at the palace. Most just came here to work, experimenting with technologies, spying on other governments and whatever other shady activities went on in these secret chambers.

One of the Grey Hats pulled a lamp closer to the device on the table. "We stole this technology from the French," he said. "An inventor named Daguerre.

This box captures images – real images. They're called daguerreotypes, or photographs."

"Impossible," said one of the Black Hats.

"No, it's quite extraordinary. The device uses iodine crystals to form a light sensitive copper—"

"It is an interesting trick," interrupted another Black Hat.

The man who stepped through the cigar smoke looked like an antique. His skin was the colour of cigar ash, and grey whiskers hung from saggy jowls. A layer of dust – dandruff, really – coated the shoulders of his frock coat. His eyes, though, were dark and sharp and fiercely alive. They glared at the other Gentlemen with such intensity that all of the men shifted back from the table.

Lucien Grant, Wild Boy thought.

He'd spied on enough of these secret meetings to know that Lucien was one of the most powerful figures among the Gentlemen, a retired army general and leader of the Black Hat military men.

Lucien retrieved a silver snuff tin from his coat pocket. His jowls wobbled as he snorted a pinch of the powder up his nose. When he spoke again his voice was as deep as a double bass.

"I cannot imagine any use for such a toy," he said. "We are soldiers and spies, not artists."

"But we are *scientists* too," protested one of the Grey Hats.

"Yes, of course. Sometimes I forget."

"Perhaps we could discuss this device with the Principal?"

Lucien scoffed. Dandruff sprinkled from his shoulders. "I hardly think this would interest the Principal."

The Principal. Wild Boy had heard the Gentlemen use that name before, and always with the same note of fear. He didn't think the person was their leader. As far as he was aware, the Principal never came to the palace.

"It is my information that the Principal intends to come to the palace," one of the men said.

A thrill ran through Wild Boy's hair. This sounded interesting.

"Your information is as good as mine," Lucien replied. "All I know is that we must assemble in the Tapestry Room tomorrow morning."

Wild Boy grinned, already looking forward to spying on that particular meeting. But what he heard next wiped the smile from his face.

"I have heard the meeting is about the children."

"The freak and the acrobat?" Lucien said. "Have they not taken up enough of our time? This is not a bloody orphanage." He chuckled, a deep rumbling noise. The other Black Hats joined in.

"Have you heard their story, Lucien?" one of the Grey Hats asked. "Clarissa's mother turned against her, *hunted* her even. And I am told Wild Boy has unique detective skills. I must admit, I am intrigued."

"Please. We are a secret organization, appointed

to safeguard the interests of Britain and her Empire. Children have no place here. I am sure the Principal intends to inform us that we cannot continue to harbour them."

Wild Boy didn't hear anything else, just a beating drum, the sound of blood pounding in his ears. Was it possible? Was the Principal going to kick them out of the palace? They had nowhere else to go.

Suddenly he didn't want to be here. They had to get back up to their room, act as if they'd never dream of causing trouble.

"Hey," Clarissa whispered.

She had taken the rat from its cage. The creature sat on her head, sniffing the air.

"Think I'll call him Hatty," she said.

"No, Clarissa … put it back."

The rat leaped onto the laboratory table, knocking over a rack of test tubes. Glass smashed and chemicals spilled across the surface. The fizzing liquid soaked the weaponized hats. It reacted with the gas inside one, causing it to shake and jolt – and then burst into the air with a gunshot-loud boom.

"That was *brilliant*," Clarissa said.

There were shouts from the next room, and stomps of boots.

Grabbing Clarissa's arm, Wild Boy yanked her from the laboratory. They raced back along the passageway and leaped through the secret entrance. As Wild Boy slammed it shut, Clarissa shoved one of the suits of armour, toppling it over to block the exit.

"Hurry!"

As they darted back into the hallway, bells began to ring around the palace.

"It's the Gentlemen's alarm," Clarissa said.

Several men charged from the other direction.

"The tapestries," Wild Boy said.

They ran faster, slapping the hanging tapestries. A cloud of dust filled the corridor, hiding them from the approaching Gentlemen.

They climbed the stairs, pelted along a corridor and up to their attic bedroom. They collapsed on the other side of the door, wheezy breaths broken by gulping laughs.

"Did anyone see us?" Clarissa said.

"Don't think so."

"Then we ain't done nothing, have we?"

"You *haven't* done *anything*," a stern voice corrected.

The voice was so forceful that it seemed to grab their jaws and snap them shut, instantly silencing their laughter.

A man sat watching them from the corner of the attic, fingers locked over the top of a cane. His face was in shadow, but still something glinted in the darkness. Something gold.

"However," the man continued after a pause, "we all know that is a great big lie."

3

ild Boy helped Clarissa up from the floor. The alarm had stopped ringing around the palace, but they could still hear the shouts of the Gentlemen charging around the corridors in search of the intruders.

As the shouts grew louder Wild Boy and Clarissa's attention remained focused on the person seated in the dark corner of their attic bedroom.

The man rose, leaning heavily on his silver-topped cane. Another glint of gold shone from a face that otherwise seemed carved of stone, so sharp were its lines and angles. The gleam came from one of the man's eyes. He had a golden eyeball.

This was Marcus Bishop. For the last four months he had been Wild Boy and Clarissa's guardian. And until that evening, Wild Boy had thought that he was the leader of the Gentlemen.

Marcus limped closer, slicked silver hairs brushing the low attic ceiling. His voice was as calm as ever, each word measured and laid neatly into place. His single good eye narrowed with disapproval.

"What have you two done this time?" he asked.

Clarissa thrust her arms in the air in disgust. "I knew you'd blame this on us," she said.

"How exactly are you not to blame?" Marcus said.

"Cos we're stuck up here," Clarissa said, hurling herself onto the bed. "All we're doing is keeping our skills sharp. Ain't that so, Wild Boy?"

Wild Boy didn't hear. His mind was still downstairs in the Gentlemen's laboratory, listening to Lucien's grim prediction. *"The children have no place here. I am sure the Principal intends to inform us that we cannot continue to harbour them."*

A knot tied in Wild Boy's stomach. These past four months, fooling about with Clarissa, had been the happiest of his life. He'd never thought it might end.

No. He was being stupid. Marcus wouldn't let them be kicked out. He was their guardian, their friend. Wild Boy had spied on him issuing orders to police inspectors, army generals, even the Prime Minister on one particularly tense occasion. He couldn't imagine anyone having more authority than Marcus.

But someone did. The Principal.

"Anyway," Clarissa said. "It wasn't us. We ain't done no snooping."

Marcus winced slightly from a pain behind his

false eye. "I am not angry about snooping. A detective and an acrobat? I *expect* you to snoop. I do not, however, expect you to get *caught*. You were lazy, foolish. You must control your emotions. Concentrate. Think."

"If we do, will you give us our own cases to solve?" Clarissa asked.

"You know that is not possible."

Marcus pulled two folded sheets of paper from his coat and dropped them on the bed. They were posters for plays, printed with the same picture of a werewolf attacking a top-hatted man and a ball-gowned lady.

Clarissa snatched one up and read it with the exaggerated horror of a showman at a fairground. "'*The Savage Spectacle of Wild Boy! The murdering boy monster that preyed on London.*'" She picked up the next sheet. "'*The Wild Boy of London. The voodoo fiend who devoured his victims' flesh and drank their blood.*'"

"It ain't fair," she said. "People thought I was a monster once too. Now they've forgotten all about me. It's all 'Wild Boy killed this' and 'Wild Boy murdered that'. I should've bitten someone. Or howled like a wolf."

She gave her best werewolf howl and fell back laughing on the bed.

The knot pulled tighter in Wild Boy's gut. Four months ago he'd proven to the police that they were innocent of murder, but not to the public. He had become famous: the Wild Boy of London.

That was why he hid in the palace, why he couldn't leave. Why he couldn't stop thinking about what he'd heard downstairs.

"Who's the Principal?" he said.

The words came out before Wild Boy could stop them. Questions about the Gentlemen's business were as forbidden as snooping around their laboratories.

Marcus looked at him. He seemed as if he was about to answer, then suddenly slammed a hand against the wall, grimacing. Clarissa stepped towards him, but he held out a palm, signalling for her to stay back. His eye scrunched shut as the pain grew stronger behind the other socket.

"Sir?" a voice called. "Sir!"

"Oh *great*," Clarissa said. "It's Gideon."

It was hard at first to see much of the man who rushed up the stairs. Small and skinny, he was hidden by an oversize tricorn hat and a coachman's coat that was almost twice his size, flowing behind him like a royal gown. Tripping on its train, the man tumbled into the attic. His hat fell off and a parcel slipped from his hands.

Clarissa grabbed the hat and hid it behind her back.

"Sir," the man said, scrambling to Marcus. "Sir, your medicines."

"No, Gideon. I am fine."

The man whirled around. He had a tight, shrivelled face, like an old sponge, and beady black eyes. It was Gideon Finkle, Marcus's coach driver.

"What have you done to him now?" he yelled, glaring first at Wild Boy, then Clarissa. "You'll kill him! You'll be the death of him."

"Oh, it's always us, ain't it, Gideon?" Clarissa said. "Maybe it was your coach driving that hurt Marcus, eh? So bumpy he banged his head about."

Gideon's lips peeled back, revealing brown, peg-like teeth. He fingered a dirty cloth tied around his wizened neck. "I've been his driver for sixteen years," he snarled.

"Should be better at it by now, then."

"Give me my hat," Gideon demanded.

"Ain't got your hat."

She tossed it to Wild Boy, who threw it back, trapping Gideon as a piggy in the middle.

"Sir!" Gideon squealed. "They're doing it again."

"Enough! All of you."

Marcus's voice boomed around the attic, and they all fell silent. He sighed a breath so heavy it clouded the air. "Can't you just get along?"

"No fun in that," Clarissa muttered. "What's in that parcel?"

With his cane Marcus prodded the parcel that Gideon had dropped. He raised an eyebrow at Wild Boy. "Care to tell us?"

Wild Boy hadn't been paying much attention to the quarrel with Gideon. His mind had still been on Lucien and the Principal. But suddenly it was here again, sharp and focused.

It was a test. He loved tests.

He crouched beside the parcel, wide eyes scouring the surfaces. "It's a dress," he said, looking to Marcus, "from a fashion shop on Bond Street. It's for Clarissa, although you only got the idea to give it to her in the last half hour."

A small smile cracked the corner of Marcus's mouth. "Care to share your observations?"

Wild Boy rose. This was the bit he really liked, a chance to show off his skills. "Gideon gave it away," he said.

"Sir, I said nothing. I promise."

"No, your coat. The mud marks tell a story."

Gideon glanced around at the back of his coat. "Ain't no mud marks."

"That's the story. Means you only drove on metalled roads between here and the shop. You ain't gone past Oxford Street to the north or Park Lane west, where it gets muddy. So you went east into Mayfair.

"Also, look at the parcel. See these dried spots on the top? That's from snow. But it's only snowed in the past twenty minutes, since midnight. What shop would open so late for you to collect a dress? Only the *very* poshest, the ones on Bond Street. And why pick it up so late? Cos Marcus only just got the idea of inviting Clarissa somewhere – somewhere she needs a dress."

"How do you know it's a dress? You didn't even touch it."

"If it's from Bond Street, it's either jewellery or a dress. Gideon didn't go crazy when he dropped it, so it ain't jewellery."

"Well, how do you know it's for Clarissa?"

"Cos I don't wear dresses. Though neither does she."

Gideon snatched the parcel from the floor. "That ain't so clever," he muttered. "I once saw a magician chop a lady in half. *That* was clever."

"It ain't *magic*," Clarissa said. "Wild Boy's a detective."

"Freak, more like."

Clarissa shot up. "What did you just say?"

"The parcel, Gideon," Marcus said calmly.

Gideon dumped it beside Clarissa on the bed, and snatched his hat back in return.

Clarissa opened the box and took out the dress. Golden sequins shimmered on red silk. Wild Boy wondered if she realized how similar it looked to her old red and gold circus outfit, the costume she had worn to perform with her mother in the circus.

"What's this for?" Clarissa asked.

"I thought you might accompany me to dinner tomorrow evening at Lady Bentick's house," Marcus said.

"I… *Where?*"

"Berkeley Square."

"No, I mean why?"

"I hoped it might teach you a few manners."

"What's Wild Boy gonna wear?" Clarissa said. "He only ever wears that coat."

Marcus looked at Wild Boy, and his Adam's apple rose and fell. He didn't need to explain. Wild Boy knew there was no invite for him. He was the Wild Boy of London.

"If I go," Clarissa said, "can I steal something?"

"Only if you don't get caught," Marcus said.

Holding the wall for support, he began to descend the stairs. Gideon scuttled after him, pausing just long enough to glare at them again, shove his hat back on and slam the door.

Clarissa banged a fist against the other side. "You're just jealous cos Marcus likes us more than you!" she shouted. She laughed, flopping back onto the bed. "What shall we do now? Wanna sneak around and steal stuff?"

A crow flew past the attic window, cawing loudly into the night. Wild Boy closed his eyes, tried not to listen, but still the dark memories came creeping back. Memories of showmen and freak shows.

The Principal *was* coming to kick them out of the palace. And they had nowhere else to go.

Clarissa sat up, brushing back her hair. "What's up with you?"

"If I tell you something, do you promise to stay calm?"

· 4 ·

"**C**larissa, wait!"

Wild Boy scrambled after her across the rooftops, his bare feet slipping on the icy surfaces. He caught up with her on the roof of the palace chapel. Anger flowed off Clarissa in waves, as if it might melt the ice. Wild Boy wondered if she would punch a chimney-stack if she couldn't get into the Gentlemen's meeting with the Principal.

"You said you'd stay calm," he gasped.

"I am calm. I'm gonna calmly punch all the Gentlemen in the face."

"Clarissa…"

"Wild Boy, they can't kick us out. They owe us. We helped them catch a killer, remember? Anyway, we can't exactly stroll about on the streets. You're the Wild Boy of London."

Wild Boy knew that much. He'd been thinking

about it all night. They needed to find out what was going on, but they couldn't just storm into the Gentlemen's meeting.

He gazed across the rooftops of St James's Palace, squinting in the midday sun. He'd snooped around enough of the palace to have a map in his mind of its various staterooms, secret laboratories and hallways. He saw it now, laid over the snow-sheeted clutter of rooftops and attics that surrounded its four courtyards.

"Where are they all, anyhow?" Clarissa said.

"Lucien said they were meeting in the Tapestry Room," Wild Boy said. He pointed to a weather vane several roofs away. "That's under that black ship."

Clarissa set off again, swinging around flagpoles and leaping over skylights. Reaching the weather vane, she stood on the edge of the roof and looked down. Several black coaches were parked in the courtyard.

"Looks like the Gentlemen are here," Clarissa said. "I could climb down and listen at the window."

"You'll get seen by the drivers," Wild Boy said, catching up.

"So how we gonna listen in?"

Still struggling to catch his breath, Wild Boy slapped a hand against the roof's chimney-stack. He remembered Marcus's history lesson about the Tapestry Room. It was the oldest part of the palace, a banqueting chamber where kings and queens had once hosted lavish feasts. It had a huge open hearth and a very wide chimney.

"Don't be a thickhead," Clarissa said, realizing his plan. "We ain't chimney sweeps." She peered over the top of the stack. "Anyhow, I'm too tall to fit in there."

"I can, just about."

Wild Boy stood on tiptoe and looked into the sooty chute. A murmur of voices rose up the shaft. The Gentlemen were down there, but he couldn't hear what they were saying. Was the Principal there too? He had to get closer.

"It's a long drop," Clarissa said. "You'll break both your legs if you fall. That's if you land that way up." She grinned. "This is the best thing you've ever done."

Usually Wild Boy was pleased if he impressed Clarissa. But all he felt now was fear. He wasn't scared of the fall, but of what he might hear.

Gripping Clarissa's shoulder, he sat up on top of the stack. His matchstick legs quivered as they dangled down the chute.

"Hey," Clarissa said. "If you die, come back to haunt me."

Wild Boy forced a smile and began to climb. Pressing his back against one side of the shaft and his feet hard into the other, he wriggled down the cramped space. The soles of his feet were as rough as pumice, perfect for gripping the coarse brick. But his legs shook from the effort, and soot sprinkled into his eyes.

"Can you hear anything?" Clarissa called.

The Gentlemen's voices grew louder. Wild Boy could pick out a few words.

"… the Principal…"

"… Wild Boy and Clarissa … threat to security…"

He shuffled lower. A pigeon nested in a space where a brick had crumbled from the wall. It watched Wild Boy with unblinking eyes as he pressed his feet either side of its hole, wedging himself tighter into the shaft.

The words grew into sentences. Lucien Grant's barrel-deep voice rose above the others.

"Perhaps you might explain to us what this is all about, Marcus?"

Marcus spoke. "As you know —"

"Know?" Lucien interrupted. "All we know is that the Principal is coming."

"Then you appreciate how serious the situation must be. This case is … *unusual*. That is why the Principal proposes to involve Wild Boy."

Wild Boy's feet almost slipped from the wall. The Principal wasn't coming to kick them out of the palace. He was coming to talk to them about a case!

Lucien scoffed. "I suggest, Marcus, that I handle this. It sounds as if it is beyond the boy's limited abilities."

"You would not think that, Lucien, if you knew

him. Indeed, I am yet to discover a limit to his abilities. I am, however, inclined to agree. This should not be the children's first case. It is a delicate situation. A dangerous one, perhaps."

Clarissa whispered something down the chimney, but Wild Boy ignored her. He knew he should climb back up. This would definitely not be a good moment to get caught. But he wanted to hear more.

Clarissa's whisper rose to a shout. "Smoke!"

He glanced down and his heart lurched.

The Gentlemen had lit the fire.

Smoke rose up the chute, choking him. He began to wriggle back up, but the pigeon – trapped beneath him – panicked and pecked his legs. He reached to swipe the bird away, but his feet slipped.

He dropped twenty feet down the shaft, screaming all the way, and landed in a cloud of ash and sparks.

Around the Tapestry Room, Gentlemen tumbled back from the table. Others rushed forward, drawing pistols from their coats. They watched Wild Boy roll from the hearth, spluttering and swearing and thrashing his arms to put out sparks.

Slowly, Wild Boy rose.

This ain't gonna be easy. He looked around the Gentlemen and forced a smile. "You won't believe this," he said, "but I was just cleaning the chimney, and — "

"Wild Boy."

Marcus rose from the table. Leaning on his cane,

he limped closer. To the others his face was unreadable. To Wild Boy the message was as clear as if printed on a poster. The narrowing of his guardian's good eye, the rise and fall of his Adam's apple and the slight clench of his jaw.

Not anger. Disappointment.

"I assume Clarissa is close?" Marcus asked.

"Get your stinking hands off me!" a voice screamed.

The door burst open and Gideon shoved Clarissa into the hall. He bowed to Marcus. "Discovered her outside, sir. She was about to smash the window. I warned you this would happen, sir. Only a matter of time with these two."

Wild Boy guessed that Clarissa had planned to cause a distraction, giving him a chance to escape. He smiled gratefully, but at the same time an icy hand squeezed his heart. He'd really messed up now.

Lucien Grant pushed closer, barging several Gentlemen while making a big show of brushing soot from his coat sleeve. But the delight was obvious in his dark eyes, the triumph barely disguised in his voice. "The children must go," he said. "We cannot tolerate this insubordination."

The room filled with shouts of support, everyone agreeing that the incident could not be ignored.

"The girl and the freak must go," Lucien demanded.

Clarissa launched forward and shoved him in the chest. "Who you calling a freak?"

She swung at punch at Lucien, but another of the Gentlemen yanked her back before it found its target. Wild Boy couldn't stop himself now; no one started a fight with Clarissa and didn't get in one with him too. Half the height of most of the men, he went in low, punching one of them in the groin, kicking another's shin, and then biting a third on the thigh.

"Get your hands off her!"

Gentlemen wrestled them to the ground. There were grunts and groans, sounds of coats tearing, Wild Boy's muffled swearing and Clarissa's manic screams.

Then a quiet voice spoke.

"Gentlemen."

The Gentlemen immediately released Wild Boy and Clarissa, springing up as if they'd been zapped by electricity. They neatened their suits and brushed soot from their faces.

Wild Boy and Clarissa lay on the floor, staring up at the person the Gentlemen had gathered to meet.

The Principal.

"Bloody hell," Clarissa said. "It's Queen Victoria."

• 5 •

Around the Tapestry Room, the Gentlemen bolted up, stiff and straight, like soldiers. Each man bowed his head, lowering his gaze from the royal visitor. A few edged forward and a few shrank back, an unspoken pecking order asserting itself among their ranks.

Impatient hands shoved Wild Boy and Clarissa to the back of the group. Clarissa was happy to hide; she brushed her hair with her hands and neatened her crumpled clothes. She nudged Wild Boy to do the same, but he just stood there staring at the leader of the Gentlemen through gaps between the men. The Principal.

He'd seen paintings of Queen Victoria at fairgrounds around the time of her coronation four years ago. They had made her look beautiful, almost like a goddess. In person, though, she looked so *normal.* She was elegantly dressed, of course, in a gown embroidered with flowers, and her hair was tied in elaborate buns around her ears. But she was shorter than the paintings had suggested, dumpy even, with a plump face, pointed nose, and eyes so deep-set they sank into her skull. She carried a parcel, which seemed strange for a Queen with two footmen following so closely.

Still, she radiated authority, even in a room full of such powerful men. Perhaps it was just the knowledge that she was the sovereign of the largest empire the world had ever known.

Lucien came forward first, knocking over a chair in his eagerness and causing the Queen to step back with a start. He bowed so low that his grey whiskers brushed his knees – an impressive feat, Wild Boy thought, for a man of his size.

"Your Majesty," Lucien said solemnly.

The Queen glanced at Marcus. For a second her polite smile changed into something more playful, childlike even. Then it was gone, replaced by the stiff formality of a monarch greeting her subjects.

Several other Gentlemen approached, although none dared compete with Lucien's bow. Instead they tried to out-greet each other with increasingly elaborate salutes.

"Royal Majesty."

"*Graceful* Majesty."

"Defender of the Faith."

Marcus came forward last. He bowed, and smiled, very slightly.

Wild Boy glanced at Clarissa, saw her eyes narrow with jealously. She, too, recognized their guardian's smile – the one he usually reserved for her.

"Your Majesty," Marcus said. "You look radiant."

The Queen reached for his hand, but stopped herself, aware of how many people were watching. "If that is your way of inquiring if we are with child again, Marcus, then we assure you that we are not. My mother sends her greetings. She asks if you find the palace adequate for your needs?"

"Perfectly adequate, Your Majesty. I cannot thank you both enough."

"Nonsense. We much prefer Buckingham Palace. Tell us, what secrets have you hidden around this old place?"

"It is best that you do not know, Your Majesty."

The Queen nodded. It was an answer she had clearly received before. "And as for our current situation, have the Gentlemen discussed the matter?"

"At length."

"Have you reached any conclusions?"

Lucien bowed again. "Your Majesty, we have—"

"None whatsoever," Marcus interrupted.

"In that case," the Queen said, "there is one secret that you now *must* share with us, Marcus."

Wild Boy watched, fascinated. He saw Marcus hold the Queen's gaze for a brief moment, a hint of a challenge. Whatever she was asking, he didn't approve.

The Queen noticed too. "Marcus, need we ask again?"

"Not at all, Your Majesty."

Marcus turned to the Gentlemen. But when he spoke, his voice was directed beyond them, to the back to the room. "Wild Boy. Clarissa. Your Queen wishes to meet you."

Panic slapped Wild Boy in the face. He shot a look over his shoulder, half-expecting to see two other people with those names waiting to greet the Queen.

"He means us," Clarissa said.

Wild Boy cursed and brushed soot from his coat. He couldn't meet the Queen like this. Clarissa nudged his arm, but he ignored her, his curses growing louder as he rubbed the hairs on his face.

Clarissa elbowed him again, and finally he looked up. The crowd of Gentlemen had parted. Everyone was staring at him, including the Queen.

"You first," Clarissa said, shoving him forward.

He took several calming breaths and shuffled closer. As he approached the Queen he kept his eyes down and attempted a bow. He'd never bowed to anyone in his life, and messed it up completely, dipping so low that the blood rushed to his head and he had to grasp the table for support.

"You know who we are?" the Queen asked.

"Bloomin' right I do," Wild Boy blurted. "I

mean, it's a pleasure to meet you, Majesty. Sorry for cussing."

"You appear to be dusty."

"Fell down a chimney, Majesty."

"Indeed."

Her expression gave nothing away. "We have heard a little of your story," she said. "Such experiences must have left you with scars."

Wild Boy felt those sunken eyes searching him, seeking the memories he kept locked at the back of his mind. Memories of the freak show, of shame and crushing loneliness. "No, Majesty," he said. "No scars."

"And this is Miss Everett?"

Clarissa rushed to Wild Boy's side and sank into a surprisingly elegant curtsy. "Your Royal Highness Majesty," she said.

"We owe you both a debt of gratitude," the Queen said. "Marcus informs us that you were responsible for the apprehension of a killer, the culprit of crimes of which you yourselves stood accused."

Still are accused of them, Wild Boy thought, although he decided not to correct the Queen.

"We took great interest in that case," the Queen continued, "and indeed in your subsequent lives here at the palace. Now we have a particular problem with which you might be able to offer some assistance. However, before we take you into our confidence, perhaps you might provide us with a demonstration of your abilities."

Wild Boy glanced at Clarissa. Another test.

"Perhaps," the Queen said, "you require a few moments?"

"He don't," Clarissa said.

She was right. He didn't.

"You've lied three times since you've been in this room," Wild Boy told the Queen. "First, you *are* pregnant. The lace around your waist has been tied half an inch looser. See where them folds from the old knot are showing? And there's a couple spots of sick on your sleeve, which you see a bit on pregnant ladies. Second, you told Marcus you're well, but when that chair fell over, your grip went tight around that parcel in your hands. Means you're scared of something. I suppose that parcel is what you wanna speak to us about, or why else would a Queen carry her own mail? And I know that you ain't taken no interest before in me or Clarissa, cos each time you lie your bottom lip wrinkles, and it did it again when you said that."

The Gentlemen stared at him, outraged by his tone. Even Clarissa looked shocked. The Queen, though, simply glanced at Marcus and nodded. Wild Boy had passed.

"Well then," the Queen said. "Perhaps you might assist us in another matter. A singular and unpleasant matter."

Wild Boy tried to look calm, but he wanted to

jump in the air. He and Clarissa had hoped they might be given a case, but they'd never dreamed it might come from the Queen. If they solved it, surely they would be allowed to remain at the palace.

"Not only him," Clarissa said. "Me an' all. We're partners."

"Indeed," the Queen replied. "Miss Everett, are you a fan of the opera?"

"Never been."

"That is a shame. We and Prince Albert adore the opera, and attend every Thursday. The Prince is currently in Bavaria, so last week we went alone to the opening of *Don Giovanni* at the Opera House on Haymarket. Have you ever attended a royal opening?"

"I think, Your Majesty," Lucien said, "that you may assume the children are entirely unfamiliar with the events of your social calendar."

"We never assume anything, Mr Grant."

The Queen's eyes remained on Clarissa. "Had you been, you would know how crowded the Opera House becomes. That evening was the busiest we have witnessed. We are hosting a ball at the palace tomorrow evening, an annual celebration of the passing of winter. Despite the fact that winter has clearly not yet passed, many people wish to secure an invitation. Thus we exchanged pleasantries with several individuals prior to the performance. As we were led to the royal box, we were accosted."

"Accosted?" Wild Boy asked.

"We can hardly describe the person other than in terms of his attire, which was the usual dress of a gentleman at the opera. All we can say for certain is that this individual removed a necklace from our person. Among the confusion, however, he escaped."

"Someone swiped your necklace?" Clarissa asked.

"We have not finished, Miss Everett. As we say, these events took place almost a week ago. Yesterday, however, a parcel arrived at Buckingham Palace. It is this item which we now hold, and which we entrust upon you."

Wild Boy accepted the parcel with trembling hands. It was heavier than its size suggested, a rectangular object wrapped in brown paper. "This ain't the paper it came in," he said. "There's no address on top, and no seal on the bottom."

The Queen nodded. "The member of staff who opens our correspondence discards packaging as a matter of course. The original paper, which had a black wax seal and a handwritten address, was thrown into the fire before the importance of its contents was established. But we hardly think the wrapping is significant. It is the contents that we wish you to examine."

Wild Boy pulled a lamp closer. He peeled away the wrapping paper to reveal a small ebony container. A square of card lay on top. Written in its centre, in black ink, was a single word.

MALPHAS

"Is that a name?" Clarissa said.

She lifted the lid. The container was half-filled with sand, or something like sand. Some of the granules were opaque, others raspberry red.

"What is that?" she said.

Wild Boy tilted the box, letting the contents spill onto the table. "It's the Queen's necklace," he said, realizing. "Someone crushed it up."

"You are correct," the Queen said. "That is what remains of the necklace's jewels. Two hundred and eighty diamonds and ninety-six rubies."

"They must've been worth a *fortune*," Clarissa said.

"Several fortunes," Marcus replied. "And yet they have been destroyed and returned with utter contempt. However, there is one jewel missing. The stone that formed the necklace's pendant – a large black diamond."

Clarissa scoffed. "Diamonds ain't black."

"This one is," Marcus replied. "That is why it is so valuable."

"So that's what you want us to find?"

"Miss Everett," the Queen said. "We would not have troubled you with anything so ordinary as a stolen jewel. We informed you that this case was both singular and unpleasant. That parcel and its contents are the singular details. Now we must show you those that are unpleasant. Please, follow."

The footmen leaped to life. One of them opened the doors as the other scuttled behind the Queen in case her dress snagged on a treasonous nail.

Marcus signalled with his cane for Wild Boy and Clarissa to walk by his side. But Wild Boy hung back, noticing something curious. All of the Gentlemen sank to their knees as the Queen left the room, except for one.

Lucien.

The man seemed to have forgotten her existence entirely. As he stared at the box and the card on top, his grey face drained almost white. Did that name on the card – *Malphas* – mean something to him?

Wild Boy grabbed the card and shoved it in his pocket. He flashed Lucien a grin, and then rushed to catch up with the others.

None of them spoke as they followed the Queen along a corridor, through a guard chamber and out to the palace's entrance courtyard. Sunlight bounced off the polished wood of the royal coach. A golden letter *R* gleamed on the cabin door.

The Queen stopped. "Wild Boy?"

"Majesty?"

"You enquired about the parcel's packaging, but not the servant who opened it. That man's name is Prendergast. It is he whom we wish you to meet."

She gestured to her footman to open the door.

Wild Boy noticed the man hesitate before stepping forward. He guessed he was about to be shown a dead body.

Clarissa came up alongside him as the door opened. At first they saw only a shape in the darkness beyond. It was a body, but it wasn't dead. It was another royal footman, in a scarlet tunic and powdered wig. The man was moving, clutching his knees and rocking on the cabin seat.

Clarissa recoiled, grabbing Wild Boy's arm. "His face!" she gasped.

It was a ghastly face. Prendergast's skin was so pale it was almost translucent. Black veins shot from his forehead to his chin, like dark, streaming tears. His eyes were so wide they bled at the sides, and his lips were shrivelled black slugs. They parted very slightly, whispering a single word to the rhythm of his rocking.

"Malphas … Malphas … Malphas …"

The Queen spoke again. "Prendergast has served the Royal Family for over ten years. He has two young sons. His wife passed away during the delivery of the second. He is a kind, innocent man."

"He's got some sort of disease," Clarissa said.

"No, no disease," the Queen replied. "We spoke with Prendergast yesterday morning, moments before he opened that package. He was perfectly well. The package was the first and only piece of correspondence that he opened. He read its card and got rid of the packaging. Then he was like this."

Wild Boy brought the card from his pocket. *Malphas*.

Marcus spoke. His voice, usually so calm, seemed suddenly flustered, broken by small swallows. "Whoever stole the Queen's black diamond and sent that package somehow did this to Prendergast. However, we suspect that Her Majesty was the intended target."

"Wild Boy and Clarissa," the Queen said, "we wish you to consider all that you have heard and seen, and search for clues that might identify the person behind this most heinous of crimes."

Instinct urged Wild Boy to turn and run. Whatever was going on, he sensed that he and Clarissa should have no part in it. But he gathered his nerve and stepped closer, listening to that name repeated over and over from Prendergast's lips.

"Malphas … Malphas … Malphas…"

Prendergast's mouth opened wider, and he whispered two more words.

"He's coming."

～ · **6** · ～

"**Y**ou really think someone wants to kill the Queen?" *yes*

Clarissa tossed a wet boot over the top of the dressing screen. It landed with a thump that rattled the mirror panels on the walls. "Imagine if we stopped that. We'd be famous."

"We already *are* famous," Wild Boy said.

"Yeah, but people would *like* us. Maybe we could stop hiding from everyone." She threw the other boot over the screen. "I bet the Queen would even invite us to her swanky ball on Thursday."

They were in the Royal Dressing Chamber, where maids and footmen had once clothed kings and queens. The room was entirely walled with mirrors, and ceilinged with them too. Some of the panels were rashy with blotches, or spiderweb-shattered where moody monarchs had hurled boots against

the glass. Marcus had suggested this as an appropriate place for Clarissa to dress for Lady Bentick's
dinner. Wild Boy didn't know if that was because it
had once been so grand or that it was now so grubby.

"I ain't said I'm going to this dinner tonight,"
Clarissa muttered. "Just trying the dress on, is all.
Probably look stupid."

"No change there," Wild Boy replied.

Clarissa cursed him and waited for his reply –
they regularly exchanged affectionate abuse. But
Wild Boy just stared at the Queen's card, running a
hairy fingertip over the word in black ink. ~~Malphas~~. Oswald

He should have been excited. If they solved this
case, they would have something even stronger
than Marcus's support; they'd have royal approval.
They definitely wouldn't need to worry about being
thrown out of the palace anymore.

But with what he'd just seen, Wild Boy didn't
exactly feel like celebrating. He sat up on the
window ledge, watching one of the Grey Hats lead
the Queen's servant, Prendergast, across the courtyard. In the lamp's harsh glare, Prendergast's face
appeared even whiter, his veins even blacker, like a
living corpse. He kept twitching, shaking. His eyes
shot around him as if he were surrounded by invisible, swooping demons.

"Who would do that to someone?" Wild Boy
wondered.

"That is the question."

Marcus limped into the Dressing Chamber. He wore an impeccable evening suit, and his silver hair was slicked with pomade. But the lines on his face had grown deeper, as if he'd aged a decade that day.

"Any news from the docs?" Clarissa asked. The physicians among the Gentlemen had spent the afternoon studying Prendergast for clues to what had caused his affliction.

Marcus shook his head slowly. "They have tested the man for every known disease. Consumption, white lead, new strains of cholera. The powdered remains of the Queen's necklace were also examined. They contained no poison, no substance that might have caused any effect upon Prendergast. The box was just a box, and the crushed jewels were just crushed jewels. Hours of study by the country's leading medical men, and the closest any have come to a diagnosis is to agree that Prendergast has been, somehow, frightened to within an inch of his life."

"Could've told them that before they began," Clarissa said. "So we ain't got no clues?"

Wild Boy shifted closer to the window, watching Prendergast being led across the courtyard. "Who's that with him now?"

"A young physician named Carew," Marcus replied. "He studied in India, specializing in rare diseases. He volunteered to take care of Prendergast."

Dr Carew looked like he regretted his eagerness. His face was lit with nervous sweat, and his spectacles kept slipping down his nose. But the doctor wasn't the only person keeping an eye on Prendergast. Across the courtyard, Lucien watched from the shadows. He snorted a pinch of snuff without taking his gaze off the doctor and patient.

Gideon was there too, wrapped in his huge coat. His face screwed up tighter than ever, and he tugged at his neck cloth as if trying to strangle himself. His small eyes were fixed on Prendergast. Did the Queen's story mean something to him too?

Wild Boy slowly turned the card over in his hand. "Malphas," he said.

"Think it's a name?" Clarissa said.

Marcus closed his eye, wincing at another stab of pain in his head. "I do not know," he said. "Are you not ready yet, Clarissa?"

"Button's stuck," she replied. "So you think this is just a boring old theft then? Whoever done it kept one of the jewels, remember? The Queen's black diamond."

"Clarissa…"

"Although why crush up the other stones if it's a theft? Sounds more like a threat, right?"

"I do not know, Clarissa!"

Clarissa's head rose from behind the screen. "Bit grumpy tonight, ain't you?"

Marcus sighed. "I apologize. It has been a long week, which I fear is about to get longer. As for your speculation, you might be surprised to learn that to assassinate Her Majesty would not be an especially difficult task. Her agenda is widely known. She rides her carriage in public, and her horses. She regularly stops in Hyde Park to converse with strangers. Any fool with a pistol could take a shot at her. Indeed, several have. It was only through poor planning that their attempts did not succeed."

Wild Boy had heard about one of those cases. Two years ago a madman shot at Queen Victoria as she rode from Buckingham Palace. The man escaped, but the Queen insisted on riding the same route the next day to tempt him to strike again. The risk paid off: the gunman was caught.

"I reckon Lucien knows something about all this," Clarissa said. "Did you see his face when he saw that card? Pink as a boiled ham."

Marcus was about to reply when a shot of pain struck his skull. He tried to hide his grimace but it reflected around the room's mirrors. He slicked back his hair, trying to gather his composure, but when he spoke again his voice was softer than usual, distant.

"I have not always been in charge of this organization," he said.

Clarissa's head rose again from behind the screen. Marcus rarely told stories about the history of the Gentlemen, and he never spoke about himself.

Wild Boy and Clarissa had asked, plenty of times. They'd searched the palace for Marcus's bedroom, but had not found it. They'd probed for information about his family, but had gotten none. Wild Boy had studied him for clues, but their guardian's clothes were always so perfectly pressed that it was hard to detect anything other than what he'd eaten for breakfast.

But now, for the first time, Marcus was volunteering information. Wild Boy shifted from the windowsill, listening carefully.

"There are secrets within secrets," Marcus said.

"You mean secrets so secret that not everybody at the secret organization knows about them secrets?" Clarissa asked.

"Precisely. Incidents that occurred before my time in charge of the Gentlemen. It is possible that this case involves one of those events, a particular event with which Lucien was involved. That is all I can say for now. But I assure you that I shall be speaking with him."

"I got a few things to say to him an' all," Clarissa said. She laughed, relishing the thought of her next encounter with Lucien Grant.

Marcus's grip tightened on the top of his cane. He watched the dressing screen for a moment, and then limped closer to Wild Boy. He spoke in a whisper. "Should I be worried?"

"Eh?"

"You know what I mean."

Wild Boy did – of course he did. He'd seen, too, how quickly Clarissa's temper had flared in the

Tapestry Room. She'd almost punched Lucien in the face before she was dragged away. Clarissa had always acted tough; that was how they got by in their world. But lately the anger had grown worse.

She never spoke about what happened at the circus – her mother had turned against her and hunted her with dogs. Nor did she mention her father, who had abandoned her years before. She pretended that both subjects were miles from her thoughts. But sometimes Wild Boy got the feeling they were so close that they almost crushed her.

"I'm coming out!" Clarissa called. "Wild Boy, if you mock me I'll break your arms."

Wild Boy hopped from the windowsill, fully intending to mock her. But as Clarissa stepped from behind the screen, the words stuck in his throat.

She looked beautiful.

Her hair shone like fire, her eyes sparkled, and her pale skin was delicate rather than unhealthy. Marcus told them that princesses and queens had been dressed in this room, but Wild Boy couldn't imagine any of them looking better than Clarissa.

She shifted in the dress, acting uncomfortable. "What do you think?"

Wild Boy shrugged. "Looks all right."

Marcus limped closer. For a second, all of the pain and tiredness eased from his features, and he smiled. It wasn't just a hint of a smile. It was a big, broad grin, and it warmed up the whole room.

He offered her his arm. "Gideon is waiting with our carriage. Shall we?"

Clarissa glanced at Wild Boy. The two of them had hardly been apart over the past few months. It felt strange to be separated, even for an evening. But they both knew he couldn't come; the reason was reflected in the mirrors all around this room.

Wild Boy wanted to say something – a joke, anything to make her stay a little longer. But it was as if all the words had been sucked out of him. Seeing Clarissa like this, he realized for the first time how easy it would be for her to have another life. A life without him at her side.

He was glad to see her pull on her old boots, shoving her lock picks into one of them.

"I'll steal some posh grub for you," she said.

And then she was gone. The golden sequins on her dress shimmered in the lamplight as Marcus led her away.

Wild Boy stared at the empty corridor where the only two people in his life had just left. He turned and considered his reflection in one of the room's broken mirrors, a shattered vision of scruffy hair and sudden, desperate sadness. He knew right then that if they were ever thrown out of the palace, he would leave Clarissa. She wouldn't want him to, but he would have to, because the only place he could go would be the fairground. And he would never let her go back to that world. He would never let that happen.

This case was his chance to make sure it never did. He was convinced that if he could solve it, they could stay in the palace as long as they wanted. Everything would be fine.

Then – a scream.

Wild Boy had never heard a scream like it; a cry of pure terror that came from everywhere at once, ringing around the mirrored walls. Several Gentlemen charged past the room.

In the corridor, Prendergast had begun to scream and thrash as if those invisible demons had suddenly attacked him. Dr Carew struggled to control him as Prendergast collapsed to the ground and convulsed like a fish plucked from the sea. Black froth bubbled from his mouth, but somehow he continued to scream. A single word rushed along the corridor and swept through Wild Boy like a wind, freezing his bones.

Malphas.

The scream stopped.

Prendergast lay still.

Wild Boy edged closer. "Is he…?"

He didn't need to ask. It was clear from the look on Dr Carew's face that Prendergast was dead. Whatever had infected him had killed him.

Now this was a murder investigation.

· 7 ·

The corpse was not easy to carry.

The moment Prendergast died, Lucien Grant ordered two Gentlemen into action. They were Black Hats – military men – and Wild Boy guessed that they had carried bodies before. But those were normal bodies; limp things thrown over a shoulder. Prendergast's corpse was not limp. It was stiff as firewood, locked in the twisted, frenzied position in which he had died. The neck cords strained, and his hands were rigid and curled like cocks' claws.

Only Prendergast's head hung loose, lolling at the throat, so that his hair hung down and his eyes rolled to the limits of their sockets. Wild Boy tried not to look, but the dead man's gaze followed him as the corpse swayed with the Gentlemen's hurried march.

He tried to rush to the front, but one of the Gentlemen shoved him against the wall. He scrambled up and kept following, resisting the urge to kick the man in the legs. This was supposed to be *his* case. But Lucien had taken control, ordering Dr Carew to follow.

Dr Carew scurried alongside Wild Boy, his flushed face beaded with sweat. He nudged his spectacles up his nose, trying to gather his composure. "Mr Grant, I must protest. This patient was entrusted into my care."

"He is no longer your patient, Dr Carew," Lucien replied. "He is a corpse. The only reason you are here is because you are an expert in rare diseases. I assume that means you are qualified to conduct an autopsy?"

"Autopsy? That is quite out of the question. Any dissection of a body requires paperwork, an ordinance of medical—"

"Dr Carew."

Lucien stopped by an open door. He held his candle high as the Black Hats carried the corpse through, manoeuvering its stiff limbs through the narrow entrance.

"You are new to our organization," he continued. "Otherwise you would know one thing about the Gentlemen: we are not concerned with paperwork. Her Majesty has been threatened. We need to know what happened to this man, and we need to know now."

"Even so, I must protest."

"You have, doctor. Twice. Now get in this room."

Dr Carew shot a panicked look over his shoulder, as if considering an escape. But with Marcus away, Lucien was in charge. Clutching his medical bag, Carew stepped into the room.

Lucien lowered his candle, dazzling Wild Boy with its glare. Wild Boy tried not to react, but couldn't help shrinking from the flame that threatened to singe the hair on his cheek.

"This is my bloomin' case," he said.

"Your case?"

Wild Boy moved closer, letting the flame crackle his hair. "Unless you know something special about it?"

Lucien stepped back. "Not at all. We are all on the same side."

Like bloomin' blazes we are. Wild Boy passed through the door and into a windowless room. The brick walls were black with soot, hooks hung on chains from the ceiling, and the fireplace was almost as large as the caravan that had once been Wild Boy's home. The air was as sharp as pickle vinegar.

A waist-high wooden slab filled half of the room, lacerated with cuts and grooves. A smaller table was laid with a collection of medical instruments that gleamed in the candlelight: surgical knives, hacksaws, weighing scales and a copper microscope. They were spotlessly clean but, judging from the splatter marks Wild Boy spotted on the floor, the tools had been used.

"What is this place?" Dr Carew asked.

"Originally, one of the palace kitchens," Lucien replied. "Now we use it for something else."

The Black Hats dumped Prendergast's corpse on the slab as if it were a sack of potatoes. One of them began to cut away its clothes with the surgical knife, revealing naked, twisted limbs. Prendergast's whole body was black and white. Inky veins streaked across his arms and up his neck, shattering the poor man's face.

Lucien reached over and closed Prendergast's eyes. "Doctor," he said, his voice rumbling around the room. "Tell us what happened to this man."

The force of his order offered no possibility of resistance. Dr Carew sighed and set his medical bag on the table. "We shall begin with the heart."

Prendergast's ribs spread open with a wet crack. Dr Carew cranked the handle on the retractor, stifling a cough as a cloud of brown gas rose from inside the body.

Wild Boy wrapped an arm around his nose. He had seen dead bodies before, and body parts, but never watched one become the other. Sick rose up from his stomach but he swallowed it back down. He needed to stay focused, to search for anything that might help him with this case. Apart from the card with its strange name – *Malphas* – Prendergast's twisted black and white corpse was the only clue he had.

Dr Carew took a surgical knife from the table and snipped something inside Prendergast's chest. A spurt of green goo splattered across his spectacles. He wiped the glasses on his apron and continued his work.

Wild Boy was impressed. Dr Carew had seemed meek in front of Lucien, his gaze always darting over his shoulder in hope of escape. But now the eyes behind the doctor's spectacles were needle sharp, totally focused. He was clearly in his element.

Dr Carew lifted a large, dripping organ from the body and laid it on the weighing scale.

"Well, doctor?"

Lucien stood on the other side of the kitchen slab, his deep breaths rustling his side-whiskers. His hand trembled as he held his candle closer to the corpse. "I trust you have discovered something we can tell the Queen?"

Dr Carew dipped a quill in an inkpot and made a note in a ledger. "That is a perfectly healthy heart," he said. "Perhaps we will learn something from the other organs."

For Wild Boy, the next hour was one long struggle not to throw up. He watched Dr Carew extract a sausage-string of intestines, then slice open Prendergast's stomach and tip its contents into a bucket. Things got even worse when the doctor sawed off the top of the corpse's head like a boiled egg and dissected his slimy brain. That was too much for Wild Boy, who grabbed the bucket and added the contents of his own stomach to Prendergast's.

He rose, wiping his mouth with his sleeve. He expected to see a sneer on Lucien's face, but the Gentleman just stared at the splayed open corpse. Lucien's hands trembled harder as he opened his silver tin and snorted another pinch of snuff. Brown powder stained his nostril and caught in his grey whiskers. He noticed neither. Again, Wild Boy wondered if Lucien's interest in this case went beyond his desire to impress the Queen. Was something else troubling him?

"Anything, doctor?" Lucien asked.

Dr Carew looked for a place to wipe his hands, but his apron was entirely smeared with gore. He held them dripping in the air. "Strange," he said. "I see no indication whatsoever of disease."

"So what done Prendergast in?" Wild Boy asked.

The doctor stared at him, translating the question in his head. "Ah! Cause of death." He prodded part of the corpse's brain with the end of his quill. "Well, from the inflammation of the *nucleus amygdala* in the temporal—"

"In English, doc," Wild Boy said.

"Terror," Dr Carew said.

He nudged his spectacles with a finger, leaving a red smear on his nose. "It seems that Prendergast was affected by something that left him in such a state of terror that, eventually, his body could not handle the strain."

"He was scared … to death?" Wild Boy said.

"It is impressive that he survived so long," Dr Carew continued. "The man's mind must have been strong, able to cope with the fears. A weaker person would have died in seconds. Although that might have been a more desirable fate. This poor man suffered unlike any I have seen."

Lucien snorted another pinch of snuff. He exhaled, filling the kitchen with a rush of stale breath. "Might he have been given a hallucinogenic?" he asked.

"A what?" Wild Boy asked.

"A hallucinogenic," Dr Carew said. "A drug that affects the brain, causing visions that are not real. In this instance, terrifying visions. Prendergast saw his darkest memories. He was trapped in a nightmare."

"He might have ingested or inhaled such a substance," Lucien said.

Dr Carew glanced at Wild Boy. "Swallowed or smelled."

Wild Boy knew what ingested and inhaled meant, but neither made sense. Prendergast had simply opened a parcel sent to the Queen. He hadn't been drugged.

"So there could be a human agency behind this," Lucien muttered.

"Human?" Dr Carew said. "What else might it be?"

Lucien cleared his throat, as if he'd accidentally coughed out the wrong words. "What *can* you tell me, doctor? We fear that whoever did this might have targeted the Queen. That means the killer could *still* be targeting the Queen. Can you formulate a cure?"

Dr Carew leaned over the microscope, studying a sliver of Prendergast's brain. "Perhaps if I knew what he was exposed to I could develop a cure. There are tests I could conduct at the hospital. Consider this sample, for instance."

Lucien set his candle beside the corpse and leaned over the microscope.

Wild Boy hung back, feeling sicker than ever. But it was no longer the corpse that turned his stomach. It was Dr Carew's diagnosis. *Scared to death.*

For the second time that night he felt an urge to run as far away as possible from Prendergast. But, again, he forced himself to stay. He was convinced that Lucien knew something about this case. The man had obviously been waiting for Dr Carew's results. So what would he do next?

Thinking fast, Wild Boy grabbed Lucien's candle and bent the edge of its pewter tray so the wax dribbled over the side. He replaced it on the table just before Lucien turned, grabbed it and marched from the room. The Gentleman didn't notice the wax drips that marked his path.

"Keep me informed of any developments," he ordered.

"Go soak your head," Dr Carew muttered.

Wild Boy looked at him, surprised.

The young doctor shrugged, putting his ink pot and quill back in his bag. "Lucien Grant is a bullying toad," he said. "Now, I must prepare Prendergast's body for transport to the hospital. Would you lend me a hand Mr ... Master... What exactly should I call you?"

He looked up, but Wild Boy was gone.

· 8 ·

Wild Boy's coat snapped behind him as he set off on Lucien's trail. He knew he had to be careful; despite his assignment from the Queen, he wasn't allowed to wander the palace alone. Whenever a Gentleman passed, he ducked into hiding – first sliding beneath a chaise longue, then behind a dusty Ming vase that he nearly knocked over in his rush to remain unseen.

He steadied the vase on its stand, then continued his hunt, seeking out the fresh drops of black wax from among others glistening on the floorboards. He plucked a candle from a mantelpiece as the trail led him through a drawing room with pikes and spears arranged in patterns on the walls, then out to an arched cloister that framed the palace's smallest courtyard. He'd never been here before. Judging from the waist-high brambles that filled the courtyard's small central garden, nor had many others.

He crept around the cloister, through stripes of moonlight and shadow. It wasn't hard to follow Lucien's path anymore, a lonely trail of wax drops that led to an arched door in the corner of the courtyard. Wild Boy's heart thumped from the thrill of the chase, but he wished Clarissa was there. Sneaking about wasn't as much fun without her.

The door opened with a creak that echoed around the darkness beyond. Wild Boy stepped through it, eyes scanning for danger. Shelves rose on every wall, each crammed with leather-bound books and ancient-looking scrolls. Sheets of cobwebs hung like net curtains across the stacks. Cockroaches scurried over spines.

"A library," he whispered.

From the reek of stale breath that lingered in the air, it was obvious that Lucien had just been here. Wild Boy followed another drop of wax, and then another. His frosted breaths hung in the air like ghosts, and his trembling hand caused the candle-light to skitter across the stone-flagged floor. He heard footsteps and stepped back against one of the bookcases.

The steps grew louder, echoing around the cold stone gloom.

And then – *thud*. The library door slammed shut.

Wild Boy released a breath he didn't know he'd

been holding. Lucien was gone, but why had Wild Boy come here in such a hurry? Lowering his candle, he followed the trail to the rear of the library, where multicoloured moonlight streamed through stained glass.

Four wax drops dotted on the floor, marking the spot where Lucien had stopped. It wasn't hard to see which book had interested him: the only one with its dust unsettled. It was halfway up the shelf and bound in pigskin.

Wild Boy moved closer, reading the title on its spine.

He drew a sharp breath.

Encyclopaedia
Demonica

"Demons?" he breathed.

He pulled the book down, setting his candle into its space on the shelf. Slowly, he turned the pages. What he saw made his fingers tighten. The book was full of monsters. Strange, unearthly names flicked past – *Abbadon, Behemoth, Gamigin, Leviathan* – with descriptions and drawings of grotesque creatures. Parts of different animals melted into each other, faces twisted with pain. There were lions with serpent's tails, goats with wings, misshapen toads with claws as long as kitchen knives. Each drawing was surrounded by magical symbols, pentagrams and ancient scripts.

Wild Boy felt sicker and sicker with each page.

He stopped at one that was stained with Lucien's wax. Here was the most terrifying drawing yet: part crow, part man. The beast had ragged black wings, curling talons and tiny blank eyes. Its beak was open, revealing vicious barbed-wire teeth. The creature was screaming.

No, Wild Boy realized with a shudder: it was laughing.

Its name was printed in thick black type.

⚓ MALPHAS ✕

ONE OF THE GRAND Princes of Hell AND Commander of Demons.

He comes sometimes as a crow, sometimes as a man, and sometimes in both forms at once. Destroyer of cities. Bringer of plagues. He makes his enemies witness the blackest memories of all things past.

MALPHAS

Wild Boy read the entry again, his fingers growing so tight around the page that they crinkled the parchment. He didn't believe in demons or anything like that. He'd seen enough horrors in real life. But he remembered Prendergast's face. The terror in his eyes, the invisible horrors that tormented him in those moments before he died…

"No," he said, firmly. "I don't believe in demons."

He tore the page from the book and stuffed it in his pocket. He reached to take the candle from the shelf, but stopped. His detective instincts took over, and he saw something he wasn't looking for. Spiders had spun homes in the space behind the book, but the cobwebs were broken. It didn't make sense; why would Lucien have reached that far back on the shelf?

Rising to tiptoes, Wild Boy slid his arm deeper into the space. A spider scuttled across his hand, tickling his hairs. He felt the back of the shelf, prodded the wood, tapping, testing…

The wooden panel flipped open. There was something hidden behind it.

"Ha," he said, and then bit his lip, fearing he might be heard.

Every hair on Wild Boy's body tingled. He couldn't wait to tell Clarissa he'd found a clue without her. She'd be *furious*.

Eagerly, he slid the item from the secret compartment. It was a small ebony box, similar to the one the killer had sent to the Queen. He plucked off the lid and groaned. Whatever had been in there was gone. All that remained was an outline in dust, about the size of a plum, where an object had sat.

But it was still a clue. Whatever had once been in the box, Wild Boy was certain it was important to the case. He and Clarissa would find a way to get it after she got back from Lady Bentick's dinner.

Already grinning at the prospect, Wild Boy slid the box back. He pushed the hatch shut. It closed with a hollow *thud*.

Wild Boy turned to leave, but stopped.

That *thud*.

He had heard it before.

It was the sound he'd thought was the library door closing, the *thud* he thought was Lucien leaving.

A grey hand grabbed his arm. It threw Wild Boy so hard against the shelf that books crashed down on his head.

Lucien glared at him. His arms trembled and his voice boomed like musket fire. "What are you doing here, boy? What did you see?" He leaned closer, blasting Wild Boy with stale breath. "This isn't one of your detective games! This is beyond anything you can possibly comprehend."

He pushed Wild Boy harder, causing more books to fall. Wild Boy didn't fight. He wasn't bothered about the beating; he'd taken worse, and from nastier people. What worried him then – what scared him to his bones – was the look in Lucien's eyes.

This man had led armies into battle. And yet something about this case terrified Lucien Grant. And that terrified Wild Boy too. He wanted to get away from him. Far away.

Just as Lucien opened his mouth to shout, Wild Boy hocked up a ball of spit and fired it between the Gentleman's lips. Shock caused Lucien to relax his grip, freeing vital inches for Wild Boy to swing a knee at his groin.

Lucien's eyes widened and he made a sound like a bagpipe.

Twisting free, Wild Boy kicked him again between the legs, and then again, harder. He turned and pelted between stacks of shelves.

Every instinct urged him to keep running, but he forced himself to stop in the library doorway. Whatever Lucien took from that box could be his biggest clue yet. He had to find out what it was, but he could think of only one way. One very painful way.

Lucien stumbled closer, red-eyed and roaring. "Bloody boy!"

Wild Boy clenched his fists, ready for the impact. "Come on, old man!" he yelled. "Hit me as hard as you can."

The Gentleman slammed into him like a locomotive, and they tumbled together back into the cloister. The blow knocked the breath from Wild Boy's body, but he managed to turn as he fell, so that

Lucien's head cracked against the stone ground.

Blood seeped from a cut on Lucien's forehead, forming crimson crystals in the snow. His eyes rolled as he struggled to stay concious.

Retching for breath, Wild Boy crawled closer. He rummaged through Lucien's coat, searching for the object from the box. All he found was Lucien's snuff tin. He dropped it and was about to search again, when Lucien's hand shot up and grabbed his arm.

Wild Boy tried to pull away, but the grip on his wrist was like a vice. When Lucien spoke again he didn't sound angry. His voice was urgent, imploring – desperate, even.

"Wait…" he groaned. "Marcus…"

Wild Boy stopped tugging his arm. Did he say *Marcus*?

"God's sake…" Lucien said. "Marcus … in danger…"

The fire fizzled out inside him and he slumped back to the ground. Wild Boy held onto Lucien's hand, shaking it and then shaking his whole body.

"Oi! Oi, wake up. What did you say about Marcus? What danger?"

"Hey. Hey, you!"

A Black Hat marched from the drawing room. He saw Wild Boy crouched over Lucien, saw the blood in the snow. His face creased in horror. "Alarm!" he hollered. "Sound the alarm!"

Wild Boy turned to flee back into the library,

but he knew he'd be trapped. Instead, he dived over the cloister wall and into the brambles that filled the courtyard garden. Thorns tore at his hair and scratched his face as he wriggled through the thicket. He heard a bell clang inside the palace – the Gentlemen's alarm. The cloister filled with bobbing lights, frightened questions and frantic commands.

"What happened?"

"It's Wild Boy. He attacked Lucien."

"He's still here somewhere, in the brambles."

"Surround the garden. Find him."

The Gentlemen were too wary of the thorns to come after him. Instead, they grabbed antique lances from the drawing room wall, and guarded the garden on all sides. They began to jab the weapons into the thick bushes.

"Give up, boy!" one of the men called. "You can't stay in there forever."

Snow sprinkled from the brambles, soaking the hair on Wild Boy's face. His heart was going berserk with fear; for himself, and for Marcus. He'd seen Lucien's eyes, heard the urgency in his voice. Marcus *was* in trouble, which meant Clarissa might be too.

He had to get to them. Somehow he *had* to.

Tearing his coat from the thorns, he crawled to the edge of the brambles. He was yards from the drawing room door, but one of the Gentlemen stalked closer. The man rammed his spear into the brambles.

The blade shot past Wild Boy's face, so close it sliced the hair on his cheek and dug into the ground.

The Gentleman yanked the weapon from the bush. "Anyone see him?" he said. "He's here somewhere."

Wild Boy burst from the brambles. He barged into the man, knocking him over, and charged for the door.

"There!" one of the other men cried. "He's there."

Wild Boy darted back into the palace, through the Drawing Room and along a hallway. Several Gentlemen charged towards him, rushing to investigate the alarm. Wild Boy screamed at them, waving his arms.

"Outside! A monster! It's eating your pals."

The men ran faster, right past him. Wild Boy kept going, past the Tapestry Room and down corridors, until he reached the Guard Chamber that led to the entrance courtyard and out of the palace.

He had to get to Marcus and Clarissa.

Through a window, he saw Dr Carew laying Prendergast's corpse in a cart and covering it with a tarpaulin. Wild Boy turned, considering the antique rifles and flintlock pistols hanging in diamond patterns on the Guard Chamber wall.

He made a decision.

• 9 •

"**W**e have spoken before about controlling your emotions."

Marcus's fingers locked tighter over the top of his cane. The carriage jolted as it rode over cracks in the road, but somehow the Gentleman remained still, not one silver hair slipping out of place. "You must learn to think less with your fists and more with your head."

"Can't think with nothing at the moment," Clarissa replied. She curled up more tightly on the seat, exaggerating a shiver. "Brain's frozen solid."

Marcus laid his coat over her, and she sank beneath its thick fur trim.

"Anyway," she said. "All that stuff at the palace was Wild Boy's fault."

She bit her lip, fighting a smile. Although she had lived on the same fairground as Wild Boy for three years, she'd only really known him for four months. Even so, she'd never felt closer to anyone else. It was a strange relationship. She would stand beside Wild Boy in any fight – through anything – and yet they delighted in landing each other in trouble. She would never snitch on him for something he'd actually *done*, but she was quite happy to make up stories about things he hadn't.

"It was all Wild Boy," she said. "In fact, I think I saw him steal a—"

"Enough, Clarissa. You both need to learn restraint."

Clarissa tensed. She didn't take well to being scolded, even by Marcus. She sank deeper beneath the coat, hiding the flush she could feel spreading across her cheeks. "You ain't my father," she muttered.

The carriage jolted again, and a strand of hair slipped over Marcus's golden eye. He brushed it back with a gloved finger. "You should not dwell on what happened with your father or your mother."

"You don't know nothing."

Clarissa felt bad for snapping. The fact was, Marcus knew everything about her past. That was his business. But just knowing about things was different from living through them. He hadn't been there when her father ran off with one of the freak show performers, and he hadn't watched it drive her mother crazy, turning her into "Mad Mary Everett", that bitter witch. He wasn't chased by her hunting dogs. He had no idea how that felt.

Clarissa curled up even smaller on the seat. She couldn't remember the mother she once loved. All she could picture were those raging eyes. She could still hear that hate-filled cry when her mother discovered her helping Wild Boy escape. "*Get them. Get both of them.*"

"That woman's dead to me," she said.

Eager to change the subject, she threw back the coat and grinned at Marcus. "You and Wild Boy are much more fun anyhow, even though Wild Boy's a thickhead."

Marcus opened his mouth to disapprove, but she cut him off. "He ain't as clever as you think, you know. I mean, he is, but he ain't. He's no cleverer than I'm good at circus skills, is he?"

She prodded her guardian's knee, seeking a response. The smallest of smiles cracked Marcus's stony face, but it was enough.

"You are equally talented," he conceded. "That is why you *both* must learn to master your emotions. Your past is your past. That is where it should remain. If not, it will control you."

Was it that easy for Marcus? Clarissa wondered. What did she really know about her guardian's past? Even Wild Boy hadn't been able to detect much. Eventually they'd given up trying to find out. They were both just happy he was on their side.

"I cannot protect you for ever," Marcus said.

"Stop saying that," Clarissa replied. "Course you can. Anyhow, once we crack this case for the Queen, you won't need to. She'll probably make us lords."

"That is utter nonsense. But you are correct in thinking that solving this case would prove your value to the Gentlemen. That is why we are visiting Lady Bentick this evening."

Clarissa sat up. "Eh? I thought this was some fancy dinner to teach me about society."

The carriage slowed. With the end of his cane, Marcus parted the curtain to look outside. "Clarissa, I have no desire to teach you about society. Certainly a few manners would do you no harm, but on the whole, society is a dreary place for which you are far too interesting."

"You mean we're on the case right now?"

"We are following a lead."

"Wild Boy didn't say nothing about no lead."

"It is not something of which he is aware. I wish it to remain that way until I have more information. There is a possible…" He paused, choosing his words carefully. "A possible connection between the Queen's story and Lady Bentick. It is a delicate matter that requires careful handling. I arranged this dinner to make enquiries. Wild Boy would have insisted on coming, and we both know that he could not."

"He'd probably have jumped onto the back of this carriage if he knew."

"Precisely."

She laughed at the idea, but talking about Wild Boy was even more painful than Marcus's probing about her past. This was the first time they'd been apart, even for a few hours. She had considered staying with him, but hadn't wanted to let Marcus down. And, well, it felt nice to wear a posh dress, even though she'd never admit it.

Now she didn't regret coming – not one bit. No way she was keeping this secret. Wild Boy would be *so* annoyed when he found out she'd investigated the case. She'd tell him the moment she next saw him, and she couldn't wait.

The carriage stopped. The door swung open with a rush of cold air. Gideon looked inside, beady eyes peering from beneath a heap of snow-covered capes and coats. He bowed to one side, making it clear the greeting was only for Marcus. "We're here, sir."

They had arrived in a square of townhouses set around a private, railed-off garden. Most of the buildings looked the same – dark and stern, with polished marble steps, and stone columns guarding doors. Beyond tall windows, Clarissa glimpsed servants carrying silver trays and crystal decanters through hazes of cigar smoke.

One house was different. Scalloped arches at the front were carved with intricate floral arabesques, and lit by hanging brass lamps. The larger, central arch framed a brass-studded oak door with ivory elephants on either side.

"Lady Bentick's house," Gideon said.

A servant stepped from the door, dressed in a saffron turban and white tunic brocaded with gold. He looked like the Indian magicians Clarissa had seen around fairgrounds, but she didn't need Wild Boy's detective skills to tell her that the man wasn't really Indian. He had white skin and seemed ill at ease with the turban, raising a hand to hold it in place as he dipped into a low bow.

"Mr Bishop," he said. He nodded at Clarissa. "Fräulein Bishop. Her Ladyship is expecting you."

Clarissa looked at Marcus. "Fräulein Bishop?"

"This evening," he replied in a whisper, "you are my niece from Bavaria."

"Bavaria?"

"So you do not have to talk. Lady Bentick has an old fashioned habit of being offended by foul-mouthed children. Remain silent and try not to steal anything while I make the necessary enquiries regarding our case."

They were led into an entrance hall that was even more extravagant than the front of the house. Clarissa wondered if Lady Bentick had got a deal on white marble. Almost everything was carved from it. Marble arches led to corridors on either side, and a sweeping staircase rose from the centre, with a balustrade of carved arabesques. The floor was chequered marble – black and white squares all over – and stone thrones stood on either side of the door.

Stuffed peacocks watched from recesses around the hall, with fanned tails and glaring marble eyes. Bronze lamps burned coconut oil, giving the air a sickly sweet smell that made Clarissa gag.

"Strange place," she said. She tried to whisper, but it came out too loud and echoed around the bare walls.

The turbaned servant scowled at her as he sank into another bow. "Her ladyship will be with you momentarily," he said.

The man retreated down one of the corridors. Clarissa watched as he issued orders to two other servants in Indian costume.

"What's with the Indian stuff?" she asked.

"Lady Bentick and her husband lived there," Marcus said. "They became obsessed with the place."

"Where's her husband?"

"Highgate Cemetery."

"My darlings!"

Lady Bentick came down the stairs, moving slowly to exaggerate the drama of her entrance. The trail of her muslin gown was so long that it still had several steps to descend as she tottered towards them across the chessboard floor. She held out her arms to show off the fat gemstones set in her rings.

"Oh, my darlings," she repeated.

Earlier that evening, when Clarissa had met the Queen, she'd been surprised by how modestly the sovereign was dressed. *This* was what she expected.

Lady Bentick was drenched with jewels – necklaces, earrings, bracelets – as if the contents of a treasure chest had been tipped over her. Her face was hidden by a layer of make up that gave her the appearance of a porcelain doll, and a heap of grey curls balanced precariously on her head.

Marcus took Lady Bentick's hand and dipped his head to kiss her rings. Clarissa noticed him hesitate, briefly, as if to study her knuckles. She sensed that Wild Boy might have made something of that moment, but she couldn't think what.

Again she felt that she should have stayed with him at the palace. She couldn't imagine this posh old lady having anything interesting to say. But Lady Bentick was obviously stinking rich, so at least the grub would be good. Clarissa decided she'd steal some for Wild Boy and then scoff it in front of his face. That would *really* annoy him.

The turbaned servant gestured along the corridor with the sweep of a hand. "Dinner is served."

"Ah! Wonderful," Lady Bentick declared, as if the idea of dinner was a complete surprise. Marcus accepted her arm and escorted her towards the dining room.

"So are we on a case or not?" Clarissa whispered.

Her guardian glanced back at her. His golden eye gleamed and a slight smile curled the corner of his lips. The case was definitely on.

· 10 ·

"**M**ove a muscle and I'll blow your brains out!"
Wild Boy's cry rang around the palace courtyard, frightening crows from the gatehouse turrets.
He aimed a pistol at Dr Carew's head, praying the
Gentleman didn't notice the weapon tremble in his
hands. The antique flintlock was heavier than he'd
expected when he snatched it from the Guard Chamber wall, and certainly not loaded. But Dr Carew
was one of the Gentlemen's Grey Hats, a scientist,
not a soldier. Hopefully he wouldn't realize he was
being threatened with an ornament.

Dr Carew looked down from the seat of his cart.
His face flashed from panic to confusion, then back
to panic as the carthorse whinnied and stamped.

"What is the meaning of this?" he demanded.

Wild Boy didn't have time to explain about
Lucien's warning, and his fear that Marcus and

Clarissa were in danger. He just had to get to them, and fast. The gatehouse doors were open and he could see out to the street. It was past midnight and below freezing, but the city was still busy. Hackney cabs sprayed up slushy brown snow, night soil men shoveled steaming dung into their carts, and ladies of the night picked their way through the ice to clients who stumbled from supper clubs, cigar shops and gambling dens. If Wild Boy tried to get to Lady Bentick's house on foot, he – the Wild Boy of London – would be mobbed before he made ten steps.

"This is a hold-up, doc," he said. "I need that cart, which means you need to get off. Geddit?"

Dr Carew didn't get it at all. His face was deathly pale. A bead of sweat slid over his spectacle lens. "You wish to steal this cart?" he said. "There is nothing of value in it, just Prendergast's corpse."

Inside the palace, the Gentlemen's shouts grew louder.

"I ain't asking again," Wild Boy said. "You're new around here, doc, so maybe you ain't heard about me. I'm the Wild Boy of London, a cold-blooded killer. You gonna get down or am I gonna shoot you down?"

As he spoke, his eyes scoured the doctor for clues he could use against him, some form of blackmail to force him to help. But he saw nothing. Dr Carew did not drink or smoke, never gambled, and certainly did not take opium. All Wild Boy saw was the doctor's same curious reaction, that glance over his shoulder, as if searching for a place to flee.

When Dr Carew turned back, the fear was gone from his eyes. It was replaced by an intense, almost wolf-like stare.

"I know you are not a killer," he said. "Marcus said he trusts you, and I trust him. So tell me this: whatever you are doing, is it for a good reason?"

Wild Boy wanted to punch himself. He'd been so desperate to save Marcus, he'd not thought of appealing to the Gentlemen's loyalty to him.

"Marcus is in trouble," he said. "And Clarissa an' all. I gotta get to Lady Bentick's house in Berkeley Square."

"Then get in the cart. And stop pointing that ridiculous antique pistol at me."

Dropping the gun, Wild Boy scrambled over the side of the cart and under the tarpaulin. Fearing the Gentlemen might search for him, he then wriggled under the corpse. Prendergast's rigid fingers clawed at his face. The stitches where the body had been sealed had burst open. Goo seeped from inside and onto Wild Boy's coat.

Wild Boy forced himself to lie still as he listened to the Gentlemen's footsteps rush closer. They were yards away, searching the courtyard. He held his breath, scared that the movement of the tarpaulin might give him away.

"Dr Carew!" one of the men shouted. "Have you seen the boy?"

"Yes," Dr Carew answered. "Yes, I have."

The footsteps marched closer.

Wild Boy braced himself. He'd punch the man in the nose and make a run for the gates.

"He ran past," Dr Carew continued. "Into the West Guard Chamber room."

The footsteps charged away.

Wild Boy lay back and breathed again. The cart shunted forward, riding through the gateway and onto the street.

Prendergast's corpse pressed harder against his chest. The thick goo slid from its chest and stuck in the hair on Wild Boy's cheeks. Worse was the smell, the reek of decomposing flesh. Wild Boy gagged each time he gulped for air.

A sliver of lamplight shone through the tarpaulin, illuminating Prendergast's twisted mouth and grey, staring eyes. Wild Boy tried not to picture Clarissa and Marcus that way. Was that what Lucien had meant? Was whoever killed Prendergast after Marcus too?

They turned onto another street. It was quieter, darker.

"We are here," Dr Carew said.

Wild Boy dared a look from under the sheet. This was a swanky part of the city. All the townhouses around the square looked the same, with crystal lanterns twinkling in tall windows. One house, though, was different. It looked more like an Indian palace, with ribbed marble arches, hanging brass lights and stone elephants by the door.

"Bentick House," Dr Carew said.

Wild Boy spotted Marcus's coach parked outside, but where was Gideon?

"Nothing seems amiss," Dr Carew said.

"I gotta check."

"You'll forgive me, but I am not sure it is wise for you of all people to knock on a stranger's door at this hour. Wait here and I shall investigate."

Dr Carew climbed from his seat and neatened his suit. He glanced at Wild Boy, and then at his bag beside the cart seat, with his notebook and medical equipment. He grabbed the bag, shrugged. "Marcus said you were not a killer. He didn't deny that you were a thief."

Clutching the bag, he stepped up to the house and peered through the windows. Light from inside glinted off his spectacles. "All quite normal," he said. "I suggest we—"

He stepped back, staring into an alley that ran down the side of the house. "That's strange."

"What?"

"I think I saw someone."

The doctor stepped into the alley and was swallowed by the darkness.

This is stupid. Wild Boy had to make sure that Clarissa and Marcus were safe. He leaped from the cart, ran to the door and yanked the chain. He pulled again, banged a fist against the door. Why was no one answering?

Something *was* wrong.

He rushed to the nearest window and climbed onto the railing that guarded the front of the house.

The light in the window went out.

Wild Boy jumped down, staring in disbelief as one by one the lamps in the house were extinguished. Darkness spread from window to window.

Something was *definitely* wrong.

He ran to the entrance and tore one of the hanging lanterns from its bracket. He raced back to the window and hurled the light at the glass. The pane shattered, but there was no movement inside.

"Hello?" Wild Boy yelled.

No reply.

He scrambled over the rail and jumped the gap to the ledge. He tried to edge through the broken glass, but his coat snagged on a shard. Pulling it free, he tumbled inside and landed with a curse on a cold marble floor. He rose, looking down the dark corridor that led along the width of the house.

"Clarissa?" he called.

The only reply was a howl of wind through the broken window. But there was a light now, flickering dimly at the end of the corridor. Wild Boy moved closer, his heart beating harder with each step.

The corridor led to an extravagant entrance hall with a floor like a giant chessboard. Stuffed peacocks stared from niches, and a single brass lamp glimmered in the corner. A servant in an orange turban stood by it, leaning into the wall.

"Hey," Wild Boy said. "What's going on?"

The servant didn't reply. Didn't even move.

Wild Boy grabbed the man's shoulder. The servant slid down the wall and slumped to the floor, rolling onto his back. His face was like Prendergast's – chalk-white with inky black veins streaking up his forehead and under the fold of his turban. His eyes were wide and full of terror.

He was dead.

Wild Boy staggered back, wrapping an arm around his mouth to stifle a scream.

He bashed into someone else, whirled around in fright.

It was another dead servant. The man's tunic had been taken off, revealing black veins on his arms and hands. A third servant lay beyond him, in the entrance to another corridor, convulsing on the black and white squares.

Wild Boy rushed to him and sank to his knees. He tried to control the man, struggling to pin down his thrashing limbs. "What's happening to you?" he gasped. "I don't know what to do. I don't know how to stop it."

The servant's hands rose to protect his face, as if he were being clawed by a tiger. His eyes stared into the darkness, at nothing and everything.

"No!" he screamed. *"No, not that! Not again!"*

Wild Boy had never heard a cry like it, felt the terror of whatever horrors tormented the man's mind. He slid back, scared that whatever had caused it might get him as well.

The screams stopped.

The man lay still.

The house was silent.

Then, a creak.

Wild Boy stepped back against one of the corridor doors, hidden by its marble frame.

Another creak. Someone was coming this way.

Wild Boy sprang from the doorway, swinging a fist. But he was too slow. A hand grasped his arm and twisted it behind his back.

"Hey," hissed a familiar voice.

A freckled face glared at him from the gloom. "What are you doing here?" Clarissa said. "Why weren't you in the drawing room?"

Wild Boy stared at her, his mind flooding with conflicting emotions – relief that she was safe, and confusion at what she'd just said. Relief won and he grabbed her in a tight hug.

She shoved him away. "What's wrong with you? I waited for you in the drawing room, like your note said. Bet I missed dessert an' all. If it was anything with custard, I'll kill you."

"Clarissa," Wild Boy said. "What are you talking about? What note?"

"The note the servant slipped me. Said to meet you in the…"

Her mouth stayed open but no more words came out as she finally saw the corpses.

"Clarissa," Wild Boy said, "where's Marcus?"

"Wild Boy … what's happening?"

"Where is he, Clarissa?"

"This way!"

They ran to a door at the end of the corridor. Clarissa rattled the handle. "Why's it locked? It wasn't locked before."

She grabbed her picks from her boot and began to work on the door.

A wisp of black smoke floated through a gap around the frame. It curled like an eel, twisted up to the ceiling, thinned, disappeared. As Wild Boy watched it, a knot in his stomach pulled so tight that he could barely breathe. Right then he didn't want to go inside that room. Because he knew what he would see…

· 11 ·

It was like a vision from a nightmare.

Wild Boy was so horrified that at first all he could do was stare. Candles flickered on a long dining table, illuminating the faces of two figures sat at the end. One was an old lady with rings on most of her fingers and a string of pearls around her neck. Her skin was as white as the china plates, but shattered with black veins. The dark lines shot down her arms too, and over her hands, one of which still gripped the table, even though the lady – Lady Bentick – was clearly dead.

Next to her, at the side of the table, was…

"Marcus!" Clarissa cried.

Black veins throbbed across his face. His hands were raised, ripping silver clumps of hair from his scalp. Muscles twitched and tugged in his cheek. His golden eyeball had slipped from his face and fallen to the floor. Candlelight glistened in the empty socket.

Rushing to him, Clarissa tugged his hands from his hair and took them in her own. Marcus's fingers gripped hers so hard that one of her knuckles cracked, but she let him hold on.

Tears slid down Clarissa's cheeks. "Wild Boy? We can help him, can't we? We have to help him."

Wild Boy's mind was flooding with panic, and his legs suddenly felt so weak that he gripped one of the chairs for support. He stepped over another victim – a servant with his face buried in the rug – and crouched beside Marcus.

Drool slid from Marcus's mouth and dripped to the tablecloth. His single eye danced with madness.

Clarissa wiped the spit from his lips. "Marcus?" she said. "Can you hear me? Me and Wild Boy are gonna fix you. We're gonna fix you right up. Ain't that so, Wild Boy?"

Wild Boy remembered what Dr Carew said at the palace. Prendergast had survived for so long in that state because his mind was strong, able to fight the horrors it saw. Marcus was fighting them too, but for how long?

No, there had to be something they could do. What had Marcus taught them the previous night? *Control your emotions. Concentrate. Think.*

Dr Carew had said that if they found out what caused this, he could make a cure. Whoever had poisoned Prendergast – whoever killed him – had also been here. He'd slipped Clarissa a note. There had to be some clues to help catch him.

Think!

Wild Boy stepped over to the French windows at the back of the dining room and looked into the moonlit night. In the garden, statues of Indian gods glistened with ice, and peacock-shaped holly bushes shivered in white blankets. Beyond rose the green and white wall of a hedgerow maze. The snow was thick and undisturbed, with no trace of footprints. Judging from the seal of ice around the frame, these windows hadn't been opened in days. No one had entered or left that way. It didn't make sense. That was the only other exit.

Think. Think!

His breathing slowed. Despite his panic and heartache, Wild Boy felt the thrill he needed to feel as instinct kicked in and his senses began to work.

He moved around the table, his eyes roving among candlesticks, crystal glasses and plates of lamb chops. Marcus and Lady Bentick must have been talking after Clarissa left the room; neither had touched their drinks or eaten anything.

Wild Boy stopped beside Lady Bentick, his eyes drawn to her hands. It seemed strange that only one hand gripped the table. The other was curled and stiff, as if it had been torn from its grip. A small scratch broke the skin on one of her knuckles.

"A ring," Wild Boy realized. "The killer took only one of Lady Bentick's rings."

But this wasn't just theft, or her pearls would be gone too. This was a very *particular* theft.

Wild Boy grabbed a candle from the table and turned to the wall above the fireplace. An oil painting showed Lady Bentick and her husband seated in an Indian palace, surrounded by turbaned servants. Lord Bentick wore a ceremonial robe and a chestful of medals. The Lady wore even more jewels – necklaces, earrings, bracelets.

He raised the candle higher. Despite all her jewellery, Lady Bentick wore just one ring, as if to draw attention to its brilliance. It was set with a single, very large gemstone.

"A black diamond," Wild Boy said.

The killer had taken one of those rare stones from Queen Victoria, and now from Lady Bentick. It was a link between the crimes. But he sensed something else here, a clue he'd not yet seen.

"We have to get Marcus to the palace," Clarissa said.

Wild Boy stepped over the dead servant, returning to Marcus. Clarissa didn't know about his fight with Lucien. "We ain't welcome at the palace no more," he said.

"What? Then what are we going to do?"

"We gotta get the killer, find out how he's done this. Dr Carew said if he knew what caused it, he could make a cure."

He could hear the desperation in his voice. But they had a clue now, a link between the crimes. Black diamonds. "Dr Carew's around here somewhere," he said, "and Gideon too. They'll get Marcus some place safe."

They each put an arm around his shoulder and lifted him from the seat. Marcus was over six feet tall, but somehow they found the strength. Their guardian's feet dragged along the floor as they pulled him from the dining room and along the corridor, weaving around the dead servants. Exhausted from the effort, they sat him on one of the marble thrones.

Clarissa reached to open the door, but Wild Boy held it shut.

"Wait," he said.

He'd just seen something important. He turned, looking back down the corridor. His lips cracked open and a small gasp came out.

"That servant," he said.

One of the servants in the corridor was missing his tunic. Wild Boy had noticed before, but had been too horrified by the man's appearance to see the clue. It didn't make sense; no servant would remove his coat in the middle of service. Someone had taken it from him after he died.

The killer. But why?

The answer struck Wild Boy like a whip crack. He charged back along the corridor, crying out. "He's still there. The killer's still in the dining room!"

He heard glass smash. Cold air rushed at the hair on his face. He reached the dining room in time to see the candles go out as wind swept through the shattered French windows.

He stepped inside, trembling all over with anger.

A white tunic lay on the floor, but no servant. The man who had been there, face down, was gone. He had hidden right next to them, listened to their every word.

Clarissa rushed in. She saw the tunic and immediately understood. She shoved Wild Boy in the chest. "How could you not see?"

Instinct urged Wild Boy to retaliate. But the real fight wasn't yet lost. The killer couldn't be far away. He stepped through the broken windows and onto the patio, scanning the snow for prints.

The moon emerged from behind the clouds. The peacock bushes threw long shadows across the silver snow. A crow settled on the hedgerow wall of the maze and cawed loudly into the night.

A hunched figure darted from the side of the house.

"There!" Clarissa said.

Barging past Wild Boy, she leaped the patio steps, landed in a roll and charged towards the maze after the killer.

~❧ ·12· ☙~

Wild Boy raced after Clarissa, ignoring the sting of the snow against his bare feet. He jumped the patio steps and dodged between sculpted bushes. Freezing wind whipped his eyes, watering his vision. He slipped over, came up swearing.

Ahead, the killer moved across the snow – a dark, hunched figure. He seemed to crouch as he ran, hiding his shape. Wild Boy glimpsed the flap of a coat or cloak. Then the killer was gone, disappearing through the entrance to the hedgerow maze.

"Hurry!" Clarissa yelled.

Wild Boy kept moving, sinking into the snow up to his knees. The green and white maze wall rose over him, twice his height. Icicles hung from a wrought iron arch that framed its entrance, gleaming like the teeth of a monster. That entrance was the only way in or out.

"Wild Boy?" Clarissa's cry grew fainter as she ran deeper into the labyrinth. "I can't find him."

Wild Boy looked back, praying that Dr Carew or Gideon would come to help. Where were they? He knew he should stay here and trap the killer in the maze. But he couldn't just stand here, not while Clarissa was in there with him.

He ran into the maze.

The high hedge walls blocked the moonlight, but he could just make out footprints in the snow; the killer's marks trampled by Clarissa. He tried to climb one of the walls to see across the maze, but he couldn't get a foothold in the thicket and thumped back to the snow.

"Clarissa?" he called.

"Wild Boy? Where is he?"

She sounded closer at first, then further away.

Wild Boy ran along twisting paths, following the broken tracks. Wind rustled the moon-slivered hedges, and shadows shifted along the ground. Something moved behind him. He whirled around, but all he saw was a flurry of snow falling from one of the walls.

He kept going, taking one bewildering turn after another. The gaps between the hedges grew narrower, the maze walls closing in. The only sound was the wind moaning along the path.

A scream.

"Clarissa!" Wild Boy yelled.

She was just yards away but they were separated by a hedge. He ran at it, tearing at branches to force his way through. He heard her cry out again, thought he saw someone run past on the other side. He pushed harder, until he tumbled out onto the path.

In the moonlight he saw three shades of red: rusty hair, bright silk dress and crimson blood spreading across the snow.

"Clarissa!"

His cry rang around the maze as he rushed to her. Her breaths came out in slow, frozen clouds. Her hair was wet and sticky with blood.

"He hit me …" she groaned "… from behind."

Wild Boy tugged off his coat and slid it under her head. He didn't bother telling her he'd get help; Clarissa was the toughest person he knew. And now there was only one set of footprints to follow.

He looked at her and saw it in her eyes. *Get him.*

And then he was running again, the wind rushing at the hair on his chest. His eyes scanned the ground, fixed on the killer's trail. He turned, turned again, and came out in a clearing in the centre of the maze.

A thin mist filled the heart of the labyrinth, but it was lighter here, where the moon shed its rays. Ice glinted on a small pagoda in the middle of the clearing. A crow sat beneath its onion dome, watching Wild Boy, not moving.

The snow was thicker here too. The killer's tracks

were knee-deep sinkholes leading towards the pagoda. But halfway, they stopped.

Wild Boy turned, confused. The maze's walls were too far for the killer to have jumped. So how could the prints just stop?

He crouched, examining them. They were different from others he'd followed. Those had sloped forwards, shaped by the killer's movement. But these marks leaned backwards too. That made no sense, unless the killer had stopped and retraced his steps.

At that moment Wild Boy knew two things: that he had walked into a trap and that the killer stood right behind him.

He tried to move but something crashed against the back of his skull and he stumbled to his knees. A crimson cloud drifted over his shoulder. A mist of his own blood, freezing, floating.

A boot kicked Wild Boy forward. It pressed on his head, forcing his face deeper into the snow. He couldn't breathe.

A hand gripped his hair and yanked him up. Gasping a lungful of air, Wild Boy reached for the edge of the pagoda, hoping to pull himself away. The boot kicked his arm so hard that the force flipped him over. Agony roared up his shoulder and out of his mouth.

Still the crow did not move.

A long shadow fell over Wild Boy. He tried to see who was there, but his vision was blurred by pain and wet hair.

The killer's voice was muffled, as if he was covering his mouth. "You disappoint me, Wild Boy. I thought you were a brilliant mind."

Disappointed him? Well at least that was something…

No – don't give in. He'd never given in, no matter how bad the beatings got. He wasn't about to start now. He couldn't fight, but maybe he could keep the killer talking long enough for Gideon or Dr Carew to get here.

"Who are you?" he groaned.

"You know that."

"Know who you *think* you are. Some ugly demon."

"*The* demon. Malphas, the Prince of Hell. Destroyer of Cities. But no, that is not me. I am merely his Servant."

"Don't … don't believe in demons."

The killer laughed, a sound like an Alsatian barking. "Ask Marcus. Now he has seen the power of Malphas. Imagine the horrors that torment his mind. Surely he has witnessed more evil than a hundred men. *Caused* more evil, in the name of his Gentlemen." The killer spat the word like it was poison. "For that he deserved to die."

"He ain't dead."

"Not yet, perhaps. But it is only a matter of time until his heart fails and the terror claims his life too."

With a boot, the killer rolled Wild Boy onto his front. "And you? What will you see when you taste my terror, freak? Tell me, what miseries has someone like you experienced?"

Talk to him. Get him close to see his face.

"Can't hear you… "

"Then I suggest you listen harder, for this is the important part. You know what I seek?"

"Black diamonds. Why?"

"You will know soon enough. For now, your only concern is the *next* black diamond. It is in a place to which I am unable to gain access. A dangerous place. With your combined skills, however, you and Miss Everett stand a greater chance of success. You shall acquire it for me."

"I'll get it. I'll shove it up your—"

"I am running out of patience."

Yeah, and out of time. Wild Boy heard a shout, someone coming. He had to keep the killer talking. He was about to speak, but then something made him shut up.

"I have a cure that could save Marcus," the killer said. "Do you believe me?"

Wild Boy did, instantly. It wasn't just the tone of the killer's voice – cold and deadly serious. He simply understood what the killer knew he would. This man had been in the dining room after Clarissa left. But the poison, whatever it was, hadn't affected him.

He had a cure.

"Give it to me and I won't come after you," Wild Boy said. "I swear, no one will. I'll send the

Gentlemen in the wrong direction with every clue. I ain't one of them, and I ain't no copper neither. You give me a cure for Marcus and you and I got no quarrel."

Another barked laugh. "Your guardian would be disappointed to hear you say that."

He was right, but Wild Boy didn't care. He looked out for his friends, no matter what. He was about to say so, but the killer spoke again.

"If you bring me the next black diamond, I will give you the cure."

"I don't believe you."

"But you will try anyway. It is the only hope, and not just for Marcus. Without him you have nothing. How long would a freak like you last on the streets? How long would Clarissa remain by your side? Finding that diamond is *your* only hope."

How did this man know so much about him? It didn't matter. All that mattered was that he was right. "Where?" Wild Boy asked. "Where is it, the diamond?"

The killer leaned closer, blocking the moonlight. With one hand he pressed Wild Boy harder into the ground. With the other he wrote in the snow. He lifted Wild Boy a few inches to see the word.

OBERSTEIN

Wild Boy burned it into his mind. It meant nothing to him, and yet it meant everything. "I'll do it," he gasped. "I'll get the next black diamond."

The killer released him, and Wild Boy slumped back to the ground.

"Then we will speak again," he said.

PART II

Secrets
WITHIN
Secrets

· 13 ·

Wild Boy opened his eyes.

He lay on a damp mattress, looking up at a ceiling that seemed ready to collapse at any moment. Much of it *had* collapsed. Chunks of plaster had fallen to reveal bug-eaten timbers and broken tiles. Snow had melted through from the roof, and needle-thin icicles dangled over Wild Boy's head.

The room reeked of gin and damp and rotting wood. Wind rushed through a broken window, rattling the last shards of glass that clung stubbornly to the frame. Thin walls shook from a commotion next door. Wild Boy heard cheering and stamping, and the slap of a fist against a face. It sounded like a boxing match.

"Where am I?" he groaned.

His coat was wet from the snow in Lady Bentick's maze, and the back of his head throbbed where the killer had struck. Another pain there was sharper and more vicious, like a bird pecking the wound. Something tugged at his skull, causing his head to twitch.

He tried to rise, but a hand held him down. Its skin was pasty and wrinkled. Its nails were encrusted with blood.

"Don't move," Gideon grunted.

Wild Boy saw him now in a mirror on a wall. He saw, too, what tugged at his head: a needle and thread.

Gideon made a final stitch above Wild Boy's ear, sealing the wound. Leaning closer, he bit the end of the thread. There was at least a bottle of gin in his breath.

"That should hold it," he said.

He gave the end of the thread an unnecessary tug, causing Wild Boy to gasp with pain, and then sat beside the remains of a fire. He lit a clay pipe from the pulsing embers.

"Who done it?" he said.

Wild Boy sat up, an effort that exhausted most of the energy left in his arms. He touched the wound, feeling stitches that were tight and precise. It was an impressive job, even though it felt as a nail had been hammered into his skull.

"Where's Clarissa?" he asked.

"She's fine. Outside. I said, who done that to Marcus?"

Gideon's face screwed up even tighter as he drew on his pipe, as if he were sucking in needles. Wild Boy realized that he must have seen Marcus in that state, too. Black-veined, tormented by his own mind. What had the killer called it?

The terror.

"What happened to him?' he asked.

"Lucien and his Black Hats showed up," Gideon said. "They took him away. To a hospital maybe, or an asylum. He was still alive. If you can call that living."

"I gotta see Clarissa."

Suddenly Gideon bolted up, grabbed Wild Boy and pinned him against the wall. "You think this is all about you, don't you? You're Wild Boy! The great detective genius! You think this is all your story and don't mean nothing to no one else."

His eyes were red and blurred. Veins bulged beneath his neck cloth.

"I've served Marcus for sixteen years," he said. "I owe that man everything. He saved me once. You've known him for, what, four months? You think it was hard for *you*, seeing him like that? So I am asking you again: *who done that to him?*"

He pressed Wild Boy harder against the wall. Instinctively Wild Boy lashed out, head butting him and sending him tumbling back beside the fire.

Sparks crackled up the chimney.

Gideon clutched his nose, but blood leaked

between his fingers. He scrabbled towards Wild Boy, about to attack, but stopped, seeming to realize that fighting wouldn't help Marcus. Instead, he turned and neatened the cloth around his neck.

"None of the Gentlemen wanted you," he said. "They said you were trouble. But Marcus stood up for you. He said you and Clarissa could do amazing things. Said you would be great one day. He protected you, defended you. Saved you over and over, and you had no idea."

The pain grew sharper in Wild Boy's head. "You said he saved you too?"

"That ain't none of your business. Your business now is saving him back. So you better be amazing, like he said. Do you find a way to save him."

Gideon leaned closer to the fire, breathing in the smoke. "Do you remember what the killer said to you?"

Wild Boy did, every word. The killer offered a deal, a cure to save Marcus in exchange for the next black diamond. He'd even given him a clue to find the diamond. A single word. *Oberstein.*

He suspected Gideon might know what it meant; the man had spent years with Marcus, and Marcus knew everything. But could he really help the killer? Marcus wouldn't want that, not for anything.

He watched Gideon place a cooking pot over the fire, only just realizing something about this place. "This is where you live?" he asked.

Gideon shrugged. "Seemed like the best place to bring you. Not many Gentlemen or coppers come here. We're in the Rat's Castle."

The Rat's Castle. It was one of the roughest inns in London, yet just a knife's throw from Lady Bentick's house.

Wild Boy looked around the frigid room. The bed sheets were stiff with dried sweat, and the mound of empty bottles under the bed was so high that it raised the mattress. Surely Marcus had offered Gideon a home in the palace. Why did he choose to live here then, in squalor?

Gideon's coat sleeves were rolled up, and Wild Boy spotted a faded Indian ink tattoo on his sinewy arm – crossed swords over a crown. He'd seen the symbol on soldiers that visited the fairground. Had Gideon been in the army? Wild Boy realized how little he knew about the man, even though they'd quarreled almost every day over the past four months.

A Bible sat on a chair beside the bed. He flicked it open where a crease on the spine suggested it had been read. A passage was circled on the page.

Though your sins are like scarlet, they shall be white as snow...

Gideon snatched the book. "That ain't none of your business either. You and I are friends as long as you're saving Marcus. If you ain't got a plan for that, you can take your chances on the streets. You got that?"

"Yeah, I got it."

"Go get Clarissa. You need to eat."

Wild Boy swung his legs from the chair, testing their strength. His head whirled as he walked to the door. The walls moved in crazy circles.

He turned back. "You ever heard of some place called Oberstein?" he asked.

Gideon looked up from the cooking pot. His face changed from rage to something like fear. "Why you asking that?"

"You know it or not?"

"Yeah I know it," he said. "But it ain't a place, it's a person. Oberstein's a jeweller, got a shop on Bond Street."

A jeweller? Well, that answered something at least. Wild Boy went outside to find his friend.

•14•

Wild Boy stepped outside, squinting in the midday sun. He was on a wooden balcony that overlooked the courtyard of the coaching inn, a rickety rat trap of shedlike rooms and greasy doorways. Everything glistened with ice and grime.

Noise came from all around him, beery singing from a tavern below and grunts and cheers from the boxing match next door. The courtyard's square of snow was speckled with colour. There were yellow holes where punters had relieved themselves, steaming brown dung, and flecks of red from fights. Wild Boy didn't need his detective skills to tell that a snow-covered lump in the corner was a man, short and squat and buried by the snow where he had died.

A flurry of snow sprinkled from the tavern roof. Despite everything, Wild Boy smiled. He'd known where Clarissa was the moment he stepped outside.

Always up high.

Still shaky on his legs, he walked to where a barrel was collecting rainwater from a broken drainpipe. The barrel was full, the water frozen solid. He climbed on top of it and gripped the pipe, but his head whirled and his feet slipped on the ice. Just as he was about to fall, a hand shot out from above and grasped his wrist.

Clarissa hauled him onto the roof and wrapped him in a tight hug. Then she released him and shoved him in the chest. "It's your fault!" she said. "You should've seen the clues. You should have saved Marcus."

Wild Boy crouched, pressed a palm to the tiles to steady his balance.

Clarissa towered over him. Her dress was torn, and its sequined sleeve snapped in the wind. A bandage around her head was spotted with blood. A trickle had escaped from beneath; a red tear sliding down her face.

"What do we do now?" she asked. "We don't have another plan, Wild Boy. Now the Gentlemen are after us and Marcus is gone. We only ever had him."

A rush of wind swept across the rooftop, swirling up snow and dislodging tiles. It carried Clarissa's rage away with it, and she sat beside him on the roof.

They huddled closer, enjoying the feeling of being together. From up here they could see across the patchwork of rooftops that spread towards the river. Factory chimneys protruded from the riverbank, belching brown smoke. In the other direction rose the tall, elegant architecture of Mayfair. Church towers jutted up here and there, their white stone streaked with dark grime.

Wild Boy pictured Marcus as they'd last seen him. He wanted to tell Clarissa about the killer's deal, but she wouldn't think twice about accepting it. He had no idea what danger was involved in finding the next black diamond. And he knew Marcus wouldn't want them do to it, not even to save him.

Was there another way? His mind kept spinning. Pain pounded his skull. He couldn't gather his thoughts.

"What clues do we have so far?" Clarissa said. "The killer is collecting black diamonds. He stole one from the Queen and then from Lady Bentick. But why, and why'd he save me at Lady Bentick's house and no one else?"

Wild Boy had wondered about that. He sensed it might be an important clue. "You still got that note he gave you?"

"Said to destroy it," Clarissa said, "so I threw it on the fire as I left the dining room. I thought it was from you, remember. Ain't we got nothing else?"

Wild Boy slid two papers from his pocket – the Queen's card and the page from the *Encyclopaedia Demonica*. He handed them to Clarissa and she read about Malphas, that laughing crow with those blank eyes and barbed-wire teeth.

"A demon," she said. "Destroyer of cities."

"No," Wild Boy said. "The killer's crazy, thinks he's working for a demon. But he's a real person, all right."

"What did he say? Anything that can help us?"

"I'm... I'm not sure."

She shifted closer, pressing against him. He felt her body tremble.

"I'm scared, Wild Boy. We won't make it on the streets, not us."

Somewhere across the roofs, a crow cawed. Wild Boy's wound throbbed harder. He saw a flash of his nightmare – crows and a fairground field, a caravan and a showman.

Clarissa was right. They wouldn't make it on the streets. Not together.

The crow called louder.

"I... I was lying," Wild Boy said. "I did hear the killer."

"What? What did he say?"

"We gotta steal a black diamond."

·15·

BOND STREET

It seemed almost impossible that the squalour of the Rat's Castle, where dead bodies were left where they fell, existed just a few streets away from this – the most exclusive road in the richest city in the world. Here were London's poshest clothing boutiques selling mink muffs, fox-fur mantles and beaver-pelt opera hats. Footmen in powdered wigs stood like dusty statues by coaches that were decorated with crests of dukes and counts and viscounts and marquesses. Behind jewellery shop windows, breathtaking displays of gemstones reflected the midday sun in the colours of the rainbow.

The sweep of shops was broken halfway along the street where one building stood detached from the others, and two floors taller. Plasterwork columns climbed its façade, and sculptures framed its tall windows: twisting stone wreaths and fat-cheeked cherubs blasting bugles. While the other buildings had been scrubbed of the green-black grime that encrusted most of London's buildings, this one had been left to its mercy, so that the cherubs appeared as demons clinging to withered leaves.

"That's it," Gideon said. "That's Oberstein's place."

Wild Boy had guessed as much. It was the only building here that matched the killer's description. *Dangerous*.

They watched from the roof across the street. Gideon had led them here by breaking into the shop below and sneaking up the service stairs. That had been the easy part of their plan. Now they had to get into Oberstein's building, steal a black diamond and get out alive.

It had no shop sign and nothing on display. The windows were hidden behind steel shutters. The only door, bolted and made of iron, looked as if it were designed to guard offenders at Newgate rather than greet the shoppers of Mayfair. Two burly guards stood by it; they had long leather coats and arms as thick as their necks.

Clarissa stood beside Wild Boy, balancing on the edge of the roof. "You sure that's Oberstein's place? Don't look like no jeweller."

"That's because it *ain't* like no jeweller," Gideon replied. He lit his pipe, blew a cloud of smoke. "From what I've heard, Oberstein used to cut stones for the most powerful folk on the planet: kings and queens. Indian maharajas, Chinese emperors, even old Bonaparte himself. Every toff in the world wanted to be seen in that shop."

"So what happened?" Wild Boy asked.

"No one knows. Around a decade back, the place just went dark. The shutters were closed and the door bolted. See them guards? Those are Swiss mercenaries. They make Lucien's Black Hats look like toddlers."

Wild Boy wondered how Gideon knew so much about the guards' military pasts. Then he remembered the tattoo on his arm, the army symbol.

"What are they guarding?" Clarissa asked.

"Can't say," Gideon said.

"A black diamond?"

"Can't say that neither. All I know is stories. Some say the place is haunted, or rigged with traps. Hard to know what's true. Place has become a legend among crooks. A spook story, bit like you two."

"We ain't scared of traps," Clarissa said. "Wild Boy can spot 'em a mile off."

Wild Boy wished he were so confident. The truth was, that building gave him the creeps. It seemed unreal. Every bit of ice and snow had melted from its ledges. Water trickled down the bricks, mingling with the grime and dripping darkness onto the pavement. A faint haze around the walls quaked the air.

"Marcus spoke of a feller once," Gideon said,

drawing on his pipe. "A thief who tried to get into that building. Wanted to prove he was the best at his job. Marcus thought he was too."

"I know what you're going to say," Clarissa said. "He was never seen again, right?"

"Oh no, he was. In lots of places. His head was found on top of St Paul's Cathedral. Sawn off at the jaw."

Clarissa stepped back from the edge. "What... What about the rest of him?"

"His arms were found in Notre Dame, in Paris, his legs outside a mosque in Constantinople, and the rest of him turned up in a temple in Calcutta, I think. Could just be a story though."

Wild Boy noticed some drivers whip their horses harder as they rode past Oberstein's building, and how a few shoppers crossed the street rather than pass its shuttered windows. Had they heard the same stories as Gideon?

"I ain't so sure about this," he muttered.

Gideon grabbed his wrist. "You ain't got a choice," he growled. "If you don't get that black diamond, Marcus dies. Ain't no risk we won't take."

He let go of Wild Boy's arm. "Besides, what happens to you if he dies? Think about that, eh?"

Wild Boy had thought of little else. That was what scared him. He knew he wasn't doing this for Marcus. Marcus would never want them to help a killer. He was doing this for himself.

"Let's get on with it," he said.

Gideon dropped a canvas bag by Clarissa's feet. For the first time, Clarissa didn't scowl at him. She simply nodded, a begrudging acceptance that, for once, they were on the same side.

"I'll be ready in five minutes," Gideon said, trudging back to the door to the service stairs. "You'd better be ready too."

Clarissa opened the bag. It was filled with items Gideon had brought from the palace – a rope, candles, a tinderbox and a pronged tool like four butcher's hooks welded together.

Clarissa tied the end of the rope to the tool's base. "Grappling hook," she said, swiping it through the air.

Wild Boy searched her face for any hint of a smile. Usually Clarissa lived for this sort of thing, a chance to cause some trouble. But right then he saw nothing in her expression other than a fierce determination to save Marcus.

He wished they could talk more, but there was no time. A wind was rising, whipping snow across the roofs. Clouds began to dapple the buildings in shade. Their plan relied on bright sunshine, to dazzle the guards. It had to happen now.

He peered over the edge of the roof. Below, Gideon had begun to ride his carriage along the street. He yanked the reins with deliberately clumsy jerks and bellowed at the shoppers as if he was drunk.

"Look out, toffs!" he yelled. "I'm coming through."

As he neared Oberstein's building, he turned the horses. The carriage slammed against a lamp post, sending him tumbling from the seat to the pavement.

That was the cue.

"Now!" Wild Boy said.

With a sweep of her arm, Clarissa sent the hook high into the air, carrying the rope across the street. It disappeared over the top of Oberstein's building, from where they heard the gentle *clink* of it landing.

She pulled the rope until the tool's claws caught the parapet of Oberstein's roof. Rushing back, she lashed the other end around a chimney stack, forming an uphill tightrope across the street.

She jumped up and stood on the rope as easily as if it were a foot-wide beam. She strapped Gideon's bag over her shoulder. "Ready," she said.

On the street, the guards shouted at Gideon and tried to pick him up. But he just grinned and rolled his eyes, acting too drunk to understand. The distraction was working. The guards hadn't seen the tightrope.

"Go!" Wild Boy said.

Clarissa was already off, so fast she was almost running. Her silk dress shimmered as she raced up the sloping line.

Wild Boy watched, holding his breath as if breathing might somehow knock her off balance. Clarissa vanished onto Oberstein's roof and then reappeared holding the grappling tool. She hooked its claw onto her dress, fixing herself to the line, then swung her legs over the edge of the roof and climbed down. Her fingers dug into cracks in the stone while her boots sought footholds on the cherubs' cheeks.

A shout came from the street.

Wild Boy's breath finally came out in a stream of curses. One of the guards had seen the rope. The man charged across the road and into the building below.

"We can still do it," Wild Boy muttered, trying to convince himself. But he couldn't help wondering if that was the guard that had sawed the thief's body to bits.

"Hurry, Clarissa…"

She was going as fast as she could down the building, like a spider. The rope slackened with her descent, then grew tight again as she climbed to the windows on the next floor down. She hooked the grappling tool around the rivet where the shutter met the wall. Now the tightrope sloped downwards to the third-floor window.

Clarissa forced the window open and climbed inside. She signalled to Wild Boy to follow.

Wild Boy peered again over the edge of the roof. The ground rushed up at him and his knees turned to jelly. The stitches in his head began to throb again. He felt dizzy and weak.

Footsteps stomped up the stairs. The guard would be here in moments.

Crouching, he pulled off his coat and draped it over the rope. He had to jump and let it carry him, but his arms shook so hard that the whole line quivered.

The guard stumbled onto the roof, coughing and wheezing. He saw Wild Boy and his face flushed an even deeper red. Veins bulged in his temples. He reached for a weapon in his coat.

Wild Boy closed his eyes and jumped.

He expected to start sliding, but instead he hung from the line. He filled the freezing air with more curses, wiggling his arms. "Come on," he urged. "Come on!"

The coat jerked and he began to slide. Cold air rushed at the hair on his face and chest. His shriek of fear turned into a cry of victory as he shot towards Oberstein's building. "It's working," he yelled. "It's bloomin' working!"

But now Clarissa's face changed from a smile to a scream. She reached from the window, pointing to something across the street; something terrible.

On the roof, the guard cut the rope.

The line sagged, and for a second Wild Boy felt as if he was floating. Momentum carried him forward and he slammed against the wall. One hand scrabbled at the brickwork, hoping to hold on. The other gripped his coat tighter, praying it might still somehow save him, even as it slid from the rope.

And then it did.

Instead of falling he remained against the wall, dangling from the sleeve of his coat. Above, Clarissa clung onto the other sleeve. Her hair hung down and her freckles looked as if they might pop off her cheeks.

She began to pull him up. "Stop screaming," she grunted.

Wild Boy hadn't realized he *was* screaming, but now that he did he screamed even louder and didn't stop until he had clambered through the window and tumbled to the floor inside Oberstein's building.

"Well," Clarissa said, "they definitely know we're here."

Wild Boy lay on his back, trembling as much with fear as relief.

They were inside.

Now came the hard part.

• 16 •

"**T**his don't look so scary."

Clarissa pulled the window shutters closed, but sunshine sneaked between the wooden slats, giving just enough light to see the room they had broken into. "It's just an ordinary bedroom," she said, sounding disappointed.

The fire was unlit, but the air was warm, prickling the hair on Wild Boy's face. The walls were decorated with faded green paper and golden fleurs-de-lis. Heavy woollen drapes enclosed a four-poster bed. The door was open, inviting them into a long, dark corridor.

"Come on," Clarissa said. "Let's find the black diamond."

She moved towards the door, but Wild Boy held her back, sensing danger. It was an instinct he'd learned to trust, and so had Clarissa.

"What is it?" she breathed.

He still wasn't sure. His breaths slowed as he scanned the room. He saw a sheen of dust on the door handle. He saw a dead fly, dried and shrivelled, on the bed. He saw how the fleur-de-lis, bright against the dull green wallpaper, were unevenly spaced. And above, he saw a pinprick of light on the ceiling.

His hand tightened on Clarissa's arm. "Don't move," he said.

"What do you see?"

"That light up there. What's it coming off? There's something we ain't seeing."

"Don't be a thickhead, you see everything."

Not now I don't. "You got a light in that bag?"

Clarissa brought a candle from Gideon's bag, a black wax stump. She lit it with a tinderbox and raised it to the gloom. As the light spread they saw that the air was filled with jewels.

Dozens of crystals hung on impossibly thin threads, so transparent they were invisible without the reflection of the light. The crystals were suspended at different heights. Some kissed the rug. Others dangled at eye level. Some even hung from the canopy of the bed.

Clarissa held the candle close to the nearest crystal. The light bounced off its facets, speckling the walls. "These ain't for decoration, are they?" she said.

She tilted the candle and prodded the jewel.

"No," Wild Boy said. "Don't!"

Psst. Something fired across the room and shot into the candle. A hiss of steam rose from one of the fleurs-de-lis.

The candle quivered in Clarissa's hand. A small shard of glass was stuck in the wax. "A dart," she said.

Wild Boy plucked a hair from the back of his hand and let it flutter over the dart's edge. The brown strand split in two as it fell. He'd never seen anything so sharp.

"Why would someone do this?" Clarissa said.

"Protection," Wild Boy guessed. "Oberstein's scared of something."

He watched steam drift from the fleurs-de-lis and began to understand why the room was so warm. "There's machines in the walls," he said. "I reckon each stone sets off a dart if it moves."

"It's impossible," Clarissa said. "No way through the room."

Wild Boy took the candle and raised it high, studying the suspended stones. His gaze moved among them, searching for the best passage; the wider gaps between the jewels and the dead ends where the spaces were too slim to pass. A map formed in his head, a twisting path through the maze.

"Follow me," he said.

He pressed the hair down on his face, fearing it might brush the stones. Then he stepped through the gap. He tried not to think of punctured organs, knives slicing through butter...

"You sure you know what you're doing?" Clarissa asked, edging carefully behind him.

Wild Boy didn't reply, for fear of unsettling the stones. He kept moving, inch by inch, following the map in his mind. Clarissa followed as they shuffled forwards, backwards, ducked to slide under one jewel, turned sideways to move around another.

"Almost there," Wild Boy said.

There were only two threads left between him and the bedroom door, but the gap between them was less than a foot wide.

"You ain't gonna make it," Clarissa warned.

He could do it. He was sure of it. He breathed in, held the breath and moved. A hair on his nose sprang up and brushed one of the crystals.

Psst.

Wild Boy closed his eyes, waiting for the impact. None came. Sliding a hand to his back, he felt a tear where a dart had sliced the fabric of his coat.

He sighed with relief.

Several threads swayed.

"Jump!" Clarissa cried.

Psst. Psst. Psst. Psst.

Glass darts shot across the room as they leaped into the doorway. Wild Boy rolled over, feeling for rips in his coat or cuts on his limbs.

"You all right?" he gasped.

Clarissa rose, brushing back her hair. Wild Boy expected her to grin, or say something cocky. Instead she turned and yelled along the corridor: "Hey, Oberstein! We're still alive and we're coming for your black diamond."

A moan echoed back from the darkness.

"That don't scare me," Clarissa said in a voice suddenly full of fear. She helped Wild Boy up from the floor. "Who was that?" she whispered.

Wild Boy didn't think it was someone, but rather *something*. The air was filled with a haze of steam, and the whole building trembled. His feet felt warm against the carpet runner.

"We gotta watch out," he said. "Come on."

· 17 ·

Wild Boy led the way down the corridor. None of the lamps on the walls were lit, but he didn't need them. He'd spent most of his life locked up in dark rooms, so he was used to it. He saw several closed doors along the passage, between shelves crammed with books.

"Which door should we take?" Clarissa said.

"None of them. Don't open any."

"How are we gonna find the black diamond if we don't even look?"

"Those ain't the places to look. None of these doors have been opened in months. See the dust on the handles?"

"Reckon there are more traps inside?" Clarissa asked. "That would explain all the machinery in the walls. What's got Oberstein so scared? All this security can't be just to protect some jewels."

Wild Boy stopped at one of the bookcases and leaned close to read the titles on the spines. His hairs bristled. All of the books were about the same subject: *The Hierarchy of Demons, Occult Philosophy, Banishing Evil Spirits*.

"Demons," he said.

"So how we gonna find the black diamond?" Clarissa asked. "Ain't no other way out."

There was always another way out, Marcus had taught Wild Boy that. You just had to look hard enough. He turned, letting his eyes and instinct take over.

There.

"The lights," he said.

He rushed to one of the lamps on the wall, then another. All of them had full bowls of oil except one, which was almost empty. Only that lamp had been used. It was only there that someone had needed illumination.

He sank to his knees and pulled back the carpet.

Underneath was a hatch.

Clarissa joined him and they lifted the trap door. A blast of steam rose into their faces. The cavity beneath the floor was filled with pipes and pistons, as if a locomotive engine were squeezed into the space. A bronze pole, rutted with grooves, hung from the machinery and into the darkness below.

Clarissa struck another flint from her tinderbox and lit a candle. She waved the flame through the hole. Whatever was down there made her gasp.

"What is it?" Wild Boy said.

"Jewels!"

She swung through the trap door and into the dark.

Wild Boy lowered himself awkwardly through the hole, clinging onto the pole. His hands scraped against its metal ridges. "This looks like a screw," he said, as he reached the floor.

"It ain't the only one," Clarissa replied.

The candlelight gleamed off a dozen shafts that rose from floor to ceiling around a small, wood-panelled room. Each screw ran through the centre of a metal disc, like a giant cog but with sharper teeth.

The poles surrounded a table, and the table was covered in jewels.

Clarissa rushed to it, guiding her light around the stones. There were pearls as large as hens' eggs, fat blue sapphires, and emeralds bigger and greener than Wild Boy's eyes.

At any other time, Clarissa would have shoved them in her pockets. But now she was only interested in one jewel. She grabbed a handful of the stones and hurled them against the wall. "None of 'em are black diamonds," she said.

Wild Boy hadn't looked. He stared at the poles, then one of the walls, where he spotted a dark splatter mark. A thought occurred to him so terrible that it took him several seconds to find the courage to say it out loud.

"These poles ain't screws," he said. "They're saws. Clarissa, that thief Gideon told us about. Wasn't his head *sawn* off?"

"Oh my God…"

The jewels began to shake.

Spits of steam rose through cracks in the floorboards, scalding Wild Boy's feet. The screws began to turn; first slowly, then as fast as toy tops. The cogs whirled up and down the shafts, their teeth glinting blurs. Now the screws started to move, sliding back and forth along grooves in the ceiling.

Hot air rushed around the room as the blades whirled from all directions. One of them fizzed past Wild Boy so close that it trimmed the hair on his cheek. He tumbled back, then rolled over as another saw screamed from the side.

"How do we turn them off?" Clarissa yelled.

Through the saws Wild Boy spotted a wooden panel hanging crookedly on the wall, as if it had been replaced in a hurry. Was there a hidden lever?

"Clarissa!" he called. "See that panel? You gotta get to it."

Clarissa ducked another blade. It spun over her head and chopped off the top of her candle. The flame fluttered, and the room plunged into darkness.

"I can't see!"

"You can do it, Clarissa. Remember what Marcus said. You gotta concentrate. Think!"

Wild Boy didn't see everything that happened

next; it was too fast. He glimpsed Clarissa flip over a saw, duck under another, spring up and dive between two more.

A saw came at him from behind, another from the front. One of them tore his coat at the back. Another whirred at his belly, slicing the hair, kissing his skin. He closed his eyes.

The saws stopped.

"Wild Boy? Wild Boy!"

He tried to reply, but all that came out was a gasp. A few more seconds and he'd have been cut in two.

Clarissa lit another candle. Her hair had been cut short on one side, and her dress had new tears, but she wasn't bleeding. The panel in the wall hung open; a lever had been forced up among a clutter of pipes and machinery. "Got it," she said.

Wild Boy edged delicately away from the saws and moved through the blades to her side. One of the stitches on his head had come undone and warm blood slid under his hair. But he couldn't stop grinning.

Then something happened that lifted away the pain.

Clarissa grinned too.

"Easy," she said.

Wild Boy was about to reply when another trap door opened beneath them and they fell through.

The drop was short, to a steep wooden slide. They hit it hard and shot down its polished surface. Before they could find their screams, they crashed through another door and tumbled across a cold stone floor.

The ground floor.

The shutters were sealed across the shop front. The only light came from a fire that smouldered on the other side of the room. But all around them things gleamed. And hummed. And steamed.

Pipes covered two of the walls. They rose from underground, hissing and steaming at their joints. The air here was even hotter, like a warm sponge, dampening the hair on Wild Boy's face. Steam misted the glass of several display cases, empty relics from the chamber's previous life as Oberstein's jewellery showroom.

One case, though, was neither empty nor steamed. It seemed to have been cleaned moments before they tumbled into the room. Inside was a velvet cushion, and sitting on the cushion was...

"The black diamond," Clarissa said.

Wild Boy was amazed by *how* black it was, as dark as a lump of coal and almost as big. But still, somehow, the jewel gleamed. Black beams scattered across the showroom from a thousand polished surfaces.

Clarissa moved towards the case, but again Wild Boy held her back. He'd sensed from the moment they landed in this place that they were not alone.

Four silhouetted figures watched from the shadows. One of them stepped closer, eyes glinting in the darkness.

·18·

Steam hissed from one of the pipes fixed to the wall of Oberstein's showroom.

One of the figures silhouetted stepped through the mist, seemingly untroubled by its heat. As the man came closer, the glow of the fire caught his face. The flash of bright, shiny green did not make sense at first.

No, it was not a face.

"A mask," Clarissa said.

The mask was smooth, like a doll's face, and fixed around the person's head with leather straps. It was made of dazzling green jade. The eyes that stared through it were grey and glazed and entirely without emotion. Wild Boy could hear the man's heavy, steady breathing.

He had no weapon, nor did he need one. He was not tall but his neck was as thick as a tree trunk. His hands were the size of frying pans, and the muscles in his arms were so large their contours showed through the sleeves of his long leather coat.

The guards from outside were here too, one armed with a pistol, the other with a knife. They stood over Gideon, who had been forced to his knees beside the fire. Gideon stared into the barrel, fidgeting furiously with his neckcloth. Wild Boy hoped he didn't try anything stupid. The guard looked worryingly eager to use that pistol.

A third, smaller, guard remained in the shadows in the corner of the showroom.

Wild Boy moved closer to Clarissa. He felt her arms tremble, but knew it was from anger, not fear. For the first time since Lady Bentick's house she had enemies to fight.

Her eyes flicked from the masked man to the black diamond, and then back to the man. "Are you Oberstein?" she demanded.

The masked man replied with a slight tilt of his head.

"Nice to meet you," Clarissa said. "We've come for that black diamond."

The man replied with an even slighter shake of his head. With a sweep of a leg, he kicked a hessian bag across the floor. It slid to a stop beside Wild Boy's feet.

"Watch out," Clarissa said. "Could be another trap."

Wild Boy didn't think so. If this man wanted them dead, all he had to do was signal to his guards. Cautiously he unbuttoned the bag. For a moment he just stared.

"Wild Boy?" Clarissa asked.

The bag was filled with jewels. Blue, green, pink and blood red, packed so tightly they strained the bag's seams. A card lay on top, with a single sentence written in ink.

"*Take them and leave,*" Wild Boy read.

The message was so unexpected that he didn't know what to say. He'd never been interested in wealth, so he was surprised how tempted he was by the offer. With such a fortune, he and Clarissa could live where they liked, however they liked. They wouldn't need the Gentlemen's protection. They could probably buy a palace of their own if they wanted to.

Clarissa barely glanced at the bag. Her glare remained on the jade-masked man. "You ain't too chatty," she said, "so maybe you don't hear too good neither. We're only here for *that* stone. The black diamond."

The man's eyes narrowed. Another hiss of steam escaped from one of the pipes, and he used the distraction to glance at the guard in the shadows.

A curious thought occurred to Wild Boy. So far nothing in this place had been as it seemed. Why should this situation be different?

"What do we do?" Clarissa whispered. "Ober-stein's gonna kill us if we go for the diamond."

"No he ain't," Wild Boy said.

"How do you know?"

"Cos he ain't Oberstein. Are you, mister?"

The man breathed deeper into the back of his mask.

Wild Boy moved closer, seeking clues to confirm what he already knew. "It don't make sense," he said, "that someone so obsessed with safety should show himself so fast. And think of the things you'd expect to see on someone who's spent a life study-ing jewels up close, cutting and polishing. Squinty eyes, hunched back, scars on their hands. You ain't got none of them, mister. Real straight back, in fact. You *do* have soot marks on your fingers from shoveling coal into whatever furnace gets all these pipes steaming. Why would the master of this place stoke his own furnace when he's got all these guards to do it? No, you ain't Oberstein."

He looked beyond the masked man, to the guard in the shadows.

"You are," he said.

The figure stepped into the firelight. The person was so small that Wild Boy thought it might be a child, until a long coat fell away to reveal an old woman, frail and hunched. Her face was round and wrinkled like a walnut, and grey hair hung in wisps from her liver-spotted scalp. Dark spectacles hid her eyes. Her ragged, sack-like clothes were more suited to the slums of Seven Dials than the wealthiest establishment in Mayfair.

She spoke in a pained, rasping voice. "You see a lot, young man. There you have me at a disadvantage."

She removed her dark glasses. She had white, dead-fish eyes.

Another attempt to speak ended in a hacking cough that echoed around the empty showroom. She must have known the masked man would move towards her, because she waved him back with a flap of a hand. Another flap caused one of the other guards to lower his gun, although the man's grip remained tight around the weapon.

The woman came closer. Shrivelled hands reached for Wild Boy's face. "May I?"

Wild Boy forced himself to stay still as she slid rough hands over his forehead, cheeks and chin. She felt hair where other people had skin, but she didn't flinch.

"You know who I am," he said.

The lady – *Oberstein* – stepped back. "Of course. You are the Wild Boy of London, world famous villain. You and Miss Everett were seen entering this building. You were not expected to be seen again. You are lucky to be alive."

"It ain't luck," Clarissa said. "We beat your stupid traps. Now we're taking that black diamond."

"I am afraid not, Miss Everett. That stone belongs to another."

"Yeah? Who's that?"

"You would not believe me if I told you."

"I wouldn't be asking if I didn't wanna know."

"Nevertheless, I urge you to accept my offer. In that bag are enough jewels to place you among the ten wealthiest individuals in the world. I suggest that you take them with my congratulations, and leave. We will also release your friend, Mr Gideon."

"And if we don't?" Clarissa said.

Oberstein's wrinkles eased, as if she had suddenly become comfortable in her own body. "Then you will still leave," she said. "In several bags."

Wild Boy and Clarissa moved closer, fingers touching at their sides.

"However," Oberstein continued, "I am curious. May I ask why my black diamond interests you?"

"Our friend is sick," Wild Boy said. "Been given some sort of poison that's gonna kill him. Whoever done it has a cure. Only, he's after black diamonds, and yours is —"

"No!" Oberstein cried.

The old woman gripped her chest as if she'd been shot in the heart.

This time the masked man wouldn't be ordered back. Taking Oberstein's shoulders, he helped her to a chair beside the fire. He crouched beside her and held her frail arms until the worst of her pain passed.

"Did you hear, Spencer?" Oberstein wheezed. "Did you hear what the boy said?"

Clarissa made a dash for the stone. But the guard raised his firearm and she stepped back.

"I applaud your efforts, Miss Everett," Oberstein said, recovering enough to sit up. "But I am afraid they are in vain. Your friend cannot be cured."

"Shut your head," Clarissa said. "Why would you say that?"

"Because he has not been poisoned."

"What's happened to him then?"

"He has been cursed."

The woman was crazy, Wild Boy decided. But that didn't mean she couldn't help them. "Whatever's going on, you know about it, don't you?" he said.

"I do. More, perhaps, than any other person alive."

"Then here…"

He kicked the bag towards her, scattering a rainbow of jewels across the showroom floor. "You gave them to us, so now we're giving them back. That's what we'll pay you to tell us everything you know, anything that might help us save our friend."

"Ah," Oberstein said, "now we have an understanding. Then I suggest you make yourselves comfortable while an old lady tells you a story. Then you will understand the true nature of your enemy and, I am afraid, how futile your attempts are to save your friend."

·19·

"The story begins with a man named Geoffrey Dahlquist, the eleventh Earl of Cravenhill," said Oberstein. "Have you heard of this man? I do not suppose you would say if you have. But you would certainly remember him. Lord Dahlquist was a bear of a man, as strong even as my bodyguard, Spencer here. Spencer? Take my hand. Ah, that's it. Now, where was I?"

"Dahlquist. You were talking about some bloke named Dahlquist."

"Yes, Wild Boy, *Lord* Dahlquist. Dahlquist was, to many people, a fine individual. A family man, devoted to his wife and young son. A pioneering doctor who financed two hospitals. He was a philanthropist, a Master Mason and a skilled angler. Then, around sixteen years ago, Lord Dahlquist left England with his family and purchased a diamond mine in the south-west of India, near the village of Kollur. Do any of you know of Kollur?"

"None of us know nothing you're talking about. What's this history lesson got to do with what happened to Marcus?"

"Keep listening, Miss Everett, and you shall find out. That mine at Kollur was rich in diamonds. There were enough stones in those hills to make Dahlquist the wealthiest man on the planet. But he had no interest in wealth, of which he had enough through his family line to satisfy several lifetimes. Nor did he care for ordinary diamonds. All Lord Dahlquist wanted was a black diamond, and that mine at Kollur was one of the few in the world that yielded those rarest of stones."

"Why'd he want a black diamond so bad?"

"It was not for himself that he sought this stone. It was for his master."

"Master?"

"The Devil, Miss Everett. Or at least *his* devil. You see, this fine philanthropist and father was also a devil worshipper. Around that time, I recall, it was quite fashionable among the aristocracy: séances, occultism and the like. Only, for Dahlquist it became an obsession. In a cave in those mines, he conducted rituals to a demon god named Malphas."

"Malphas?"

"I can tell from your tone, Wild Boy, that you recognize this name. Malphas is, according to mythology, a Prince of Hell. A hideous creature that tortures victims with their darkest memories. He is known, too, as the Destroyer of Cities. Dahlquist believed that Malphas had sent him to that mine to seek its heart. A black diamond.

"He hired guards and forced the villagers to work as slaves. His rules were simple. Whomever among them found a black diamond was promised freedom and a fortune. Whomever did not, within a year, would be killed."

"No, he can't do that."

"He did do it, Miss Everett. No one was exempt. Not women, not children. Dahlquist paid the guards with whatever *other* diamonds the mine yielded, so naturally they drove the villagers mercilessly. No shade, no water, no rest. Many of those poor souls died of exhaustion or dehydration. Others, of despair. Bones showed through their skin. Their hands were raw with blood and blisters from the pick. They lay on the rocks for just a few hours each night, but few could sleep because of the agony in their limbs."

"But how could he do that?"

"Because, Wild Boy, those lives mattered little to him."

"Did the villagers find a black diamond?"

"Yes, after nine months one of them did. It was unquestionably the largest and most perfect example ever found: over three thousand carats. Dahlquist had it cut quickly and crudely by a jeweller in Golkonda, but even in that primitive state it was by far the most valuable gemstone in the world. He gave the stone a name, too – the Black Terror."

"Terror?"

"What did he do with it?"

"Ah! Now that is the question, Miss Everett. The stone became the heart of a statue of Malphas that stood in his cave. A hideous creature, half man, half crow. Dahlquist believed that the stone was the very soul of the demon it lived inside."

"What about the villagers? Were they freed?"

"No. For the villagers of Kollur, things grew even worse. From that day, Lord Dahlquist had them brought to him, one villager each night, and he sacrificed them to his demon. It was nothing short of a massacre. The floor of the cave sloped to an underground stream, so the blood flowed away. I am told it came out along the valley in a waterfall the colour of rubies. Also, that Dahlquist forced his poor young son to watch the executions. A truly *devoted* father."

"That blackguard."

"That is putting it mildly, Mr Gideon."

"Please tell me there's a happy ending."

"Miss Everett, I cannot. There was at least some satisfaction for those villagers. It came from the man who found the Black Terror, a young man named Sameer. You see, for all his evil, Lord Dahlquist regarded himself as a man of honour, and he kept his promise.

He granted Sameer his freedom and a fortune. First he tortured him for several days, disfiguring him to such an extent that no one would approach him, let alone listen to his tale. But Dahlquist underestimated the strength of one man's determination for justice. Spencer? Spencer, you must hold my hand. Ah, there you are. Now, where was I?"

"Sameer…"

"Yes, Sameer, thank you, Mr Gideon. Once he had recovered, that remarkable young man carried his new fortune in a bag. He used a small amount to pay for his passage to Calcutta, and the rest to secure a meeting with the Governor General of India. At that time the Governor General was Lord William Cavendish Bentick."

"Lord Bentick?"

"I sense that name also means something to you, Wild Boy."

"His wife was killed by the same thing that infected our friend. The terror."

"Yes, yes, that makes sense, as you will see. Lord Bentick himself passed away four years ago. As Governor General, he was charged with the task of balancing the British government's books in India. The man was obsessed with milking profit from the country. I heard that he considered demolishing the Taj Mahal to sell the marble. But I am told that he was a decent man. I would like to think that was why he sent soldiers to rescue those villagers, and not because he recognized the value of the black diamond that Sameer had described. But I cannot say for sure. I do know that the battle was short and bloody. Dahlquist's men were mere bodyguards, no match for the trained soldiers that Bentick sent.

"Once the guards were defeated, the soldiers entered Dahlquist's cave. I spoke with one of them once – an old man now, older than myself. Do you know what his memory was of that cave? The smell. It stuck in the soldiers' mouths, made some of them physically sick. Can you guess what that smell was?"

"It was the hearts."

"Quite right, Mr Gideon. A fine guess. It was the villagers' hearts. Dahlquist laid them on an altar as offerings to his demon. In that heat, the organs rotted in days. They swarmed with so many flies that they each resembled the Black Terror itself."

"This is horrible. Was Dahlquist there?"

"Yes, and a ghastly sight by all accounts. He had not left the cave since the day the Black Terror was found. His skin had turned pale and his veins almost black."

"Was he killed too?"

"He was, as he tried to protect his statue of Malphas. But before he died, Lord Dahlquist swore a curse on any person that touched the Black Terror. He vowed that Malphas would have revenge on those people. After that, the demon would strike at the heart of the British Empire."

"None of this can be true. Curses, demons..."

"And yet, Miss Everett, you have witnessed it with your own eyes. The curse of the Black Terror."

"But why does no one know about this?"

"Because they could not, Wild Boy. As you know, many Indians resent your country's growing power over theirs, even without mad aristocrats butchering whole villages. There would have been rebellion, revolt. Lord Bentick was ordered to make the story disappear. The villagers' bodies, found in mass graves, were dug up and burned. Those of the guards were incinerated too."

"And Dahlquist's?"

"That I do not know. There is a story that his body burned with black smoke. Other accounts claim it disappeared. Stolen, or hidden perhaps. His wife and son vanished too. Into hiding, a life of shame."

"And the Black Terror? What happened to that?"

"That is where I enter the story. This was soon after I moved into this building, although at that time I owned only this showroom and the vault beneath our feet. I was not at the top of my profession. I do, however, believe that I was its most skilled practitioner. It was my eyes. They saw things in those stones that other jewellers did not, even the craftsmen of Amsterdam. It is not an exaggeration to say that I cut double the number of facets onto a stone than any of my rivals. Thus my jewels shone twice as bright.

"But I do not think that was why the Black Terror was brought to me. Rather, it was because of my reputation for discretion. I was one of very few women in my profession, a fact that I believed would discourage clients from seeking my business. Wherever possible, I kept my identity secret, acting through agents and intermediaries. That secrecy attracted the organization that had acquired the Black Terror and buried its story so deeply. Secrets, you see, are *their* business."

"You mean the Gentlemen?"

"Indeed. It was the Gentlemen who brought the stone into my life."

"It was Lucien Grant, wasn't it? He knew about Malphas."

"It was. Mr Grant's instructions were clear. The Black Terror was to be kept in my vault for ten years. No one else was to know of its existence. After that, I was to cut it into separate parts, bestowing each with a new name and provenance. It would be as if Lord Dahlquist's Black Terror, the heart of Malphas, had never existed."

"You did this even though you knew the stone's history?"

"No, I discovered that later. But had I known, I would still have accepted the commission. I lived for my craft, Wild Boy. That stone … I would never see its like again. I could not resist the chance to become *part* of its history. So I followed Mr Grant's instructions, and the stone remained in my vault for a decade. During that time, my star rose. I received commissions from the very highest levels of society. Kings, emperors, maharajas of Rajasthan. But I recall little of that work. Of those years, I remember only the Black Terror. You see, I too grew infatuated with that stone. I used my new wealth to uncover its history. It was not easy, for it was a story that the Gentlemen had worked hard to erase. Lord Dahlquist's title had been expunged. His family had vanished. Few would speak of the man or his crimes."

"How'd you know so much about it then?"

"I said few. I had my sources. Spencer, hold my hand tighter. There, like that. Ah, I remember the Black Terror so well! Often I would sit for hours, staring into its black abyss. That stone, over which armies had clashed and hundreds died… At times I felt like a priest worshipping at its temple."

"Or like Dahlquist in his cave."

"Perhaps, Miss Everett, perhaps. But I knew the time would come when I would be separated from the stone. Worse, I would have to cut it into pieces.

"And then the day came. I will never forget the scream as the saw first bit into the Black Terror. It was as if the cries of every villager of Kollur came from it at once. Well, cutting and polishing a single diamond takes several weeks. But a black diamond is the hardest substance known. Cutting and shaping those stones took me six months. That whole time I felt as if I were cutting out my own heart.

"I divided the stone into four separate jewels. They were my finest work, and my greatest regret. One, the stone you see here, was given to me by the Gentlemen to buy my silence in the affair. Another was given to Lord Bentick."

"He had it put in a ring for his wife. The killer took it."

"Of course, Miss Everett. And the third stone I set into a necklace for the Queen."

"Wait. What about the fourth? There's still another piece of the Black Terror?"

"I cannot tell you what happened to that stone – the largest of them all. Like the others, it was given to the Gentlemen. I do not envy whoever has it now. It is clear that Malphas has come for the owners of the other stones, just as he came for me."

"You ain't got the terror, not like Marcus."

"No. The demon left me in a state I regard as far worse. You see, the day after I completed the commission, I lost my sight, never to look upon my stone again. That, I believe, was my punishment for cutting it but not for keeping it. For that crime the demon will yet return for my life."

"That's why you shut yourself up, built these traps."

"It was. However, if those defences failed against two children, then I must assume they will also fail to stop Malphas."

"We ain't ordinary children."

"Miss Everett, I do not need eyes to see that. But while it is admirable that you wish to save your friend, I fear you have a greater concern. Have you asked yourself why the killer is collecting the black diamonds?"

"The Black Terror. He's trying to get it all back together."

"Precisely, Mr Gideon. And when the whole stone is reunited, the demon will be strong again."

"No. We don't believe in demons."

"That is irrelevant, Miss Everett. *Someone* is acting out Lord Dahlquist's curse. And remember, the curse is sworn not only upon those who took his stone. Once the four stones of the Black Terror are together, Malphas will be strong again, and the demon will strike at the heart of the British Empire."

"What does that mean?"

"My guess is as good as yours, Wild Boy. Malphas, the Destroyer of Cities."

Wild Boy felt as if a wind had rushed in from outside, chilling him to the bone. He knew what Oberstein meant, but he prayed it wasn't true. The heart of the British Empire. The answer came out in a whisper, a single word.

"London."

"Indeed," Oberstein replied. "So you see, whatever is happening has only begun. Soon, thousands will experience this thing you call terror. After sixteen years, Lord Dahlquist and his demon are finally having their revenge."

·20·

Wild Boy could always tell when someone was lying. His eyes homed in on ticks and traits, subconscious gestures that were as clear to him as if the person had hung a sign around their neck declaring their guilt. The way someone's voice rose or fell by a note as they delivered their deceit, a narrowing of an eye, an almost imperceptible flare of a nostril.

He saw none of these things in Oberstein.

Really, he didn't need to look. He could hear it in her voice as she told the history of the Black Terror, the weight of emotions pressing on every word. The story was true, or at least she believed it to be.

By the time Oberstein had finished speaking, Wild Boy and Clarissa were gripping each other's arms. Clarissa's eyes remained on the black diamond, but she was no longer determined to steal it. Now she was scared of it.

Gideon was affected by the story, too. It seemed almost as if it had physically pained him to hear it. His face had screwed up even tighter, and he gripped his neck cloth so hard that he gagged.

"So," Oberstein croaked, her voice weak from her long tale. "You understand how little chance your friend Marcus has of survival. He is marked to die by a demon."

"No!" Clarissa insisted. Her cry was so loud that the guard raised his pistol. "That can't be true."

Oberstein let out a noise like a bark. Wild Boy realized she was laughing.

"Perhaps," she said, "if you see the stone, you will understand its power. Spencer, bring me my stone."

Her masked bodyguard shook his head, refusing to leave her side. He whispered something but Wild Boy couldn't make out the muffled words.

Oberstein raised a hand and stroked Spencer's mask. "My dear, please. Bring me my stone."

Still the man hesitated, but he was clearly bound to obey her command. The bones in his knees clicked as he rose. He glared at Wild Boy and Clarissa, his grey eyes swirling like storm clouds. Wild Boy wondered if Spencer had built all the traps around this building. How hard had he worked to protect his mistress? And how deeply did he now despise the people who had broken through his defences?

Spencer strode to the cabinet. With a single swing of a fist, he smashed its glass. Blood spotted his knuckles, but he didn't seem to feel the pain. He reached into the case and picked up the black diamond.

As he placed the jewel in Oberstein's hands, light from the fire gleamed off its faces, like a black sun shining darkness. It was a true piece of treasure, a mesmerizing thing. Wild Boy couldn't imagine how stunning the Black Terror had looked when it was whole.

But the jewel and its history appalled him. He brought the Queen's card from his pocket, stared at that name in dark ink. *Malphas.* He remembered the eyes of the demon, glowing with darkness just like that stone.

No, he told himself. *You don't believe in demons.*

He just had to study the clues, like Marcus had taught him. Someone had poisoned Prendergast and then Marcus and Lady Bentick. He didn't know how the killer had done it, but he sensed it was the answer he needed to unlock this case.

One of the guards snatched the card from Wild Boy's hand and eyed it suspiciously, as if it might be a weapon. Ignoring Wild Boy's protest, he strode across the showroom and tossed the card onto the fire. A puff of dark smoke rose from the flames and drifted past the old jeweller's face.

Oberstein's fingers curled around the stone, and a hiss came from her mouth, like one of the pipes releasing steam. It sounded like relief and regret at the same time. "My finest work," she said. "You see, Wild Boy? You see the power of this stone? It is truly the heart of Malphas."

The jeweller's hands sank, as if the stone had suddenly doubled in weight. She sucked in air, like the last breath of someone drowning. Her shaking grew more violent and her chair scraped against the floor.

"Wild Boy?" Clarissa said. "What's happening to her?"

Behind the jeweller, the two guards also began to shake. One of them collapsed, his pistol firing as it clattered to the floor. Spencer fell back from Oberstein in shock, and Clarissa and Gideon dived to the ground. Chips of plaster sprayed from the ceiling.

Wild Boy didn't know what was happening, only that this was his chance to get the black diamond. Running to Oberstein, he caught the stone as it slipped from her hands. He shoved the jewel into his coat pocket, but his cry of triumph turned into a shriek of horror.

He stepped back, staring…

Darkness flowed through Oberstein's veins. Black lines slithered over her arms, up her neck and across her wrinkled face. Her eyes changed too. Suddenly they saw again – nothing real, just the imaginary horrors the terror had unleashed in her mind.

She swatted at invisible swooping creatures. "No!" she shrieked. "Not again, not my eyes. Do not take my eyes!"

"It's the terror!" Gideon cried. "The demon came for her, just like she said."

Spencer sank to his knees beside his mistress and enveloped her shaking figure in his huge arms. A tear fell from the bottom of his mask and onto Oberstein's cobweb hair.

The guards had been struck with the terror too. One was dead, the other lay on the floor beside him, thrashing and drooling.

"How did it happen?" Clarissa gasped, staring at Oberstein. "One moment she was talking and then … how could the terror have got her too?"

"Oberstein!" a voice called from the street. "Open this door."

"It's Malphas!" Gideon shrieked. "The demon's come for me now!"

Wild Boy rushed to the shutters and looked through the slats. Outside, Lucien Grant pounded on the door. Dr Carew was there too, his pale face full of fear. Beyond them were a dozen Black Hats. From the way their hands hovered close to their coats, Wild Boy guessed the men were armed.

"Oberstein!" Lucien called. "We are searching for the fugitives Wild Boy and Clarissa Everett. Send them out or we will force entry."

Clarissa stood over Spencer. "How do we get out of here?" she said. "All this security, you gotta have an escape."

Spencer shot out an arm and grabbed her neck.

A sound like a tiger's snarl came from behind his mask as his fingers tightened around her throat.

Wild Boy grabbed the guard's pistol from the floor and aimed it at Spencer's masked face. He had no idea how to fire it, but he had to help Clarissa. "Let her go," he said.

Spencer glowered at him, but his grip on Clarissa's throat didn't ease.

"You can still save your boss," Wild Boy said. "There's a cure and we can get it. We need it for our friend too, so we're on the same side. But no one's gonna get it if we're caught by them men out there, understand?"

Spencer's eyes narrowed. His hand relaxed and Clarissa fell from his grip. He looked at Oberstein with eyes full of anguish, then leaned close and whispered something into her ear. He rose and stomped towards the back of the showroom.

Another crash on the door. It was heavier this time, rattling the pipes on the walls.

"They're using a battering ram," Gideon said. "They'll be through in seconds."

He snatched the pistol from Wild Boy, set the lock to half cock so it was ready to fire. He shoved the weapon into his coat. "Time to go."

• 21 •

The bodyguard Spencer unhooked a lantern from the wall and led the way down a steep stone staircase.

The air grew even hotter, drying Wild Boy's mouth. The walls trembled; warm water dripped on his head. Whatever was in the basement was glowing. He heard groans and gasps and feared for a moment that Spencer was taking them to meet the demon Malphas in hell.

The heat grew more intense as they reached an underground brick chamber. An iron furnace stood against the wall. Amber light leaked from its joints and a dozen pipes rose from the top. Each pipe split in two and split again, crawling like ivy over the basement wall and up through the ceiling. Steam hissed from their joints, and puddles bubbled on the stone floor.

"Is that what powers all the traps around here?" Clarissa asked.

Ignoring her, Spencer stomped to an iron door that was covered with a clockwork confusion of dials, cogs and springs. His hands glowed in the lamplight as he rotated one of the dials a precise number of clicks.

The cogs began to turn. One caught the other, movement spreading across the surface. Wild Boy heard the *clunk, thunk* of sliding locks.

From above, a thundering crash. One of the pipes dislodged from its bracket, spitting steam across the basement.

"It's the Gentlemen's battering ram," Gideon warned. "We gotta hurry."

Spencer pulled open the vault door and they followed him into the next room. For a moment, Wild Boy forgot all about the Gentlemen upstairs, or even the black diamond in his pocket. He stared at shelves crammed with treasure: crystal peacocks with sapphire-studded tails, silver daggers in jewel-encrusted sheaths, golden sceptres, diamond tiaras.

Clarissa grabbed his arm. "Look."

Cut into the opposite wall was an entrance to a tunnel. Beams supported the walls; a rail track ran along the floor. An iron mine cart sat in the tunnel's mouth.

Spencer turned a valve on a gas pipe fixed to the tunnel wall. He lifted what was left of the lantern's candle – a tiny black stump – and held it to the pipe, causing a streak of fire to rush through the tube. Flames spat from holes along its length, illuminating a long, sloping passage underground.

Another crash from the showroom above.

"That's the front door breaking," Gideon said. "The Gentlemen will be down here any minute."

Wild Boy heard Dr Carew call out for him, then cries of horror as the Gentlemen discovered Oberstein and her guards struck with the terror.

"Get in the cart," Wild Boy said.

He grabbed Clarissa and pulled her in with him. Spencer climbed in front, his thick frame squashing them back. Gideon clung to one of the sides.

"Let's go," he said.

Spencer pulled a lever on the side of the cart. They rolled down the track – slowly at first, then gaining speed. Warm air rushed through Wild Boy's hair as the cart moved faster, past orange blurs of gaslight. One of the flares crackled the hair on Wild Boy's cheek, and he sank deeper into the cart, clinging onto Clarissa.

Looking back, he saw the tiny, top-hatted shapes of the Gentlemen in the tunnel entrance. He felt the black diamond in his pocket, and for the first time since the events at the palace, he smiled. Gideon had said that Marcus was still alive, so now they could use the black diamond to save him. Everything would be all right.

He turned back to face the tunnel, and the smile fell from his face. Fifty yards ahead, part of the ceiling had collapsed.

Spencer yanked the brake lever. Sparks sprayed up, but the cart didn't slow down.

"Hold on!" Wild Boy cried. "Everyone hold on!"

The front wheels hit the rubble, and the cart flipped up. Its rear end crashed against the tunnel ceiling, and its front slammed onto the ground. It slid, vertical, down the track, speed and slope keeping it moving. The cart fell forwards, then to its side, all within seconds. Only Spencer remained silent. Wild Boy, Clarissa and Gideon kept screaming, even as the tunnel levelled and they finally scraped to a slow, creaking stop.

Gideon pulled himself up against the tunnel wall. His coat was torn and his face was lacerated with cuts and grazes. "Everyone alive?" he grunted.

Wild Boy helped Clarissa out. Behind them, Spencer rose to his knees. A jagged crack ran down the centre of his mask's smooth jade. As Spencer tightened the mask's straps, Wild Boy glimpsed the face underneath. Livid red scars and black welts covered his skin. They looked like burn marks.

Clarissa leaned against the tunnel wall, cursing as she discovered new cuts around her limbs. "We're still alive, Lucien!" she shouted back up the tunnel. "We've got the black diamond and we're gonna save Marcus, then you'll see what … what … what is *that*?"

Something rushed after them down the tunnel. A wall of blackness came closer, extinguishing the flares as it approached.

"It's the demon," Gideon said. "It's coming for me!"

As the darkness drew nearer, its surface swirled like a storm cloud tumbling through a dark sky.

"Smoke?" Wild Boy said. "It's smoke!"

He remembered the black smoke at Lady Bentick's house, and then again after Oberstein was struck with the terror. "It was *smoke* that poisoned them," he said. "But what made the smoke?"

"Worry about that later," Clarissa said. She grabbed his arm, dragging him along the tunnel. "Everyone run!"

They charged down the passage, tripping over, staggering up. Wild Boy glimpsed over his shoulder and saw gas flares snuff out as the smoke rolled closer. Now another, then another.

"I see the end of the tunnel!" Gideon cried.

They reached the last gas flare. The bottom of an iron ladder hung from a shaft in the tunnel roof. Spencer grasped the lowest rung and heaved himself up, squeezing into the tight shaft. He reached down and grasped Gideon's hand.

Clarissa hoisted Wild Boy up next. "Go!" she screamed.

Gripping the iron rungs, Wild Boy climbed. Clarissa followed so close behind that her head bashed his feet. Below, the last light in the tunnel went out. The black smoke rose up the shaft.

"Faster!" Clarissa yelled.

Spencer curled his back against a metal grille that sealed the top of the shaft. It rose up, then crashed down so hard that Wild Boy almost slipped from the ladder.

Wild Boy climbed into daylight, then rolled over to help Clarissa. The black cloud rose beneath her, tickling her feet, but the smoke was fainter now, dissipating into a thin haze.

Clarissa stopped, half in and half out of the shaft. "My foot," she grunted. It was stuck between the ladder and the wall. "Can't get it out."

The smoke rose higher, engulfing her head.

"Hold your breath," Wild Boy said. "Don't breathe it in!"

Wisps of smoke circled them, like swirling crows. Wild Boy swatted them away, but they parted and rejoined, swirled closer.

"Wild Boy!" Clarissa gasped.

He shook his head, warning her not to talk. Leaning into the shaft, he gripped the ladder and pulled, trying to force it from the wall.

Come on. Please…

His breath came out in a scream and her foot finally came free. They scrambled away from the shaft as the last wisps of smoke floated from underground and disappeared.

"It's gone," Wild Boy said. "Are you all right?"

"I … I think so."

Wild Boy rose, blearily taking in their surroundings. It looked like a building site, hidden from the street by wooden hoardings and corrugated sheets. But the only building works were shacks that vagrants had constructed of crates and planks. Around them the ground was strewn with snow-sheeted rubble.

Wild Boy felt his coat again, making sure the black diamond was safe. He stumbled towards Spencer and Gideon at the hoardings. From the way Gideon tugged at his neck cloth, he could tell that the danger hadn't yet passed.

He peered through a gap in a hoarding. Several Black Hats marched along the street, led by Lucien. They were searching for the exit to Oberstein's tunnel. They banged on doors and stormed into shops, roaring at anyone in their way.

"We gotta get somewhere safe," Gideon said. "Over there, see?"

He pointed to a boarded-up building across the street. Scraps of paper fluttered on its walls where posters had been torn away. It looked like an exhibition room or a theatre.

It was a good place to hide, but Wild Boy wasn't sure he could make it that far. He leaned against the hoarding to steady his spinning mind. The wound in his head throbbed, but something else was wrong.

It felt as if all the blood had been drained from his body.

A crow swooped at him, attacking with its claws. Wild Boy staggered back, whirling his fists. He looked up, but the crow had gone. All he saw were swollen clouds covering the sun.

"Hear what they say! Hear what they say about Wild Boy!"

He turned, crying out. It was his freak show boss, Augustus Finch. Scars gleamed across the showman's face as he came closer, grinning under the shadow of his crooked top hat. He floated over the rubble. *"Hear what they say about Wild Boy, the most sickening sight at the fair!"*

Wild Boy scrabbled away, fell to his backside. How could Finch be here? It wasn't possible.

"Hey," Finch said.

Wild Boy brushed back the hair on his face. When he looked again, Finch was not there. Instead, Gideon stood over him, blocking the sun.

"I asked you if you were all right," Gideon said.

Was he all right? Wild Boy wasn't sure. Maybe it was just exhaustion and emotions. He just needed… Just needed…

"Wild Boy?"

Clarissa collapsed to her knees. "I don't feel right."

Fear rushed through Wild Boy, a panic unlike any he'd known. He tried to crawl towards her, but his arms buckled and he fell to the rubble. The hair on his hands rustled in the wind. Black veins crawled up white skin.

The terror.

No! This can't be happening!

It *was* happening, and to Clarissa too. Darkness spread across her face. Her scream came as a dry rasp as she slipped to the ground.

No! Not her!

Then Clarissa was gone. All Wild Boy saw was a wooden wall, slatted and glistening with damp. It was the wall of his freak show caravan, the wall and that worm-eaten door. Above, the crows cawed like they always cawed, like they were laughing. *"Welcome back,"* they said. *"Welcome back to where you belong."*

Wild Boy curled up, cowering. Suddenly he was that boy again. Alone. Desperate. The whole world against him.

"No," he gasped. "Please…"

He slumped forward into the snow but didn't feel its cold burn. He didn't feel anything except terror, pure and absolute, taking control of every part of his body.

·22·

The creak of the wooden door resonated across the caravan, sending shock waves of fear that Wild Boy felt in his bones.

Don't cry. Don't scream. Act tough.

He slid further into the corner, beyond the ceiling lamp's searching glare. He covered his head with his arms, but he didn't need to see to know that Augustus Finch had led another crowd into the van. He could smell the gin on their breath, the stench of sweat and unwashed clothes. His mouth dried and his arms wouldn't stop shaking.

Don't scream. Don't give them the satisfaction.

If anyone touched him, he would fight back. He had to. He would fight back, no matter how bad the beatings got. It wasn't the pain that he feared, anyway. It was afterwards, when he would curl up and wish he had someone – anyone – to hold on to.

It was a loneliness so heavy that he felt it might crush him into the stage.

No. There *was* someone. Someone he'd forgotten.

Above, the crow laughed louder, a throaty, mocking laugh.

The audience pressed closer. Leering, bestial faces.

The showman grinned. The scars throbbed across his face. "Welcome home boy," he snarled. "We missed you."

And then the showman was gone, and the crowd and their laughter. All Wild Boy saw were those walls, growing larger, spreading apart. Walls with no windows and no door. No way out. A freak for ever.

He knew then that there once *was* more than this. Something had made him happy. He didn't know what, only that it was gone.

And *that* was what made him open his mouth and scream.

Wild Boy bolted up, his cry coming as a parched gasp. He pushed back his coat sleeve and the thick hair underneath. His skin was pale, but it was not white. His veins were not black.

He lay back, his heart beating as if he'd woken from a nightmare. Pain pounded in his head as if someone were trying to punch their way out of his skull. Worse was the memory of what he'd seen:

those visions from his past. The showman, the freak show, the crows… It was as if someone had kicked open a door at the back of his mind and released his darkest memories.

Then he remembered.

"Clarissa!"

He tried to rise, but firm hands held him down. At first he thought it was Gideon again, but now the pale, worried face of Dr Carew leaned closer. The doctor's spectacles glinted in the light from a fire.

"Stay still," he said. "You must rest."

No way was Wild Boy resting, not until he knew she was safe. He grabbed the doctor and yanked him closer. "Where is she?"

Dr Carew's spectacles slipped down his nose, and he gave a panicked yelp. "She has recovered," he said. "Like yourself."

A wisp of dark smoke floated past Wild Boy's face. He slid back, swatting in panic at the fumes. But it wasn't the smoke that had chased him in the tunnel. Rather, it rose from a blackened cauldron over a fire at the side of a small, windowless room. Inside the cauldron, something thick and pink bubbled.

"Wax?" he said.

The room was crammed with disembodied parts of wax statues – leather torsos stuffed with straw, carved arms, tins filled with staring marble eyeballs. Wax heads on a shelf had begun to melt. Dark streaks slid down shiny faces.

There were two doors. Through a glass pane in one, Wild Boy saw snow falling in an alley. Beyond the other, silhouetted wax figures stood on plinths, perfectly still.

"Is this a wax works museum?" he said.

"We are in its workshop," Dr Carew replied. "The museum is closed for the season. You are safe here."

"I don't understand. What happened?"

Wild Boy sipped from a mug of tea that Dr Carew held to his mouth. It was hot and sweet and soothed his dry lips. His body felt stronger already, but his mind still whirled as he tried to make sense of his memories.

"I saw my veins," he said. "They turned black, just like them others with the terror. How did I survive?"

Dr Carew dipped his quill in his inkpot and made a note in his ledger. "That is what I have been trying to establish ever since Gideon found me. I took blood samples from you and Miss Everett. They confirmed that you had both been affected by some sort of toxin."

"The hallucinothing you and Lucien talked about?"

"*Hallucinogenic*. Yes, but from what Gideon described, you and Miss Everett were exposed to only a very small amount of it." He checked his notes. "This *black smoke*."

Wild Boy remembered how the smoke had faded

by the time it caught them in the tunnel. That was why they'd survived. The other victims – Prendergast, Marcus, Lady Bentick and Oberstein – had all breathed in much more of it.

"Do you know what caused the black smoke?" Dr Carew asked.

Wild Boy shifted and looked around the workshop. Spencer stared into the fire, as still and silent as one of the wax statues. Firelight shimmered off his cracked jade mask. Beyond him, hunkered against the wall, sat Clarissa. Her head hung low and her hair covered her face like a veil.

"Clarissa?" Wild Boy said.

She didn't look up.

"She is well," Dr Carew said. A hesitance in his voice suggested that he was unconvinced by his own diagnosis. "Whatever caused the black smoke," he continued, "there is too little of it in your blood to kill you. Sadly, there is not enough to formulate a cure either. But I must warn you that it is *still* in your blood, just a little. You will continue to experience some of its effects for a short time, at least."

Dr Carew leaned closer. "Tell me, how would you describe those effects?"

Wild Boy shifted back further, uncomfortable under his stare. "What about Marcus?" he asked. "You seen him?"

Dr Carew returned to his notes. "His condition has deteriorated, but he remains alive."

For now, Wild Boy thought. He rose and crossed the workshop. The pale skin beneath his hairs was covered in bumps and dark bruises, like a rotten cauliflower. Every limb ached.

"Clarissa?"

Finally she looked up. Her eyes were pink, and salty tracks of tears stained her cheeks. He hoped she might jump up and hug him. He needed her to. But she simply gave a weak, flickering smile, like a flame struggling to stay alight, and returned her gaze to the floor.

Wild Boy understood now why Dr Carew had sounded unsure when he said she'd recovered. Whatever Clarissa saw when the terror struck had almost broken her. He tried to think of something to say, some way to help her.

"We did it, Clarissa," he said. "We got the black diamond."

No reply. Did she even hear him?

"Dr Carew said the terror is still in us, just a bit," he said. "Said maybe we'll still see some of them bad things. I ... I saw the freak show. I was back there again, alone. Did you see your mother?"

Clarissa's fists clenched so tightly that her nails drew blood from her palms. "No," she said softly. "I didn't see nothing."

At any other moment, on any other day, seeing Clarissa like this would have crushed Wild Boy's heart. But right then, as he felt his pocket, a realization struck him so hard that he felt as if it had punched right through him, bursting his lungs.

He checked his other pocket, then checked both again, making sure he wasn't mistaken. Praying he was.

He wasn't.

The black diamond. Oberstein's black diamond.

It was gone.

·23·

"**W**anna go for a walk?" Clarissa said.

Her hand was as shaky as her voice as she reached for Wild Boy to help her from the floor. Her fingers gripped his as if she was hanging from the edge of an abyss.

Across the workshop, Dr Carew looked up from his notes. "Where are you two going?"

Spencer's gaze turned from the fire, stormy eyes watching from behind his cracked stone mask. He seemed to be on the verge of rising, or perhaps even speaking. Wild Boy sensed that he, too, wanted them to stay close.

Even more reason to leave.

They walked from the workshop and through the museum's long exhibition chamber. Strips of fading daylight shone through cracks in the window shutters, spotlighting wax statues arranged in strange, imaginary scenes. On one plinth, the Duke of Wellington planted a signature boot on a prostrate Napoleon Bonaparte. On another, the French queen Marie Antoinette wore a silver-sequined mask. Courtiers danced around her disguised in cloaks and black-beaked masks. Beside them, Queen Victoria took tea with Henry VIII, the warlord Genghis Khan and the famous opera singer Jenny Lind.

Wild Boy stared at the statue of the Queen, remembering his excitement when she asked him to investigate this case: the thrill of the mystery and the prospect of solving it. He'd hoped that he and Clarissa would be allowed to stay in the palace for as long as they wanted. Only, he'd made a mess of it so far.

Marcus was still alive, but the black diamond was gone.

He didn't even know how. It had been in his pocket – deep in his pocket – after the crash in the tunnel. It had been safe.

He looked back along the exhibition chamber at the flicker of firelight from the museum workshop. Had someone stolen it while he was unconscious? Apart from Clarissa, only three people had been near him in that time: Dr Carew, Spencer and Gideon.

Was one of them the killer?

It would make sense. The killer was trying to resurrect the demon Malphas, or at least that's what the killer thought would happen when the four diamonds of the Black Terror were reunited. But one diamond was still missing, the largest of the stones. Oberstein had no idea where it was, so Wild Boy doubted the killer did either.

The killer still needed their help.

But he wouldn't get it. If the killer was acting out Lord Dahlquist's curse, that meant he planned to spread his terror across all of London. Wild Boy couldn't let that happen, not even to save Marcus. The only hope was to get that last stone and use it to catch the killer, and then make him give them the cure. They needed a new plan. But Wild Boy's mind was so foggy he could barely think.

The chamber darkened as they reached the last statues. These were raised higher than the others, to give the impression that they were leering down at visitors. A sign on the wall was scrawled in crimson writing to look like blood:

GALLERY OF GHOULS

Here were models of Britain's most notorious criminals: the crazy-eyed witch, Mother Shipton, grinning body snatchers Burke and Hare, and the murderous barber Sweeny Todd, slashing the air with his rusty razor.

On the highest plinth stood a monster covered in hair. The creature looked like a werewolf, with blood-red eyes and vicious, curling claws. The sign on its stand said:

WILD BOY
OF LONDON

Wild Boy and Clarissa stared at the figure. A few days ago they'd have found it funny. They would have blasted it with spitballs, or swapped its clothes with another wax statue. They'd always laughed about those plays in penny theatres – *The Savage Spectacle of Wild Boy*.

But things were different now. This statue and those plays were the reason they had relied so heavily on Marcus's protection. They were the reason why, if Marcus died, Wild Boy would have to leave Clarissa. She could do anything. But for him there was only one other place.

Wild Boy closed his eyes as dark memories flashed through his head, glimpses of swooping crows and freak-show walls. It was the Black Terror, still affecting his mind, as Dr Carew had warned.

Clarissa reached to him but pulled away and stepped back. "I'm sick of this," she fumed.

She shoved the model so hard that it toppled from its stand and thumped to the floor. "Even if we do get the cure, no one will thank us. They'll still make up stupid stories about you."

"I don't care about those people, Clarissa."

"Me neither." She punctuated each sentence by kicking the model on the floor. "All I care about is Marcus. He's the only one I'm giving the cure. Everyone else can *get* the terror for all I care."

Her last kick was so hard that the statue's marble eyes fell out and rolled across the floor. She stood over it, breathing hard. "Why are we even here? We've got the black diamond. How do we swap it for the cure?"

There was no point in delaying it any longer, and no good way to say it. Wild Boy had only put it off because he feared her reaction. He breathed in, braced himself. "We ain't got it," he said.

"What?"

"Oberstein's diamond. It was in my pocket. It was safe."

He expected her to explode, to swear and punch the other statues. Instead Clarissa fell silent and glared towards the workshop. When she finally spoke it was barely a whisper.

"Someone took it," she said.

She marched back along the exhibition chamber.

"Where you going?" Wild Boy called.

"To beat a confession out of one of them."

Wild Boy shouted after her, but she didn't stop. He didn't know if anything he said would make a difference anymore. Clarissa's anger had never scared him like it did then. They had always acted tough, but the terror – whatever she had seen – had turned her rage into something deeper. It was as if it had put out a light inside her and lit a darkness.

He picked up the statue and stood it on its plinth. As he stared into its empty eyes he realized that he'd never felt so sad, not even in the freak show. Back then he had nothing. Now, he had so much to lose. And he *was* losing it, minute by minute.

For Clarissa, for Marcus, for himself – he had to find the last black diamond.

• 24 •

" So which of you is the killer?" Clarissa demanded. Wild Boy raced back to the workshop, relieved to see that she hadn't started swinging her fists. He was certain that Clarissa's threat to beat a confession out of one of these men was serious. But it would be a wasted effort. Whoever was behind this was too determined and too crazy to give up merely from the threat of force.

In her anger, Clarissa hadn't noticed that Gideon was still not here. Spencer and Dr Carew sat beside the fire and its cauldron of wax, together but alone. As Clarissa strode closer, the doctor gave a frightened shriek. Spencer didn't react. Still he stared into the flames, breathing heavily into the back of his broken mask.

The workshop door burst open with a swirl of snow. Gideon hurried in from outside, muttering and grumbling. He stamped ice from his boots and shook snow from his hat and coat. Grazes on his face from the tunnel crash had turned pink from the cold.

"Where have *you* been?" Clarissa asked.

"Fetched the carriage," Gideon said. "Between here and Oberstein's place, I counted ten Black Hats and around thirty coppers, all banging on doors looking for us. People saying the Wild Boy of London's on the loose again. Just like old times, eh?"

Clarissa marched so close that flecks of her spit hit Gideon's cheeks. "You think this is funny? We ain't got the black diamond no more. So we ain't got no deal with the killer, and Marcus is gonna die."

Gideon hadn't been smiling. He was now, but without the remotest trace of humour. "I've served Marcus for sixteen years, missus," he said. "I owe that man more than you'll ever know. So no, I don't find any of this funny."

He slid off his coat and spread it beside the fire to dry. Wild Boy noticed black smears on his fingers.

"Oil," Gideon explained, quickly wiping his hand on his neck cloth. "Had to fix one of the carriage wheels where it hit the lamp post outside Oberstein's."

Wild Boy thought back to the events on Bond Street. Scenes from that morning flashed through his mind, perfectly frozen moments of time. He saw Gideon riding the carriage. Gideon tumbling off.

Gideon grappling with Oberstein's guard. But he didn't see the carriage wheel striking the lamp post.

Wherever Gideon had gone, he'd been drinking. Wild Boy could smell the whisky on his breath even from across the fire.

"Do you really believe one of us took the diamond?" Dr Carew said.

"One of you is the *killer*," Clarissa replied. "Planning on spreading your terror all over London too."

"It's possible," Gideon grunted. "Only how do we know it ain't one of you two?"

"It ain't us," Clarissa said. "We're the *good* ones."

"That so? You're the only one that walked out of Lady Bentick's dinner without the terror. Funny that. Or fishy, more like."

"The killer gave me a note," Clarissa insisted. "Told me to leave the dining room."

"Yeah?" Gideon asked. "Where's that note then?"

"I threw it on the fire."

"That's convenient, ain't it?" He cast a beady eye at Wild Boy. "You think this too, eh?"

Wild Boy stepped beside Clarissa, making it clear where his allegiance lay. He didn't trust any of these men; any one of them could be the killer. Gideon and Dr Carew had both been at Lady Bentick's mansion when the killer struck, and the doctor knew about poisons. But Dr Carew hadn't been in Oberstein's showroom when she got the terror.

What about Spencer? He still hadn't spoken, but

he *could* speak. Wild Boy had seen behind his mask, too. Burn scars. He remembered Oberstein's story of how Lord Dahlquist's body was burned by the British soldiers. And then it disappeared.

The only thing Wild Boy knew about Spencer was what he saw in his eyes. It was the same lost look he'd seen on performers at the freak shows, those who had suffered the hardest pasts. The look of someone haunted by memories. Spencer wasn't just sad about what happened to Oberstein. Something else troubled him. Something deeper.

Wild Boy doubted he'd get answers by asking politely. But a few *less* polite words might provoke Spencer into giving something away. And no one was less polite than Clarissa.

He signalled to her with a nod, and she understood. Her eyes lit up, delighted at the prospect of a quarrel. She stepped closer to Spencer.

"What about you, masked man?" she said. "I know you can hear me. How'd you get them burns on your face? Maybe when you stole Lord Dahlquist's body from the fire. That's how Oberstein knew so much about the Black Terror, isn't it? You're one of Dahlquist's pals, ain't you?"

Spencer rose. The mask's leather straps creaked as he shook his head.

Clarissa shook hers too, mocking him. "Of course you'd deny it," she continued. "I would too if I knew that crazy bloomin' killer."

"Enough!" Spencer roared.

His voice carried an accent, but it was too muffled by the mask to place.

"So you do speak," Clarissa said.

Spencer's eyes darkened and swirled, the storm gathering. Then he marched from the workshop. Moments later, thumps and crashes echoed from the museum's exhibition chamber as he took his anger out on the wax statues.

"Well," Gideon said. "You ruffled his feathers. How about Dr Carew here?"

"How about *you*, Gideon," Clarissa said.

Gideon sneered. "This'll be good. So how am I the killer then?"

"You rushed off from here awful quick. Maybe you stole the diamond and went to hide it."

"I said I fetched the carriage."

The carriage, Wild Boy thought. "At Lady Bentick's House, your carriage was outside but you weren't. Where were you?"

"That all you got on me?"

"What about that pistol in Oberstein's shop? Loaded it like you knew what you was doing. That ain't part of usual coach driver's training. But then you ain't exactly a *usual* coach driver, are you Gideon? Your tattoo is from the army. When were you a soldier?"

Gideon turned his neckcloth around his throat again, fidgeting, suddenly uncomfortable. "Don't know what you're taking about."

"I bet you don't," Clarissa scoffed.

"You said Marcus saved you," Wild Boy continued. "What does that mean? And what about that passage you marked in your Bible about sin and forgiving?"

Gideon pulled so hard on his neckcloth that he choked, coughing into the fire. He looked away, refusing to answer.

They had pushed him far enough, Wild Boy decided. Whether or not Gideon was in the army, and whatever his past with Marcus, neither might have anything to do with this case. He turned away, but Gideon's next words made him stop and turn back.

"Anyway," Gideon muttered, sitting by the fire, "this is about Lord Dahlquist, not me. I ain't got nothing to do with some village in south-east India."

A shiver ran through Wild Boy's hair. "What did you just say?"

"I said you better back off."

"No. You said '*village in south-east India.*'"

"So what? I heard it off Oberstein."

"No. She said *south-west.*"

"How could you possibly remember that?" said Dr Carew.

"Cos that's what I do," Wild Boy replied. "Marcus said you've been in India, doc. Where's that village where Dahlquist killed all them people?"

"Kollur?" Dr Carew said. "It's close to Golkonda,

an important mining community, in which—"

"Just tell us where, doc."

"The south-east. I suppose Madam Oberstein was wrong."

"Yeah," Wild Boy said, "and Gideon just got it right."

Gideon jabbed the fire with a stick, staring hard into the flames. If there had been a smile on his face a moment ago, now it was replaced by something like sadness. He brought his pipe from his coat pocket, but his hands shook too hard to open the tobacco pouch. "That don't mean nothing," he said. "What about Dr Carew? Ain't you gonna quiz him too?"

The doctor slid back from the fire as if he'd been burned. "Me?" he said, laughing nervously. "I hardly think you need consider me in your investigation."

"What are you writing in that notebook?" Clarissa asked.

"A record of the terror's symptoms. It is our only hope of developing a cure should we fail to apprehend the killer."

"How long did you live in India, doc?" Wild Boy said.

The doctor shot a look over his shoulder; that same panicked reaction Wild Boy had noticed before, as if he was contemplating an escape. When he spoke again it was with fresh confidence, as if he'd found the answer among the shadows.

"I would appreciate it if you would stop calling

me 'doc'," he said. "I am a trained medical physician, educated at Cambridge and with senior residencies at hospitals in London, Paris and Bombay."

"Bombay. That near Dahlquist's village?"

"It is not."

"What'd you do there, then?" Clarissa stepped closer. *"Doc?"*

"I specialized in rare diseases, Miss Everett. I watched people die in the most appalling ways. I witnessed atrocious levels of suffering. It is my duty as a doctor, a gentlemen and a *Gentleman* to find cures for such misery. That is why I am here, whether you happen to like it or not."

He dipped his quill in his inkpot. "Besides," he added, "it seems to me that your energies would be better spent locating the last black diamond. Then, perhaps, we will have a chance of getting the killer's cure."

"Ha!" Gideon said. He finally managed to fill his pipe and patted the tobacco into its bowl. "Answer that, mister detective."

Wild Boy didn't hear. He stared at the loose tobacco that sprinkled from Gideon's pipe. Everything else disappeared from his world as he watched the brown strands flutter to the floor.

"Tobacco…" he said.

His eyes lit up, bright and shining with excitement. How could he have not realized? His mind had been so foggy that he'd not been able to see the signpost, the obvious clue he'd missed.

"You just worked something out, ain't you?" Clarissa said.

He had. Right then he knew exactly where to find the last black diamond. He knew how to get it, and how to use it to catch the killer.

"Me and Clarissa better be off now," he said.

"Really," Dr Carew said, "it is best that we remain together."

"That's right," Gideon said. "If one of us is the killer, then we gotta settle that. If that ain't the case, we gotta solve who is."

"Only the killer would want us to stay," Clarissa snapped.

Gideon reached to his coat on the floor and pulled out his pistol. "That ain't the reason."

Wild Boy moved to protect Clarissa, but he didn't think that Gideon would fire the weapon. He noticed his finger stay deliberately clear of the trigger.

"Please," Dr Carew said. "There is no need for—"

Clarissa lashed out a foot, kicking the cauldron of wax. The iron vat toppled over and spilled its bubbling contents across the floor. Gideon slipped and dropped the firearm.

Clarissa grabbed the gun. For a second Wild Boy feared she might use it, such was the rage that flashed through her eyes. Instead, she splashed through the wax to the door, and ran out into the alley. "Come on."

Wild Boy raced after her. They peered out to the street, where Gideon's carriage sat by the museum's boarded entrance. Its horses stamped and steamed, their snouts buried in nosebags of corn as much for warmth as for food. A lamplighter struggled with his ladder through the thickening snowfall. Fat flakes fell through the lamplight, glowing like furnace sparks.

As soon as the lamplighter passed, Wild Boy and Clarissa darted to the carriage. Wild Boy grabbed a blanket from inside and threw it to Clarissa as she climbed onto the driver's seat. "You know how to drive this?" he asked.

"Course I do. Better question is, what's going on?"

"I know where we'll find the last black diamond. And I got a plan to catch the killer with it an' all."

"About bloomin' time. So where we going?"

Throughout this case there had been too many questions that Wild Boy couldn't answer. He was glad to finally have one that he could. He leaped inside the carriage and swung the door shut.

"Buckingham Palace," he said. "We gotta have a word with the Queen."

·25·

BUCKINGHAM PALACE

Marcus had once said that the grand marble arch-
way which formed the entrance to Buckingham Palace was modelled on Roman monuments to
victories in battle. As Wild Boy stared at the impos-
ing structure through the carriage window, he tried
to draw confidence from this history lesson. But he
found none.

The plan he'd hatched to get the last black diamond and catch the killer now seemed as dangerous
as it was crazy. But it had one thing going for it: it
was the only plan he had.

They had stopped beside St James's Park, close
to the Mall – the wide, tree-lined avenue that led to
Buckingham Palace. The park was empty apart from
the crows that squabbled in the bare trees. One of
the black phantoms swooped down and landed on
top of the carriage. It made no sound, but still Wild

Boy heard the grating squawks. Louder now, they caused his head wound to pulse with pain.

The crows in his mind. The terror still in his blood.

He wished they could have parked the carriage somewhere else, but this was where they needed to be; far enough from the palace to avoid being seen, yet close enough to watch it through the snow and the gathering dark. In the palace forecourt, lamp-light showed three carriages being prepared by royal grooms. One of them was the Queen's coach. The others belonged to the Gentlemen. A Black Hat Gentleman roared orders at the servants harnessing the shivering horses.

"Lucien," Clarissa said. She rubbed frost from the carriage window. "You were right, he is here."

As they watched, three footmen ushered Queen Victoria from the palace's columned portico. They tried to protect her from the snow with umbrellas and blankets, but she swatted them away. Lucien attempted to speak to her as she climbed into her coach, but he too was dismissed with the flap of a royal hand.

"What's he saying?" Clarissa asked.

"He's telling her to leave London until the killer is caught."

Wild Boy guessed the Queen would refuse. He remembered Marcus's story about how, after the failed attempt on her life, the Queen had insisted on continuing her usual routine, and even used herself as bait to catch her would-be assassin. She was clearly very stubborn and very determined.

She reminded Wild Boy of Clarissa.

This was a busy night for Her Majesty. It was Thursday evening, the night she attended performances at the Italian Opera House in Mayfair. After that, she would return to the palace to host her ball. Wild Boy could tell from Lucien's exasperated expression that she'd refused to cancel either event.

"Good," he said.

Their plan to catch the killer relied on it. They needed to speak with the Queen, but with Lucien guarding her they wouldn't even get close. They'd planned something slightly crazy to get her attention.

"They're setting off," Wild Boy said.

The royal coach rode across the forecourt, led by one of the Gentlemen's carriages and followed by another. Moving slowly, the convoy passed through the marble arch and onto the Mall.

Wild Boy handed Gideon's pistol to Clarissa. He swung the door open, swatting away snowflakes. "You remember the plan?"

"All I gotta do is keep my balance and act crazy, right?"

"That's about it," he replied, wondering if anyone was more qualified for that job than she was.

As he climbed to the driver's seat, a dark snowflake fluttered past his head, as big and black as a crow's feather.

"Black snow," he muttered.

The snowfall was speckled with them. Lit by the moon, they looked like black diamonds falling through the white. It wasn't unusual; London's skies were rotten with pollution pumped from factories. Sometimes hail fell the colour of mud. Even so, Wild Boy couldn't help fearing that it was a bad omen.

One of the horses stamped, eager to get moving.

Settling onto the carriage seat, Wild Boy dug his feet against the base of the box. He hoped the animals couldn't sense his fear. The only horse he'd ever handled was the old draught-nag that pulled his freak show van. These were powerful Arabian horses, and he was going to have to ride them fast.

He shook the reins, and the horses moved forward with such force that he almost slipped from his seat. He held on tighter as they increased their pace. Iron-rimmed wheels cut through the snow as he steered the carriage from the park and onto the Mall.

He pulled out onto the street just ahead of the royal convoy. Looking back, he saw a Black Hat driving the leading carriage, wrapped like an Egyptian mummy in shawls and scarves. Lucien was inside.

So far so good, except for Wild Boy's heart, which pounded harder than the horses' hooves. He held his breath, as if to trap as much courage inside as possible. Then he slowed the horses, letting the royal convoy catch up. He heard a cry from the Black Hat, demanding that he pull over, although it was too snowy for the man to see who he was shouting at. In response, Wild Boy slowed his carriage even more. He led the convoy to the end of the Mall, passing piles of rubble where workers were laying a new square to celebrate the Battle of Trafalgar, and then round onto Pall Mall, the street that ran along the other side of the Mall.

The road was busier here, and Wild Boy's deliberately slow pace quickly caused a jam. Other drivers joined in with the Gentleman, yelling at Wild Boy to pull aside.

From behind came a *thump* of metal on wood. Clarissa opened the carriage door and dumped the pistol on the roof.

Wild Boy's stomach began to turn somersaults. He kept his eyes on the road, his grip on the reins, and whispered a prayer to whatever god – or demon – might be listening.

Another *thump*. Clarissa swung up and landed on top of the cabin.

In the carriage behind, the Black Hat's anger changed to panic. "Get down from that roof," he demanded. "What in blazes are you playing at?"

Clarissa picked up the gun and aimed it at him. She began to hop up and down on the roof, filling the air with as many swear words as there were snowflakes. The plan was for her to act crazy, and she did it perfectly. Her hair thrashed and her feet pounded so hard that one of the panels cracked. In fact, the act was almost *too* genuine. Wild Boy was glad her pistol was too damaged by wax to work.

BOOM!

A shot roared through the sky. The horses charged forward.

Wild Boy looked back, saw Clarissa lying flat on the roof. Beyond, Lucien leaned from the window of the carriage, a pistol smoking in his hand.

"Clarissa!" Wild Boy shouted.

She slid around and jumped up. "Missed me!" she screamed. "You thickheads. Come and catch us!"

Lucien bellowed an order, and his carriage raced after them.

Wild Boy couldn't believe this was actually going well. But everything depended on the few next minutes. The Queen's coach was now guarded only by the carriage at the rear of the convoy. With the road clogged behind, they would most likely race ahead to the Opera House. Wild Boy had one chance – just one – of blocking the royal coach, and getting hold of the last black diamond.

The snow drove harder, blurring his vision. He pulled the reins, riding faster down Pall Mall. Behind, Lucien's carriage was catching up.

"Go faster!" Clarissa yelled.

"Yaa! Yaa!" Wild Boy cried.

Ahead was the arched entrance to the Opera Arcade, the tunnelled parade of shops that led behind the Opera House.

"Hold on!" he called.

Clarissa clung onto the roof rail as Wild Boy turned the carriage into the arcade. A lantern on the tunnel's low ceiling whacked her head and she fell to her knees. There were sparks and screeches as the carriage door handles scraped shop windows on either side of the narrow passage. The sounds were drowned by the rattle of wheels, the thunder of horses and the cries of shoppers fleeing for the other end of the arcade.

Lucien's carriage followed them into the tunnel. It had a clear path and was catching up.

"Hold on," Wild Boy said.

"Stop saying that," Clarissa replied.

"This time I mean it."

He yanked the reins. The carriage lurched forward, then came to a sudden, jarring halt. The momentum thrust Wild Boy further and harder than he expected. He flew from the driver's seat and thumped to the ground, landing so close to the horses that their stamping hooves snagged the hair on his cheek.

He slid back, scrambled up. It had worked. Behind, Lucien's carriage had stopped, its path in the tunnel now blocked.

Clarissa grabbed the pistol and leaped from the roof. She landed beside Wild Boy, and they ran towards the exit.

"Are we too late?" she said.

"I don't know."

"Has the Queen already gone past?"

"I don't know, Clarissa!"

They stumbled out onto the street, twenty yards from the Opera House entrance. Crowds thronged around the theatre doors, shivering faces lit by gas chandeliers in the colonnaded portico. Every man was in an opera hat, every woman in pearls. The group buzzed with excited chatter about the upcoming performance. But the chatter turned to shrieks as they saw Wild Boy.

"Look. Look!"

"It's the Wild Boy of London."

"My God, it is. It is!"

"He's got a gun."

Actually, Clarissa had the gun. She waved it in a wide circle around the street. "Get back," she warned. "Everyone, get back!"

Everyone did, desperate to escape her sweeping aim. Some of them slipped on ice and tumbled on the stairs. Horses reared and drivers cursed. A dust-cart toppled over, spilling ash across the snow.

Wild Boy tried to ignore the chaos, to focus on the street. At first he saw nothing except the snow driving at his face. Then something big and dark burst through the white curtain.

"It's her," he said. "It's the Queen's coach."

The royal coach raced closer. The driver saw Wild Boy in the street, but instead of slowing down, he gritted his teeth and lashed the horses harder.

"He ain't stopping!" Clarissa cried.

Cobbles shook beneath Wild Boy's feet. Clarissa tried to drag him from the coach's path, but he pulled back, standing his ground. His mind gave itself over to just one thought – *this coach must stop*. If it didn't, he had failed, and Marcus would die.

"Wild Boy," Clarissa said. "It ain't stopping."

He dug his feet harder into the snow.

It had to stop. It had to…

·26·

The cobbles shook harder. The horses charged closer.

Steam snorted from the animals' snouts. Wild Boy heard the jangle of harnesses even above the screams from the crowd outside the Opera House. The Queen's coach was just a hundred yards away, but still he didn't move from its path.

He wasn't scared. He was determined. He stared at the driver and hoped the man understood. *He would not move.*

Fifty yards.

The cries from the crowd grew louder. There were demands for Wild Boy to stand aside, as well as shouts for the carriage to crush him to the snow.

Thirty yards.

Then he saw it. It was just a slight change in the driver's face, resolve replaced by realization. The man understood what Wild Boy hoped he would. If the horses hit him, the driver would lose control of the coach. A coach with the Queen inside.

Twenty yards.

Finally, the driver pulled the reins, slowing the coach. The horses came to a fretful stop, so close to Wild Boy that their hot breath rustled the hair on his face. He looked up and a shriek escaped his mouth, a high-pitched mix of panic that he'd tried something so crazy, delight that it had worked and relief that he hadn't been trampled into the ground.

Clarissa moved closer, aiming her pistol at the driver. "Don't move." Her face was hot with anger, her voice a banshee shriek. "Wild Boy, go!"

Still Wild Boy stared at the horses. He couldn't believe he'd just done that.

"Now, Wild Boy!"

Snapping back into action, he raced to the side of the carriage and called to the curtained window. "Your Majesty. I gotta speak to you."

No reply. The curtain didn't even twitch.

The carriage behind the royal coach stopped and two Gentlemen leaped out. In the other direction, Lucien and his Black Hat driver staggered from the Opera Arcade. They saw Wild Boy and charged closer.

"Your Majesty!" Wild Boy yelled. He bit his lip, stopping himself from shouting, *Open the bloody door*. "I gotta speak with you. It's urgent."

Still no reply.

The Black Hat driver leaped at Clarissa in a flying rugby tackle. She jumped the dive, but Lucien shoulder-charged her and knocked her to the snow. She thrashed and screamed as the two men twisted her arms behind her back, pinning her to the ground.

Wild Boy rushed to help her, but the other Gentlemen grabbed his arms and yanked him away. Unlike Clarissa, he didn't struggle. He felt deflated. This was Marcus's last hope, their last chance to catch the killer and get the cure.

And they had failed.

For a moment Clarissa stopped thrashing and returned Wild Boy's heartbroken gaze. Then her eyes filled again with anger. She tore free from Lucien and swung a punch at his nose. A spurt of blood, a scream of pain, and Lucien tumbled to the snow. Clarissa pounced on him, screeching like an alley cat. She raised a fist to strike again.

"Miss Everett," a voice said.

Clarissa's hand froze mid-swing.

During the fighting, the driver of the royal coach had opened the cabin door. Queen Victoria sat inside, a sheepskin folded over her legs, and her hands tucked inside a mink muff on her lap. With a long sigh, she turned her head to look at Clarissa and Lucien.

"This is the second time in as many days that we have intervened in a quarrel between the two of you. One would think that you harbour ill feelings towards one another."

A collective gasp rose from the crowd outside the Opera House. Men removed their hats, and women sank into curtsys. The Gentlemen holding Wild Boy yanked him down as they dropped to their knees on the pavement.

Lucien shoved Clarissa away. He tried to wipe the blood from his broken nose, but only succeeded in smearing it across his whiskers.

"Your Majesty," he said, in a pained voice. "These children are extremely dangerous. Please allow us to protect you."

"And how would you rate that protection so far, Mr Grant?"

"They tricked us, Your Majesty."

"Indeed."

Wild Boy pulled free of his captors. "Majesty, I—"

"Wild Boy," the Queen said.

In a flash, the look on her face changed from mild disinterest to fierce authority. "Do not think for one second that we are somehow obliged to you. We entrusted you with a confidence and a responsibility. You have failed us in both regards, with quite desperate results. It is clear that you have not been found wanting in effort. Rather, we must assume that Marcus was mistaken in his assessment of your abilities. If that is the case, then there is no reason to listen to another word you have to say. Mr Grant, please remove the children from our path."

Lucien reached for Clarissa. She stepped back, her fingers like claws.

"You touch me again," she warned, "and I swear…" Then she shouted to the Queen, "We have to speak to you!"

The Queen arched an eyebrow. "You forget yourself, Miss Everett. We are not Marcus Bishop."

"And we ain't Gentlemen, *Your Majesty*."

"Even so," the Queen replied, ignoring her tone, "you would be well advised to listen to us."

"No, you listen to me."

"Clarissa," Wild Boy said.

He reached for her, but she shrugged him off. "You wanted *our* help," she told the Queen. "You and all your Gentlemen. Well, this is how *we* do things. You don't like that, you shouldn't have bloomin' asked in the first place."

As her anger calmed she realized what she'd said and added quietly, "Your Majesty."

An even louder gasp rose from the opera crowd, and mutters of outrage. Lucien erupted in a coughing fit and another of the Gentlemen was so offended that he drew a pistol to defend his sovereign.

Only the Queen remained calm, neatening the blanket over her legs. "You are correct, Miss Everett," she said. "We should not have asked for your help. We should never have expected a child to understand the concept of responsibility. You have let us down."

"I never did nothing for you," Clarissa replied. "I did it for Marcus."

"Indeed. And it is he that you have failed the most. Mr Grant, please ensure that we never see either of these children again." She slid a hand from her muff and tapped the carriage door. "Driver, we shall return to the palace. We have witnessed quite enough drama for one evening, and we have a ball for which we must prepare."

"No!" Wild Boy called. "Your Majesty, we can still save Marcus. Don't pretend you don't care. I saw how you looked at him. We still got a chance at saving him, and everyone else that might get the terror if the killer attacks London. If you leave now, then you're to blame for killing them all."

The Queen cleared her throat, a signal for the driver to hold the door open. She peered down at Wild Boy, and again he felt those deep-set eyes digging into him.

"What is it that you wish?" she asked.

"A black diamond, Majesty."

"Our diamond? It was stolen."

"No, another one. The last one cut from the Black Terror."

The Queen's eyes widened a fraction, and he knew he had her attention.

"And you know where this jewel is?" she asked.

"I do, Majesty."

"Your Majesty," Lucien protested, "this is a wild theory. Perhaps if the boy had proof we could take it more seriously."

"I ain't got proof," Wild Boy said. "*You* do."

"What nonsense."

"Ain't nonsense," Clarissa said. "Tell 'em Wild Boy."

Wild Boy turned to Lucien, praying he'd got this right. "I followed you to the palace library, Lucien. You took something from a secret compartment. It was the last diamond, wasn't it?"

Lucien snorted, causing blood to spurt from his nose. "Really? So where, pray, is this *last black diamond*?"

"It's in your snuff tin."

Lucien stepped back as if he'd been shot. Instinctively, he reached to his pocket where he kept the tin. At the palace Wild Boy had searched Lucien's pockets and found the tin, but he hadn't thought to look *inside* it.

"Mr Grant?" the Queen said.

Lucien dithered, trying to think of a way to deflect attention. Defeated, he pulled the tin from his coat. His hand trembled and at first he couldn't open the lid. It finally came away, revealing a glow of darkness like a black halo as the jewel inside caught the glare of the carriage lamp. Sitting among the tin's powdered contents was the largest diamond cut from the Black Terror. It was twice the size of the other stones, as big as a plum, and it scattered black beams across the snow.

Lucien fell to his knees. A strange noise came from his mouth. A low moan rising to a whine that, Wild Boy realized, was the sound of him sobbing.

Lucien raised the diamond high, like an ancient priest making an offering at an altar. Tears streaked his face, washing the blood into his whiskers. "Your Majesty, I can explain. This diamond... There are three others. They are said to be cursed if they are ever reunited. I had to keep one of them hidden so that could never happen. I planned to destroy it. Please, Majesty, you must believe that I acted as a Gentleman, as your sworn protector."

The Queen raised an eyebrow; her face betrayed no other emotion. "Mr Grant, we will discuss this matter another time. Have no doubt that we will. But at present we wish to have a word with Wild Boy in our coach."

"Your Majesty, I—"

"That sentence did not require a reply."

The Queen slid across the seat, clearing a space.

Wild Boy looked to Clarissa and saw the slightest of smiles flicker across her face. But this wasn't a moment to gloat. They had the black diamond, but they still had to convince the Queen of their plan to catch the killer. It was a plan that involved *her*.

He took a deep, calming breath and climbed into

the cabin. The door closed with a gentle *click*.

There was a long silence as the Queen rearranged her sheepskin. A single beam of light shone through a crack in the curtains, illuminating her plump, expressionless face and pursed lips.

She cleared her throat. "What is it that so enrages Miss Everett?"

The question surprised Wild Boy. In a way, he wished he could answer. He knew that Clarissa's anger wasn't only caused by the terror still affecting her mind. That had simply made it worse. She carried so *much* anger – at her parents for abandoning her, at the world for hunting her. It had begun as a small egg, deep inside. But it had grown and hatched as a dragon. But these were private things to Clarissa, and none of the Queen's business, so Wild Boy just shrugged.

"I don't know, Majesty."

The Queen nodded. It was the answer she expected. "You are an interesting individual, Wild Boy. You could go very far. But with Miss Everett at your side, I fear you will simply end up where you began. The fairground, or perhaps even gaol. That is, if she does not get you killed first."

"We're partners, Majesty. We come from the same place."

The Queen considered this. "Our lives are not as different as you suppose," she said. "Like you, I spent much of my childhood in isolation. Like you,

I am different by a whim of birth. Sometimes I feel burdened by the weight of responsibility placed upon me."

Her voice grew softer, losing its regal stiffness. Wild Boy realized she had stopped calling herself *we*.

"Do you know to whom I turn at such times?" she asked.

"Marcus," Wild Boy said.

"I lost my father when I was barely a year old. Marcus Bishop means more to me, the woman, than you can understand. But before I am a woman, I am the Queen." She cleared her throat again. "Tell me, what is it that you propose?"

"A trap, Majesty, with you and the black diamond as bait. You wear it tonight at your ball. We get word out that this is the last time it'll be seen. The killer will come and we'll be waiting. We get him, we get the cure."

"And you believe this to be the wisest course of action?"

"Maybe not, Majesty, but I ain't got no other course of action, and time's running out for Marcus. Dr Carew said he's got worse, that he can't hold out much longer."

Another moment of consideration, another shuffle of her sheepskin. "Very well," the Queen said. "You may continue your investigation as you see fit. I shall participate in any way you require, and the full powers of the Gentlemen shall be placed at your disposal for this evening only."

Wild Boy couldn't believe it. What a result! He wanted to hug her, and he almost did. "Thank you, Majesty."

"We have not finished. Whatever your plan, Miss Everett must play no part in it."

"What?"

"She is a storm, Wild Boy. She rages too strong. Marcus said as much, only he believed that she could be calmed. We do not share his opinion. Even making allowances for her past, we cannot allow such a person to be involved in these sensitive situations. She is free to remain at St James's Palace for as long as she chooses, out of gratitude for her assistance so far. But she is no longer to be involved in the affairs of the Gentlemen, or any future cases that you might be asked to investigate."

Wild Boy could hardly stand to listen. It was as if the words caused him physical pain; he leaned forward and groaned. He wanted to jump from the carriage and return to Clarissa's side. But something made him stay.

The Queen was right.

Clarissa had become a danger, to herself and others. He couldn't bring himself to say it out loud. All he could do was repeat what he had already said. Only this time it came out softer, less certain.

"We're partners."

"Not anymore. Of course, you are free to refuse our offer. But you would not be able to aid the Gentlemen in catching the person who has committed these atrocities. Thus, should they fail, you would become responsible for the death of your guardian and, perhaps, many others."

She let the threat hang in the cabin, making sure he understood its weight.

Wild Boy understood all right. The weight was so heavy he thought it might crush him into the seat. He gripped the door handle as the terror attacked his mind again, the poison still in his blood. He heard crows cawing, saw flashes of feathered wings.

"Wild Boy?" the Queen said.

"I can't make that choice."

"These are the choices that important people *must* make. Now is the time to decide if this is all just a game to you or if your skills are worth more than the childish satisfaction of your curiosity. Which is it to be?"

The carriage door opened.

Clarissa grinned at Wild Boy, deliberately ignoring the Queen. But her smile fell away as she saw the look in his eyes. Misery. Pain, even. Had the Queen refused his plan?

Wild Boy didn't speak. He didn't know what to say. He prayed she would understand, but knew she wouldn't.

"Mr Grant," the Queen said. "Your men are to assist Wild Boy with whatever he wishes. We place our full trust in him to catch the individual responsible for these outrages and obtain the cure for the victims that remain alive. We shall ride back to Buckingham Palace, where you shall join us with the black diamond and every man available to you, except for two."

Lucien was as baffled as Clarissa. He stared at the Queen, trying to formulate a response. In the end he focused on the only detail he felt he could question.

"Two, Your Majesty?"

"Yes. Those men shall accompany Miss Everett to St James's Palace, where she will be placed under guard for the duration of the evening. She is no longer to have any involvement with the affairs of your organization."

"What?" Clarissa said. "Wild Boy, what's happening?"

Still he couldn't look at her. His voice cracked under the weight of emotion. "Clarissa, I gotta do this alone."

She laughed, convinced it was a joke. "Don't be a thickhead. We don't do *nothing* alone. We're partners. You told her that, right?"

"I ain't got no choice, Clarissa."

"Yes you do, you tell her no. Hey, look at me."

Finally he did, through watery eyes. It was all he could do to shake his head and offer a few feeble words of hope. "I'll catch the killer, Clarissa, I swear. I'll get the cure and save Marcus. He'll make things right."

"Miss Everett," the Queen said. "Wild Boy has chosen—"

"You shut your face, you bloody cow!"

Clarissa's scream was so loud that snowflakes fluttered away from her mouth. The Gentlemen seized her, but this time she didn't struggle. Even as the men picked her up and shoved her into their carriage, she just stared at Wild Boy through the window.

The snow settled against the glass, thickening until Wild Boy could see her no more. "I'm sorry," he whispered.

He leaned forward, the twisting pain growing worse in his stomach. He knew that something had just happened to their friendship. It was something he had chosen to do. It was something he *had* to do. And because of it, nothing would ever be the same between them again.

·27·

One hour until the ball began.
One hour to set a trap to catch the killer.

Wild Boy raised his head, letting the snow settle in his hair. The cold stung his skin, but he kept staring up into the silent storm. It was nice to feel something other than pain. That look Clarissa had given him had felt like a punch to the stomach. In the half hour since, the agony had grown worse, as if the hand that delivered the blow had forced its way in and gripped his insides.

Stone angels watched from the roof of Buckingham Palace. Their faces, lit by shafts of moonlight that crept through the clouds, seemed to accuse him. *You let her down. She was your only friend and you let her down.*

Anger rose inside him, and with it came an urge to fight something. He took it out on the angels, screaming at them through the snow. "Shut your bloomin' heads!"

"Ahem."

A fussy-looking man with a pencil moustache and extremely tight breeches stood beneath the palace's columned porch. He regarded Wild Boy with the look of a man who'd just tasted something foul. "Are you Wild Boy?"

Was the question a joke? Wild Boy held his coat open, giving the man a flash of the thick hair that covered his torso.

The man's eyes widened. Then his lips screwed tighter, as if the foul taste had grown worse. "Her Majesty informs me that you are in charge this evening. I am sure there is some mistake."

"No mistake," another voice replied.

Lucien Grant marched across the forecourt, wrapped in a thick coat and scarf. His grey whiskers sparkled with frost, and his nose was dark and swollen where Clarissa had struck him. Fifty bobbing lanterns followed, a string of fire threading back through the palace's marble arch. It was the rest of the Gentlemen, apart from the two left behind to guard Clarissa. Their top hats were crowned with snow from the short walk from St James's Palace.

Lucien stopped a few yards from Wild Boy. The fog of his breath was slow and steady. "Do you know how long I have been a Gentleman?" he said.

Wild Boy turned away. He couldn't handle another fight – not now.

"Thirty-three years," Lucien continued. "In all that time, I do not believe that I have done one thing that was not in the best interests of our organization or our country. I have lost a wife to consumption and a son to cholera and I have not missed a single day of work."

Wild Boy turned, surprised. It sounded like a peace offering.

"I am not a bad person," Lucien said, "despite what you might think. We simply have different opinions about what is good. I say what I believe. I am too old to do otherwise. I do not believe that you should have been involved with this case. I would have done things differently. I would have resolved this situation by now. However, here we are, and I am bound by the orders of the Queen. So shall we work together this evening or shall we remain at odds?"

Wild Boy considered telling him where he could shove his peace offering. Working with him would be another betrayal of Clarissa. But what choice did he have? None of the Gentlemen or palace staff would believe he was in charge. He needed Lucien to set them straight.

"We'll work together," he said. "Tonight only. There ain't no Black Hats or Grey Hats. Just all of us against the killer."

Lucien turned to the man in tight breeches. "You are Wiggins?"

The man squeaked an affirmative reply. Clearly he recognized Lucien.

"You are the Royal Floor Manager, in charge of royal balls?" Lucien asked.

Another squeak.

"Not tonight," Lucien said. "Tonight Wild Boy is in charge. Do you understand?"

Wiggins didn't understand, but he nodded furiously. He bowed very slightly to Wild Boy, as if dipping any lower might split his breeches. "Well then Mr...?"

"I told you," Lucien said, "his name is Wild Boy."

Wiggins gave a laugh like a yapping dog. When he saw no one else joining in, he bolted up straight. "Well then, Wild Boy, where do we start?"

Wild Boy turned, pretending to examine the forecourt. The truth was, he had no idea where to start. All he had was a rough plan to lure the killer here using the Queen and the black diamond as bait. There were three suspects: Gideon, Dr Carew and Spencer. The killer could break into the palace during the ball or come disguised as a guest. They had to be ready for both possibilities.

"How many guests are coming?" he asked.

"Two hundred and thirty," Wiggins said.

"Two hundred and bloomin' thirty?"

"Is that a problem?"

"No. No problem."

Wild Boy breathed in, trying to focus his thoughts. He remembered Marcus's words. *Control your emotions. Concentrate. Think.*

"Where do the carriages arrive?" he said.

"Here in the forecourt."

"So where do the guests go from here?"

Wiggins led the way, walking stiffly and upright, as if he had a plank shoved down the back of his tailcoat. Wild Boy followed along a hallway decorated with pink ripples on the marble walls, bronze candle stands and a plush velvet carpet that tickled his feet.

He couldn't believe how different this place was from St James's Palace. Everything here sparkled and shone – the gilt frames around oil paintings of royal families, the silver side tables and golden carriage clocks, the teardrop chandeliers that hung from oval friezes. Everywhere candlelight glinted off crystal.

Halfway along the hall, a marble staircase swept up to the first floor alongside a balustrade of twisting golden flowers.

"The Grand Staircase," Wiggins announced. "These lead to the State Apartments, where Her Majesty waits before greeting her guests."

"That is where she will be with the black diamond," Lucien said, following. "Where do the guests go from here, Wiggins?"

Wiggins led them into a long gallery. Kings and

queens watched from oil paintings, their faces dimly lit by moonlight that filtered through a snow-covered skylight. Wiggins scuttled ahead and opened the doors. He cleared his throat and bowed, flourishing his hand as if he was presenting a Wonder of the World.

"The Royal Ballroom."

It was the largest and most lavish room Wild Boy had ever seen, a world of red and gold – strawberry wallpaper with golden mosaics of griffins and hydras, candlesticks tied with silk ribbons, gilt window frames and a huge golden fireplace. Crystal chandeliers as large as cathedral bells poured light onto a dance floor framed by red velvet benches. Beyond, a string orchestra was setting up on a small stage.

Wild Boy rested a hand against the door frame as the gaudy colours began to swirl. He saw red and gold sequins, something that wasn't real. It was Clarissa, dancing on her high wire, dazzling in her circus costume.

He covered his head as the image changed to Augustus Finch. That scarred, savage face. "Hear what they say!" Finch shrieked. "Hear what they say about Wild Boy!"

Lucien touched his shoulder. "Are you all right?"

Wild Boy shook the hand away, harder than he had meant to. Lucien stepped back.

Clear your head. Concentrate.

"We'll keep all the guests in this ballroom," Wild Boy said, looking to Lucien. "Get some of your Gentlemen to dress as servants. They can be among them, serving drinks."

"Serving drinks?" Wiggins complained, his voice reaching a falsetto. "Drinks are served in the refreshment room."

"There ain't no refreshment room tonight," Wild Boy said. He stopped himself from shouting at Wiggins, aware that he needed the man's help.

"But these events are structured in a particular way," Wiggins protested. "The husbands collect the programmes, and then there is the polonaise, and the…" He sighed. "Do you know what *any* of this means?"

"No, I dunno what anything you're saying means, mister. Don't know about high society, dinners or dances or nothing like that."

"Then what does someone like you know about?"

"Catching killers."

Wiggins was about to speak, but the words caught in his throat. His posture slumped, as if the plank had suddenly been swiped from his back. "Did you say *killers*?"

"Thank you, Wiggins," Lucien said. "That will be all for now."

Wild Boy was glad to see the floor manager scuttle away. He wished Lucien would do the same. This was going to be hard enough without him breathing his stale breath down Wild Boy's neck. At least they had agreed to work together. But Wild Boy felt so weak. It was as if, without Clarissa, he was only half a person.

Lucien checked his pocket watch. "Ten past eight. The guests arrive in fifty minutes. So, Wild Boy, where do we begin?"

·28·

"The staff," Wild Boy said. "We'll start with the staff."

Buckingham Palace usually kept a staff of around a hundred men and women. Tonight, every one of them was a potential danger. The killer could sneak into the palace disguised as a royal footman or a groom. So all but ten of the staff had been given the night off. That left three maids to attend the Queen, four servants to train the Gentlemen in their disguises as waiters, two for guiding carriages and Wiggins – the Royal Floor Manager – to announce guests as they arrived.

These men and women were gathered in a line on the dance floor, together with the members of the string orchestra. Wild Boy had to be sure they could all be trusted, and that they were sharp enough to spot trouble.

As he walked along the line, each of the servants stepped back and drew a breath. They had been told the Wild Boy of London was here, but had all assumed it was a joke.

Wild Boy stopped by one of the grooms. His gaze roved around the man's clothes and then lingered on his leathery face. He saw a missed button on his shirt, and a white spot below his left ear. Shaving cream.

"Eyes ain't too good, are they?" he asked the man.

"I cannot afford spectacles."

Wild Boy glanced at Lucien. A servant with bad eyesight was no use in a hunt for a killer. Better he was out of the way. Lucien gave a signal, and the groom was invited to enjoy an evening's rest from his usual duties.

Wild Boy continued his inspection, examining the servants and musicians in the glare of the ballroom's chandeliers. "He's all right... She's good..."

He stopped at a pretty parlour maid who was only a little taller than he was, and leaned close to smell her arm.

"You stink of perfume," he said. "And you've cleaned your nails. Meeting your lover tonight in secret, right?" He looked at the other servants along the line. "Anyone know who the lover is?"

They shook their heads furiously.

"Could be the killer in disguise," Wild Boy said, thinking aloud. "Using that way to sneak in."

The girl, too stunned to respond, allowed herself to be led from the ballroom.

That left eight servants and the orchestra. Wild Boy smiled at the group and one of the musicians fainted. "Maybe get rid of him an' all," he muttered.

"We have forty-five minutes," Lucien said. "What next?"

All of the Gentlemen stood behind him, waiting for instructions.

Think. Concentrate.

"Windows," Wild Boy said. "Everyone follow me."

At first no one did. Instead they all looked to Lucien, seeking confirmation of the order.

"Don't look at me," Lucien barked. "Do what the boy says."

The Gentlemen followed Wild Boy around the ballroom, examining latches and locks and peering out to window ledges. The patio doors were framed by heavy red curtains that were bunched in drapes, like stage curtains opening for a show. The show was snow – *lots* of snow pattering against the glass and settling thickly beyond the porch.

Wild Boy selected ten of the Gentlemen. "You lot are window patrol. All of these windows gotta stay locked. No one gets in or out. Look here, where the snow's piled up on the ledges outside. These windows open outwards. That snow means no one's opened them, so no one's got in that way."

"But how on earth will we catch the killer unless he gets inside?"

"We gotta *see* the killer to catch him," Wild Boy said. "If we keep these windows closed, then he's got to come in through the ballroom door, same as the guests."

"What if a lady swoons?" one of the men asked.

"Let her swoon. Better than getting the terror."

He felt another twist in his gut. He knew he should have been enjoying this, a chance to order the Gentlemen about. But without Clarissa it felt so wrong.

Don't think about it. Stay focused.

He shouted to Wiggins in the doorway. "Any secret passages into this room we should know about?"

Wiggins scoffed. "Why would there be a *secret passage*?"

"I dunno, usually one, ain't there?"

"Not in Buckingham Palace there is not."

"All right." Wild Boy jumped onto one of the velvet benches beside the dance floor and addressed the Gentlemen who weren't checking the windows. "You lot are on candle duty. Whatever causes the terror burns with black smoke, we know that much."

"But what is it that burns?" one of the men asked.

"Don't know that yet. Maybe fiddled candles or some sort of oil. We gotta check every light in this place, anything with a flame. Make sure they ain't got nothing suspicious about them. They should be orange-almond–oil candles, like these, and smell sweet like marzipan. Any ain't got that smell, come and get me. Oh, and don't go breathing its smoke."

"Or what?"

"Or you'll see your worst nightmares and die."

"I… Oh."

Wild Boy jumped down, spoke to two others. "You and you, guard the fire. No one throws nothing on the flames. Anyone tries, grab 'em. Could be the killer."

"Forty minutes till the guests arrive," Lucien said. "The artist is here."

A short man was brought forward, dressed in a flowing white shirt with lace ruffles and a starched collar so high it tickled his cheeks. When he saw Wild Boy he screamed for five seconds, then lit a thin cigarette.

"I am here to see *you*?" he asked.

"Can you draw?" Wild Boy said.

"Draw? I am Franz Winterhalter. I have exhibited at the Salon de Paris."

"Good for you. I'm gonna describe two people and I want you to draw their faces. Only we gotta work fast."

"I assume this is a joke?"

Wild Boy stepped closer and plucked the cigarette from the man's lips. It was something he'd seen Marcus do to signal impatience, and it worked. The artist's eyes bulged and he coughed smoke.

"Do I look like I'm joking?" Wild Boy said. "Lucien tells me that if you do this, then you're the right man for the Queen's next portrait. So are you gonna get out your pencils or should we send for someone else?"

The artist nodded several times. "Only, I sketch in ink, not pencil."

For fifteen minutes Wild Boy described Gideon and Dr Carew to the artist in as much detail as he could. The drawings wouldn't be perfect, but they'd at least give the servants an idea of who to watch out for. He didn't bother to describe Spencer. Surely his mask or burned face would be enough to give him away.

Winterhalter set to work with his inkpot and quill.

"Twenty-five minutes," Lucien said. "Where is the Queen's jeweller?"

The next man brought forward was tall and thin, with a single strand of hair slicked across an otherwise bald head. He carried a small cushion with a tiara for the Queen, a nest of pearls with the last black diamond set in the middle. Beneath the chandeliers, the jewel shone brighter than ever, dazzling Wild Boy's eyes.

"I understand this is a delicate matter," the jeweller said, in an appropriately delicate tone. "But please tell me, is this diamond Oberstein's work? I cannot imagine anyone else cutting a stone with such skill."

Wild Boy glanced at Lucien, who shook his head so firmly that his jowls wobbled. No one could know anything about that stone.

"Thank you," Wild Boy said to the jeweller. "Thank you for doing this."

The jeweller handed the tiara to one of the Gentlemen, and was led away.

Twenty minutes.

Wild Boy followed the Gentleman carrying the tiara, out of the ballroom, through the gallery and then up the Grand Staircase. The corridor on the first floor was as extravagant as the rooms below, with golden stucco squares on white wallpaper, like frames without paintings.

Two Gentlemen guarding a door snapped to attention. "Password," one of them demanded.

The Gentleman with the tiara said, "Clarissa."

The door was unlocked and one of the maids accepted the jewelled headpiece. Beyond her, Wild Boy glimpsed the Queen at a dresser, considering her own reflection in the mirror. A sad, lost look filled her eyes, which had sunken even deeper into her face. Was she was thinking about Marcus?

The Queen spotted Wild Boy in the looking glass, and her face changed in a way that only he would notice. Just a slight narrowing of her eyes and purse of her lips, but its meaning was clear.

Catch the killer or you are finished.

The door closed and the lock turned. Wild

Boy should have been reassured. The Queen was guarded in a room with no windows. But minute by minute his confidence was crumbling.

The plan was for the Queen to emerge at ten o'clock and descend to the ballroom to greet her guests. That gave the Gentlemen an hour to find the killer. If they failed, Her Majesty would appear in her tiara, presenting the killer with a target and the Gentlemen with their best chance of catching him. But Wild Boy knew that Lucien would never place the Queen in such danger. He wouldn't even give her a choice. If they hadn't caught the killer by ten o'clock, she would remain right there, in her room.

That meant they had one hour – and only one hour – to find the killer.

Downstairs, a rush of panic swept around the ballroom as the Gentlemen made their final preparations for the guests' arrival. Some donned their disguises: the white coats and gloves of royal servants. Others rechecked windows and lights. They had turned the ballroom into a mini-fortress. If everything went as planned, the killer would *have* to enter the same way as the guests. Surely he would be seen.

But still, Wild Boy couldn't shake the feeling that he'd missed something.

His heart sank deeper as the artist presented his sketches, unveiling them as if they were paintings at the Royal Academy. Neither ink drawing caught the likenesses of Dr Carew or Gideon. Hoping they might still help, Wild Boy asked one of the Gentlemen to show them around.

The Gentleman stared at the drawings. "What are these for?" he asked.

"To help spot the suspects."

"I am not sure these will help."

"Have you got a better idea?" Wild Boy snapped.

The man stepped back, his face turning as red as the ballroom walls. "No, I mean… You *have* seen the invitation to the ball, haven't you?"

Wild Boy hadn't thought to ask. "Why?"

The man brought a slip of card from his pocket and offered it with a shaky hand. "I thought you were aware," he said.

Wild Boy didn't want to take it. But he *had* to look.

YOU ARE CORDIALLY INVITED TO JOIN

her Majesty

QUEEN VICTORIA

AT BUCKINGHAM PALACE

FOR A MASKED BALL TO CELEBRATE

THE PASSING OF WINTER

AND THE DAWN OF SPRING.

The card slipped from Wild Boy's hand. His legs felt so weak that he gripped the wall for support. Why hadn't he known about this? Why hadn't he asked?

"It's a *masked* ball?" he said.

· 29 ·

The ballroom walls swirled. The golden griffins darkened. Their wings spread and claws stretched as they changed into monstrous crows.

Wild Boy rubbed his eyes, and the room returned to normal. He stared at the invitation on the floor. He'd thought he was ready, thought he'd covered all the angles. But he'd overlooked the most important factor of the evening. How was he going to spot the killer at a masked ball?

The stitches in his head began to throb again. His breathing grew faster. He needed to escape this place, to get some air. He barged past several Gentlemen and rushed along the gallery and back to the palace entrance.

Outside, the snow fell harder, hissing against the forecourt lamps. Wild Boy stepped from under the porch and in seconds his hair was covered in a thin layer of white. His teeth chattered from the cold, but he didn't care. He was glad to feel something other than painful guilt and heavy responsibility.

He was in charge of this case – in charge of the Gentlemen – and yet he had never felt so alone. He tried to remember Marcus's advice, but this time the words didn't come.

"The snow is turning black," a voice said.

Lucien sheltered under the porch, smoking a cigar.

They stood in silence, watching the snow settle around the forecourt. Clusters of polluted flakes were swept by the wind, like flocks of starlings swirling among the white. Through the blizzard, a carriage light came closer.

"The first guests," Lucien said. "Are you ready?"

Wild Boy didn't feel ready, didn't feel anything other than panic. It was as if the cold had got through his skin, turning his insides to ice. "What if the killer doesn't come?" he said.

"He will."

"How can you know?"

"Me? Training, instinct. Thirty years of it. For you it is just natural. This is what you do best."

Lucien tossed his cigar, a fiery arc that hit the snow and fizzled out. "There is something you should see."

Wild Boy didn't want to go. Whatever Lucien wanted to show him, he was certain it was another problem. But then he saw something he'd never seen before. Lucien smiled. It looked unnatural, a little forced, but it was definitely a smile.

"You should come," Lucien said.

Instead of turning towards the ballroom, Lucien led him in the other direction, along a corridor lined with marble statues of Greek gods. He banged on a door at the end.

A moment passed. The door opened.

It was another lavishly decorated chamber, with green satin drapes on the walls. A fire blazed in the hearth, and the windows were steamy rather than frosty. The blast of warmth disorientated Wild Boy so that at first he didn't recognize what he saw.

There were three men. Two were physicians, with leather bags and medical equipment on a table. The third man lay on a chaise longue beside the fire.

"Marcus!" Wild Boy said.

He rushed to his guardian and crouched by his side. In the firelight, Marcus's face was as pale and waxy as a corpse, aside from the black veins that bulged from his skin. Some of the bloodlines had branched into smaller veins, and branched again. The darkness was spreading.

Wild Boy took his hand. He could feel Marcus's pulse going triple speed. He wished more than ever that Clarissa were here. She would want to see him.

"Her Majesty insisted he was brought here rather than a hospital," Lucien explained. "These physicians are the finest in the world."

Wild Boy looked at the two men hopefully, but he knew they had no way of curing Marcus. Only the killer had the cure.

"His condition has deteriorated," one of the physicians said. "His heart is struggling to take the strain of the horrors he is experiencing."

"Lucien has explained your situation," the other doctor said. "You hope to catch the killer, to get the cure. But you do not necessarily *need* the cure, you realize?"

The physician took an instrument from his bag, a steel plunger and glass vial. A bronze needle jutted from the top, capped with a cork. "Do you know what this is?"

"A syringe?" Wild Boy said.

"Precisely. You said the killer had already taken a cure, which was how he survived in Lady Bentick's dining room. That means the cure is still in his blood. If you can catch him, all we need is a sample of that blood – take it from his neck. From that, we can develop a cure of our own."

Wild Boy could hardly believe this. It felt like fire rising inside him. "You could do that? In time to…"

He was unable to finish the sentence, but the doctors understood. *In time to save Marcus.*

"We hope so," one of them replied. "That is as much as we can say. More importantly, we would have a cure in case this madman succeeds in spreading his poison over the city."

It was enough for Wild Boy. Hope. Fresh hope. He squeezed Marcus's hand tighter, making a silent promise. One way or the other he would catch the killer tonight.

Lucien rubbed steam from the window. Outside, a carriage rode through the marble arch and into the forecourt of Buckingham Palace. The ball was about to begin.

"There is one more problem," Lucien said. He turned to Wild Boy. "Our plan relies on you detecting the killer, which means you must be there among the ball. So what the Devil are you going to wear?"

·30·

"**I** present Lord and Lady Bisquith."

Wiggins bolted up even straighter as he announced the latest guests to arrive at the ball. The Lord and Lady strutted together across the ballroom dance floor, gloved hands raised and fingertips touching.

There were a few appreciative mutters, and several jealous scowls, at the sight of their masks, which were the most extravagant of the evening so far. Fans of purple feathers rose from the top of their ivory eye masks, as if a pair of peacocks had charged full-pelt at their faces.

Wild Boy fought the urge to storm across the dance floor and tear the masks away. Even for his sharp eyes, it was hard to see behind the guests' ridiculous disguises.

It was half past nine.

Almost two hundred guests had arrived. They

all wore similar cloaks – shiny and black, with large velvet hoods – but the masks came in various colours and gaudy designs. Most featured some sort of plumage, so many feathers that Wild Boy wondered whether every bird of paradise had been plucked bare. Others were studded with jewels woven with laurel leaves, trimmed with lace or decorated with crystal horns.

"The Marquess and Marchioness of Salisbury."

"Viscount Palmerston."

The guests gathered around the dance floor, muttering about the lack of conveniences for a formal ball. Others wondered why the servants, who did not quite *look* like servants, seemed ignorant of the correct manner in which to serve drinks.

"It simply will not do," said an admiral.

"I swear that waiter touched my glass," replied his wife.

"And why the devil is there a drummer-boy here?"

Wild Boy banged his drum harder, praying his disguise would work. Since he usually wore a drummer boy's coat, Lucien had suggested he play that role at the ball. His face was hidden behind a porcelain mask, and the shawl that covered his head was draped around his neck, concealing the hair.

The disguise was far from perfect. The hairs on his face bunched against the porcelain mask and poked through the eyeholes, and the rim of the hood hung too low, limiting his vision. That was a fairly big problem, since their plan to catch the killer relied almost entirely on his vision.

He felt his coat pocket, and the physicians' syringe. He was ready to strike and get the killer's blood. Aim for his neck, the doctors had instructed. The big vein called the jugular.

Around the ballroom, some of the Gentlemen examined guests as they served drinks. Others rubbed steam from windows to inspect the ledges, or lingered by candles to smell the smoke. The men were clearly on edge. They flinched at every roar of laughter from the dance floor.

Only Lucien was not in disguise. Dressed in a simple domino mask, he moved among the crowd, bowing and shaking hands. He made sure to remind everyone that the Queen, when she appeared, would be wearing the most precious jewel in her collection, a rare black diamond.

It was twenty to ten.

Wild Boy kept moving around the dance floor, banging his drum in time with the pounding of his heart. With each minute, he grew more certain the killer would come. He had no evidence, just a gut feeling that he trusted.

Come on. Where are you?

A hand grabbed his arm. It was one of the Gentlemen. The man was flustered, his forehead lit with sweat.

"Over there," he said. "Is that Gideon?"

Wild Boy leaped onto one of the benches and followed the man's gaze to a cloaked figure in the ballroom doorway.

"The Chinese Ambassador," Wiggins announced.

The Gentleman sank to the seat, dabbing sweat from his face. "I almost apprehended him," he said. "It would have caused a diplomatic incident."

"Get up," Wild Boy said. "Keep looking."

The orchestra began to play a waltz, and the dancing began. Cloaks fluttered, dresses rustled, and satin slippers shuffled around the floor. Soon the whole room was twirling. There were quadrilles, polkas, two-steps and reels. The ballroom grew hot and clammy and the windows steamed over. One of the guests tried to open the patio doors to let in some air, but a Gentleman guided him politely away.

Sweat trickled under Wild Boy's mask. He kept moving, kept whacking his drum.

Where are you? Why ain't you here?

Movement caught his eye. Lucien rushed towards the doors, responding to a signal from one of the Gentlemen. Now Wild Boy was running too, around the side of the dance floor, barging past the guests. He reached into his pocket, gripped the syringe.

He caught up with Lucien as he marched along the gallery. "What's happening?"

"Carew," Lucien replied, breathless. "Someone saw Dr Carew."

Two Gentlemen pinned a guest to the gallery

wall. But even before they removed the man's mask, Wild Boy knew it was a false alarm. The guest looked like Dr Carew, but he was too round at the waist. It wasn't him.

Lucien leaned against the wall, struggling to catch his breath. He signalled for his men to release their prisoner.

The guest staggered back. "What the deuce is the meaning of this?"

"Our apologies," Lucien said. "We mistook you for a French terrorist."

That was the story Wild Boy and the Gentlemen had agreed on should anyone ask about the security. "The Devil to you!" the guest roared. "I am no Frenchie. I was stepping out for air. And why the blazes is that drummer boy staring at me like that?"

Wild Boy leaned to Lucien. "Get rid of him."

"What?"

"He's gonna go back in there and shout about terrorists. Everyone's gonna panic."

"For God's sake, Wild Boy. That's the Earl of Gloucester."

Wild Boy didn't care who it was. The man could ruin the whole plan.

Lucien knew it too. He groaned, spoke in a low voice to one of the Gentlemen. The Earl's protests grew louder as he was led away.

Lucien checked his pocket watch. "Nine forty-five," he said. "You understand our situation?"

Wild Boy did, but he couldn't bring himself to say so. This evening had been about catching the killer before the Queen appeared. If they hadn't done so by ten o'clock, she would remain upstairs in her room. Their chance would be lost.

Time was almost up.

He tore the drum from around his neck and hurled it across the gallery. Slumping against the wall, he slid his mask up his face and rubbed his hair. He'd been trying so hard not to consider failure, but now it was impossible to avoid.

"You'll be the boss of the Gentlemen after tonight?" he asked.

"It is not guaranteed," Lucien said. "Her Majesty is yet to reprimand me over concealing the black diamond. But my appointment to the position would be the most likely outcome."

"What about me and Clarissa?"

"Do you wish me to be honest?"

Wild Boy didn't. He wanted him to lie, to tell him that they could both stay in the palace forever.

"You will both have to go," Lucien said. "I cannot have Miss Everett undermining me. I would ask you to remain with us, but I doubt you would consider doing so without her or Marcus."

Wild Boy closed his eyes. He wouldn't stay without her; that would be a betrayal too far. Nor could he stay *with* her, not for long at least. She could do anything she wanted, but not with him at her side.

"Hear what they say about Wild Boy! The ugliest freak at the fair!"

He heard the showman cry, the mocking crows. They were louder in his head, getting closer.

"Sir? Mr Grant!"

Another Gentleman rushed from the ballroom, red-faced and flustered. "We have another situation," he said.

Lucien waved the man away. "Whoever you have apprehended this time, I pray you've acted with more discretion."

"Haven't apprehended anybody, sir."

Wild Boy sat up. This didn't seem like the other false alarm. Something had happened.

Sliding his mask back into place, he followed Lucien back to the ballroom. The heat of the room hit him like a furnace, drying his throat. The dancing was in full swing. Couples whirled around the floor, whooping with tipsy laughter.

Through the moving bodies, Wild Boy spotted several Gentlemen exchanging angry words by the patio doors. Lucien saw them too, and now they were both running again, dodging through the dancers.

"What is the situation?" Lucien asked as they approached.

"The patio doors," one of the men replied. "Bentley was supposed to be watching them."

"Bentley escorted the Earl of Gloucester to his carriage. What is it? The doors are locked."

"No, sir. Outside – look."

Wild Boy rubbed steam from the glass. There were marks in the snow. They were faint, but they were definitely marks. Someone, or something, had been there just moments ago.

"Could have been a fox," Lucien said.

Shifting his mask to see better, Wild Boy leaned closer to the doors and examined the groove around the frame. The ice seal was broken.

"It ain't no fox," he said. "This door's been opened. Someone's broken in."

· 31 ·

"**W**e must protect the Queen."

The words came almost as a whisper from Lucien's mouth as he stared at the marks beyond the patio doors. The tracks of an uninvited guest.

Wild Boy turned and scanned the dance floor. He suspected that whoever had sneaked into this ball-room was *still* here. He was certain he could find the person, but not if Lucien and his men charged around causing panic.

He grasped Lucien's wrist, kept his voice low. "We gotta stay quiet."

Lucien glared at the hand on his arm as if it had just fractured whatever fragile peace existed between them. "You forget yourself," he said. "It is our primary duty to protect the Queen."

Ain't my primary duty. Wild Boy was here to save Marcus. He almost said as much, but stopped himself. "Look at them candles on that stand," he said. "Two of 'em are out."

"So?" Lucien said. "The wind extinguished them when the killer opened the door."

"Right. But they were all lit at the same time, and now the other three have burned for about ninety seconds longer."

"How can you be sure?"

"Cos I know this sorta stuff. Now listen, we were in the gallery before that and no one passed us. Here in the ballroom the windows are guarded and your men are on the doors. No one's gone out in that time. So whoever broke into this ballroom is still in this ballroom, geddit?"

Lucien got it. He watched the guests swirling around the dance floor. "Good God," he said. "If the killer knows he is caught, he might act irrationally."

"Right, like grab one of these toffs."

"What do you propose?"

"Block the doors, don't let no one out. Gimme five minutes and I'll find him."

"There are two hundred and thirty people here."

"Two hundred and thirty-one now."

"All right," Lucien agreed, with a sigh so heavy it rustled his whiskers. "Five minutes. But after that we shall tear this room apart to find him."

Wild Boy didn't doubt that. But he had to try it his way, to think like Marcus had taught him. Only he wished he'd asked for ten minutes rather than five.

He opened the patio door and slipped outside.

A porch protected him from the worst of the weather, but the cold was still vicious, like a wire in his nose. The fog of his breath formed ice crystals that hung in the air before being swept away by the wind. Through the heavy snowfall he saw naked trees swaying at the side of the palace garden.

His pulse quickened. He had a feeling that he was being watched.

He stepped out from under the porch and looked across the side of the palace. Stone angels stood guard on the roof, black against the dark sky. With their wings raised, they reminded him of the demon Malphas.

Stop messing about, thickhead.

Returning to the porch, he tore off his mask and dropped it by the doors. He crouched and examined the marks in the snow. They were just fragments of footprints – the point of a toecap, the indentation of a heel, a curling groove from the side of a sole. As Wild Boy stared at them, they began to move. He knew it was only happening in his head, but it seemed so real. The pieces of the jigsaw slid across the snow and slotted together. In the moonlight, he saw a single complete footprint.

He blinked and it was gone.

The moment lasted barely a second. But there was no mistaking the tapered, flat-soled print and sharply pointed toe of a Wellington boot, the calf-high leather boots named after the duke that wore them so often.

A clue. But was it enough?

He peered through the glass doors, studying the ballroom. In ten seconds he had seen that fifty-three of the guests wore Wellington boots.

Gotta try harder than that.

He looked down, and the puzzle came back together. He realized now that something was missing from the footprint. Most wealthy men wore either old-fashioned breeches, pulled tight by a strap under the boot, or fashionable French-style trousers. There were no marks from a bootstrap in this print. So the intruder wore trousers.

He shot back to the door. Of the fifty-three men in Wellington boots, eighteen wore trousers.

Still not good enough.

There was something else about the marks. The largest fragment was almost half complete, from the centre of the sole to the point of the toecap. He could tell from the depth at the centre that the intruder had crouched to pick the lock, transferring his weight to the ball of his toes. But the print continued two inches *beyond* that point. Either the intruder had unusually long toes or his boots were too big. But why would someone choose to wear oversize boots?

Unless he hadn't chosen.

Unless the boots were stolen.

The patio darkened as the moon slipped behind clouds. It didn't matter. Wild Boy had seen enough. Whichever of those eighteen suspects wore over-sized boots was the intruder. Hopefully the Gentlemen could escort them from the dance floor without attracting too much attention.

For the first time that evening, Wild Boy smiled. That had gone surprisingly well.

He opened the door and stepped inside.

Then he realized he'd forgotten to put his mask back on.

"It's the Wild Boy of London!" someone screamed.

"He's come for the Queen!"

Another scream, and another, and then lots of screams at once. Guests stumbled back, tripping over one another in their desperation to escape from the ballroom. Some of the men stood in front of their wives and adopted boxing stances. Others thrust their partners in front of them as shields. Lucien pleaded with the guests to remain calm as they demanded to be released by the Gentlemen blocking the open doors.

The orchestra hurled their instruments at Wild Boy from the stage. Violins and harps crashed down near his feet, but he ignored them. His eyes remained fixed on the guests, searching for the intruder.

"For God's sake!" someone cried. "There's a monster loose!"

"Get a shotgun!"

Wild Boy ignored everything, still seeking out the Wellington boots from among the fast-moving feet. He saw one pair, dismissed it, saw another and another...

His eyes locked onto a pair that looked too large for their wearer, and wet from the snow. He could only see the back of their owner, a cloak and hood swaying as the person jostled among the guests at the doors. Just for a second Wild Boy glimpsed a mask beneath the hood. It was covered in silver sequins.

He began to run.

It was a mask he'd seen before, on the statue of Marie Antoinette at the wax works museum. The boots were stolen too, he realized, from the wax figure of the Duke of Wellington. It had to be the killer. *It had to be.*

The screams grew louder as he charged across the dance floor.

"Spread out!" someone yelled. "He can't eat us all."

Wild Boy ran for the killer, bracing himself to leap at him. Then he saw something he could barely believe. With extraordinary speed, the figure dropped low, launched forward and twisted between the legs of the Gentlemen at the door. The guards saw but couldn't give chase without letting the rest of the group into the gallery.

"He got past!" Wild Boy cried. "Move!"

The guests fled from the doorway, scattering in every direction across the dance floor. The Gentlemen saw him coming and stepped aside, letting him out of the ballroom. Ahead, Wild Boy saw rustles of cloak as the uninvited guest raced along the gallery and up the Grand Staircase.

He couldn't believe it. Surely the killer wasn't *still* going after the black diamond? The Queen was guarded by six men.

He reached the stairs in time to see the hooded figure stumble, wet boots slipping on marble steps. Wild Boy willed his legs to go faster, closing the gap. He yanked the syringe from his pocket. A cry came from his mouth, savage, guttural. He didn't care how he did it, he had to get the killer's blood.

He expected the intruder to keep running, but the figure stayed at the top of the stairs. Eyes behind the sequined mask watched him run closer. They were burning eyes, filled with fury.

And then Wild Boy stopped too.

All of his anger was suddenly sucked from him, replaced by surprise.

He recognized those eyes. He recognized them but it was the last person he expected to see.

Then he heard a shout from behind.

Two Gentlemen charged up the stairs, shoving him aside in their rush to reach the intruder. The cloaked figure fled again, taking the last three steps in a single jump and then turning along the corridor at the top.

Still Wild Boy just stood there, staring.

Glints of light reflected off the Gentlemen's pistols, breaking his trance. Now he was running again – no longer after the intruder, but after the Gentlemen. He shoved the syringe back into his coat.

"Wait!" he yelled. "Don't shoot!"

BOOM!

He came to a gasping stop in the corridor.

No. No, no…

Wisps of smoke floated past his head, tinged with the smell of gunpowder.

"Don't move!" one of the Gentlemen warned.

He'd fired a warning shot. The intruder had stopped mid-escape, with one leg out of the window at the end of the corridor.

Wild Boy rushed forward, barging past one of the Gentlemen. The man slipped and fired his pistol at the ceiling.

Plaster sprayed down. The two Gentlemen fell to the floor, covering their heads, and the intruder tumbled back inside and onto the carpet. The furious cry that came from behind the mask was as familiar to Wild Boy as the angry eyes that glared at him from the floor.

He leaned against the wall, the gunshot ringing in his ears. "What the hell are *you* doing here?" he asked Clarissa.

·32·

Clarissa didn't know whether to hug him or to punch him.

In the end she decided to do neither, and sat in a sulk on the ballroom bench. She tucked her hands under her thighs, hoping that might stop them from lashing out as fists when Wild Boy spoke.

She hadn't said a word as the Gentlemen led her down to the gaudy ballroom where the toffs had been dancing. All those lords and ladies were moved into the long room with the paintings on the walls, so now it was just her and Wild Boy and stinking Lucien Grant. The other Gentlemen, dressed as servants for some reason, were in the picture gallery too, trying to keep the toffs from complaining. This ballroom seemed even bigger with just the three of them here. There was so much red and gold that Clarissa wanted to be sick.

She knew she had to speak, but part of her wanted to stay silent. That part of her wanted the killer to win, to punish the Queen and the Gentlemen. And to punish *him*.

She dug her hands harder into the seat as Wild Boy came closer. All she could ever see were his eyes, but she knew them so well and she could tell he was hurting. Was he still suffering, like she was, from those visions left by the killer's poisonous smoke? She pulled her hands from under her legs, about to reach out to him.

But then Lucien Grant whispered something and Wild Boy nodded, and she knew they had become friends. She felt another stab of betrayal: that knife in her heart.

"Clarissa?" Wild Boy said. "Why are you here?"

He looked confused.

Good. For once he doesn't get to know everything.

Lucien glowered at her. He was trying to look scary, but she was pleased to see that he stayed several steps away. He was shiny with sweat from running around in a flap. Clarissa gagged from the stench of his body odour.

"Miss Everett," Lucien said, in a deep voice. "Perhaps I might present you with a few facts?"

She swirled a ball of spit in her mouth, ready to present *him* with a faceful of phlegm if he came closer. But then he said something that made her swallow it back down.

"You were at all of the crime scenes."

"What?"

"What is more, Wild Boy informs me that a key detail of this case is based upon an account provided by yourself. You state that you were given a note by the killer at Lady Bentick's house, which you supposedly threw on her fire. And now you are here, caught by our trap. You see where this is leading?"

Clarissa almost burst out laughing until she saw how serious Lucien was. He thought *she* was the killer?

She looked at Wild Boy. "Do you think this an' all?"

Wild Boy threw his hands in the air and groaned. "Course I don't, you bloomin' thickhead. But you gotta say what's going on, Clarissa. This is serious."

She fought a grin. Of course he didn't think it was her. Still, she wasn't about to forgive him. "Why don't you work it out with your new *pal*," she said.

"He ain't my pal. You are."

Unable to control herself, she shot up and shoved him in the chest. "You left me."

She only meant to push him, but his knees buckled and he collapsed to the floor. Wild Boy was tough – the toughest boy she knew – but he'd gone down like an old man. He turned away, but Clarissa saw him grip his head. It *was* the terror.

Lucien went to help Wild Boy up, but she barged him aside.

"Here," she said. "Sit down."

"I'm sorry, Clarissa," he said. "I didn't have no choice. Marcus is gonna die. Maybe all of London too."

She didn't want to argue with him, not like this. But he was wrong. "You had a choice," she said. "We could've done it together. Instead you left me just like…"

She bit her tongue.

"Just like everyone else?" Wild Boy said.

"Like a thickhead, was what I meant. Sit down, will you."

"I'll sit down if you tell me what you're doing here."

She helped him onto the couch and was pleased to see his grimace replaced by a weak smile.

"How long did them Gentlemen manage to keep you locked up?" he asked.

She sat beside him, and immediately felt better. It was strange, like they'd been apart for weeks rather than hours. She felt whole again.

"Long enough to let 'em know what I thought of them," she said. "Then I went out the window. I wanted to catch the killer and save Marcus myself. I knew you were setting up a trap here, but I thought I could go back to the museum and make one of the suspects confess. So I ran all the way there. It was snowing harder and I didn't have boots, cos I took 'em off to climb down the palace wall. My feet felt like they were on fire, and I was still only in this dress. It was cold, but I was tough."

Wild Boy nodded, and she was pleased he believed her. In fact, it had been so cold that she'd nearly given up her hunt and returned to St James's Palace.

"Were all three of them still at the museum?" Wild Boy asked. "Gideon, Dr Carew and Spencer?"

"None of 'em," she said. "I sneaked around the back and into the workshop. Wasn't no one inside. Then I heard the front door, so I crept there and looked out. I saw someone carrying a body and putting it next to another in a carriage. The bodies weren't shaking. I thought they were dead."

Lucien stepped closer. "Who did you see, Miss Everett?"

"I ain't telling *you* nothing."

She turned to Wild Boy. "I couldn't see the bodies. It was dark and there was too much snow. Whoever carried them wore a hood and one of them crow masks from the wax statues in the museum, the ones dancing with that French lady queen. I knew it was the killer. I just knew. I dunno where he got the carriage from though. There was other stuff in there an' all, a sack and some bowls. He must've been somewhere to get it all. I knew he planned to kill all of London once he had the black diamonds, so he had to have a hideout. I thought I could catch him there. That would really show you.

"So I pinched a mask from the museum too, in case I got seen, and a cloak and these boots to keep warm. As the killer rode away, I jumped on the back of his carriage."

She saw Wild Boy's eyes light up, and knew he was impressed.

"Except he didn't go back to his hideout," she said. "He rode near here and stopped at the park. He didn't hang about long, neither. He just jumped down, grabbed his sack and ran for this palace."

"And the men inside the carriage?" Lucien asked. "Which two were they?"

Clarissa felt her face redden. She hadn't thought to look inside the carriage.

Lucien turned away, trying to control his anger, but failing. His voice boomed around the ballroom. "For God's sake. The fate of an entire city is at risk, and she didn't even look in the damned carriage."

"Shut your head," Wild Boy said. "She was chasing the killer."

"Yeah," Clarissa said. "He was fast an' all, faster even than me. He ran right along the wall of the palace garden, round to the back. Then he went up and over in a flash. By the time I got over, I couldn't see him no more through the snow."

She remembered how scared she'd been then, but decided not to say. She knew it would invite another sneer from Lucien, and she was struggling to control her anger at the man. She wished she could tell Wild

Boy more. She'd followed some wind-rustled foot-prints towards the patio and peered through steamy windows into the ballroom. But there had been so many guests, it was impossible to spot the killer.

"You came in here looking for him?" Wild Boy asked.

"Only I never saw him. Then you came in without your mask, and everyone started to panic. I thought the killer must've sneaked out of the ballroom, so I tried to go after him. But them Gentlemen chasing me had guns."

She kicked one of the candle stands, causing its light to skitter around the dance floor. The truth was, she'd simply wanted to escape without getting shot. She wished she had confronted the killer outside when she had the chance.

"I suppose I failed," she said.

"No," Wild Boy said. "You got closer than any of us."

"Really?" Lucien said. "All I can see is that Miss Everett has hindered our operation. Our plan is now in ruins and the killer is nearer than ever."

She was pleased to see Wild Boy ignore him. She recognized the look on his face – that sparkling, wide-eyed look he got when he saw a clue. Or heard one.

"I said something important, didn't I?" she said.

"Maybe. I gotta check on it."

"I'll come with you."

Wild Boy's eyes flicked to Lucien, and the Gentleman shook his head. Clarissa understood. She had been banned from their stupid operation. She wasn't allowed to help him any more. She hoped Wild Boy would insist. The Queen had put him in charge, after all. But he said nothing more as he and Lucien walked towards the patio doors. Him and his new partner. His new pal.

The knife drove deeper into Clarissa's heart.

·33·

" **I**f we can believe her story," Lucien said, "then the killer is here."

Wild Boy tried not to react. He and Lucien had agreed a truce. But if the Gentleman made one more comment like that about Clarissa, they'd become enemies again in exactly the time it took to swing a punch.

He knew he'd upset Clarissa again by leaving with Lucien, but he had no choice. She wasn't allowed to be involved in this case.

No, he reminded himself, he did have a choice. He'd chosen to catch the killer.

"I shall have more men guard Her Majesty," Lucien said. "Moving her would be too dangerous. God alone knows where the killer is hiding in this palace. The rest of the Gentlemen will begin an inspection of the guests. Perhaps those sketches you had drawn will come in handy after all."

Wild Boy nodded vaguely. He opened the patio doors and wind rushed in, blowing his hair and putting out candles.

"Where are you going?" Lucien asked.

"I gotta check on something."

"What?"

"I only saw Clarissa's prints out here before. No others."

"So she is lying," Lucien said. "Hardly a surprise."

"She wasn't lying about nothing," Wild Boy said. "But one bit of her story was just a guess."

"Which part?"

"That the killer came inside the palace."

He stepped outside and closed the door. It was unbelievably cold. Beyond the porch, the snow fell thick and fast. Flocks of polluted flakes swirled among the white. As they settled they speckled the garden with dark spots.

The porch had protected the prints that Clarissa made by the patio doors, but there were no other tracks beyond it. Whatever marks the killer had left in the garden had been scrubbed away by the wind.

No way Wild Boy could track the killer in these conditions. Instead he needed to think like him. The killer had come here for the black diamond. But the stone was with the Queen, in a room that he couldn't possibly reach.

"What would I do if I were him?" Wild Boy said.

I'd make the Queen move.

But the Gentlemen would never move her with the killer nearby.

Unless they had to.

What if something happened, an event so dangerous that the Gentlemen were forced to move her from the palace?

Some sort of attack on the building.

For that, the killer would have to be close. Clarissa didn't see him anywhere outside the palace, which was why she thought he sneaked inside. So if he wasn't inside the palace and he wasn't outside the palace...

Wild Boy looked up. Through the snowfall he saw the statues at the edge of the roof. He remembered how he'd felt that one of those winged figures was watching him.

"He's *on top of* the palace," he said.

Now he was moving again, searching for any way the killer might have reached the roof. He saw ivy leaves in the snow, torn from a creeper that climbed the palace wall. He ran to the wall, felt the creeper's wooden trellis. It was like a ladder, rising to the top of the building. Several leaves were crushed into the trellis, and one of the wooden rungs had snapped under a weight.

The killer's weight.

Get up there now.

Gripping the rungs, he began to climb. Wind

whipped his back, and his feet slipped on snow-wet leaves. He clung on, gritting his teeth. His heart was going like the piston of a steam engine, pumping fear and adrenaline through every vein. The killer was close. He could feel it. *He was close!*

Reaching the top of the ivy, he hauled himself onto the roof. A fierce wind rushed across the surface. He didn't dare stand up for fear of being swept back over the edge. Instead he crawled forward, struggling to make sense of what he was seeing.

He was on the ballroom roof, looking towards the top of the gallery. A dull orange glow rose through the skylight, but there were other lights there too. Flickering lights.

A dozen fires burned in bowls around the skylight, their flames rising and writhing, dancing like dragons. Silhouetted against the lights was the squatting figure of a demon. It was hunched and ragged, with a crow's face and a black scythe beak.

No, not a demon. It was the killer, wearing one of the masks from the museum. Wild Boy reached to his coat pocket for the syringe, but suddenly he couldn't move. He'd been struck by a realization so horrifying that it froze him to the spot.

The gallery.

That was where the guests were gathered.

His legs began to work again, and he sprang up and charged across the rooftop. "No!" he cried. "Don't do it!"

A blast of wind knocked him back, and pain shot between his ears. He covered his head, trying to fight the visions that flashed again through his mind. Those freak show walls, those laughing crows.

He heard glass smash, and knew he was too late.

He scrambled towards the flames as they snapped higher.

The killer was gone, leaving behind fires and shattered glass. Wind rushed through the broken skylight, sweeping black smoke down into the gallery.

Below, all of the guests shook with terror. Their skin had turned white, and black veins streaked across their faces. Some collapsed to the floor, dead or dying. Others curled up cowering or fell back against walls. Paintings crashed to the ground. The night filled with screams.

Wild Boy staggered back, away from the black smoke. His legs buckled and he fell to the roof. "No," he gasped.

He had to stay focused. The Gentlemen guarding the Queen would have heard the cries. Right then they'd be rushing her from her room to her carriage.

And the killer was waiting.

Scrambling up, Wild Boy ran to the other side of the roof. He saw Lucien in the palace forecourt, roaring orders at a groom to prepare the Queen's coach. But where was the killer? He must have got down there somehow.

There!

A rope hung from one of the statues and down the front of the palace. Wild Boy rushed to it, sank to his knees. No time to worry about the height. No time to worry about anything.

He grasped the line and swung over the edge. His bare feet scrabbled at the wall, seeking a grip. He let his hands slip on the rope, descending in short, stuttered bursts, blown by the wind.

Come on. Faster…

He slid past the second-floor windows, then the first. Below, the groom rode the Queen's carriage towards the palace entrance. Wild Boy glimpsed someone else move behind the coach. It was the killer. He had sneaked inside!

Get down there now.

He was still too high, going too slow. He looked down, a desperate plan forming. Directly beneath, the wind had driven a bank of snow against the wall. Wild Boy hoped it was thick enough.

He let go of the rope.

He fell twenty feet, screaming the whole way, and thumped into the white cushion. He rose, shaking snow from the hair on his face.

Four Gentlemen rushed from the palace, escorting the Queen to her coach.

"No!" Wild Boy yelled. "The killer's in there!"

His voice was lost to the wind.

Lucien opened the coach door. The glare of his lantern caught the Queen's tiara. The black diamond sparkled darkly among the pearls. The Queen protested, but this time Lucien wouldn't be dismissed. He ushered her in, slammed the door and barked to the driver. "Go!"

The carriage didn't move.

"For God's sake, man, I ordered you to—"

The words stuck in Lucien's throat. The driver was in no position to go anywhere. He had been struck by the terror.

"Lucien!" Wild Boy called, staggering closer. "The coach. He's in the coach."

Lucien threw open the coach door. "Your Majesty!"

No reply from the darkness inside.

Wild Boy arrived, wheezing and shaking.

Lucien's hand trembled so hard he could barely hold his lantern as he raised the light to the cabin. "My God," he said. "My God…"

The killer had gone. So had the Queen's tiara and the last black diamond.

Queen Victoria, though, was still there.

Shaking and muttering.

Black and white.

Struck by the terror.

• 34 •

Things quickly went from panic to chaos.

All but a dozen of the Gentlemen had been in the picture gallery when the skylight fell and the terror swept upon them. The rest now struggled to deal with the victims whose lives the poison hadn't yet claimed. They pinned down convulsing limbs, injected opiates into black-veined necks, tipped brandy into screaming mouths, anything to calm the frantic bodies.

Nothing worked.

The victims were moved back into the ballroom, where they struggled and thrashed on the dance floor like marionettes controlled by madmen. The chandeliers swayed from the volume of the screams, rocking the walls with light.

The Queen was carried to the royal physicians, who wrapped her in blankets, fed her laudanum solution mixed with treacle and waved lights at her eyes. But the doctors knew that nothing could be done for her, not without the killer's blood. Not without the cure.

Watching from the doorway, Wild Boy wasn't surprised that the Queen had survived. She was strong, like Marcus, and able to cope better with whatever horrors rampaged through her mind. Like Marcus, too, she was quiet. She muttered instead of screamed, a very *royal* way of living through your darkest fears.

Wild Boy's coat was soaked from the snow. He couldn't stop shivering. One of the doctors tossed him a blanket and he pulled it around him, wishing he could sink into it and never come out. Everything had gone wrong. The black diamonds were gone. And now, somehow, the killer would unleash his terror all over London.

A clock began to strike eleven.

Behind Wild Boy, Lucien slumped against the corridor wall. His face looked as if it had slipped down his skull. His jowls sagged lower, and his mouth hung open, whispering the same two words over and over. "My God… My God…"

He swigged whisky from a crystal decanter. The drink spilled down his shirt front but he didn't notice or didn't care. "My God…"

He dropped the decanter and charged at Wild Boy, slamming him against the door. "This is your fault," he seethed, his boozy breath blasting the hair on Wild Boy's face.

This time Wild Boy didn't fight back. Lucien was right: he was to blame. It had been his plan, his responsibility. Everything that had happened, that might happen, was down to him. The pit inside him grew deeper, sucking in air.

Lucien shoved him harder against the door. He was about to yell when the decanter was swung from behind and thumped Lucien in the side. He groaned and collapsed to his knees.

Clarissa stood over him, a wild look in her eyes. She raised the decanter to strike Lucien again, but it fell from her fingers. She staggered forward and grasped her head. Her deep moan echoed along the corridor.

"Clarissa," Wild Boy said. "Whatever you're seeing ain't real. It's the terror, the poison still in you like Dr Carew said. You gotta fight it."

She looked at him with eyes full of sadness. Then she saw Marcus lying by the fire. Clutching the wall, she pulled herself up and barged past Wild Boy into the drawing room. One of the doctors moved to stop her, but the look on Clarissa's face convinced him to step back.

She knelt beside Marcus and took his hand.

The clock stopped chiming.

"Sir!"

A Gentleman rushed along the corridor, waving

a black cloak. "We found this under the marble arch. The killer dropped it when he fled."

Wild Boy burst forward. The pit inside him filled with sudden hope. It wasn't much of a clue, but it was something. "Stop shaking it," he said. "Hold it still."

The man panicked and shook it harder.

"Stop it, you imbecile!" Lucien barked.

He took the garment and laid it on a table. "Miss Everett?" he said.

Clarissa turned, surprised by Lucien's tone. Not anger; an appeal for help.

"At the wax museum," Lucien said, "you thought the killer had been elsewhere."

Clarissa shrugged, reluctant to cooperate. Marcus's hand tightened slightly around her fingers. It was just a spasm, but it was enough to remind her that there were more important things here than her feud with Lucien.

"The killer had a new carriage," she said. "And his sack and that cloak."

"So there could be clues on the cloak to show where he went," Lucien said. "Where his hideout is." He looked to Wild Boy, their fight instantly forgotten. "Can you see anything that might tell us where? Anything at all?"

Wild Boy stood over the cloak, rubbed his tired eyes. He saw a few feathers stuck to the garment, but they were just … feathers. His senses were dulled. The magic had stopped working.

"I can't. I can't see nothing," he said.

Clarissa grabbed his wrist so hard that her nails dug through his coat sleeve. "You have to see," she said. "You *have* to."

She was barely recognizable, her mouth twisted and her eyes like hot coals. Wild Boy realized now why he couldn't spot any clues. It was Clarissa. He couldn't concentrate on anything but her. Whatever was going on in her head, whatever the terror made her see, it was taking control of her.

"Everyone get out," he said. "Just me, Clarissa and Marcus."

One of the doctors began to protest, but Lucien cut him short. "You heard what he said. Everyone out. We shall carry Her Majesty to the library next door. Doesn't make a damned bit of difference where she is right now."

There was a debate over the correct manner in which to handle an incapacitated monarch, until Lucien simply slung her over his shoulder and marched from the room. He stopped in the doorway and looked back. "Find something," he said.

He closed the doors.

For what felt like an eternity, neither Wild Boy nor Clarissa spoke. The only sound was the wind rattling the window and the crackle of the fire in the hearth.

Clarissa stared into the flames. Her wet eyes glistened. "I don't understand what's happening to me," she said. "I'm so angry all the time. It's like there's a tiger in my head. Sometimes it just sits there purring. Then it lashes out and I can't stop it."

Wild Boy stayed back, giving her space. "It's the terror," he said. "The memories are making you angry."

"No, it ain't just that. It was there before; you know it. The terror just made it worse."

"What is it, Clarissa? What did the terror make you see? Your mother?"

"No…"

"I know she turned against you. But she was crazy."

"That ain't what I see."

She looked at him, tears welling in her eyes. "I see you, Wild Boy. I see you leaving me, just like everyone else has. My mum, my dad and now Marcus."

The words hit Wild Boy like a punch to the chest so hard that he stepped back.

"You'd leave me," Clarissa said. "I see it in your eyes. If we don't save Marcus, that's what you plan. You'll think you're helping me, and no matter how many times I say don't, you would eventually. That's what makes me so angry, that you would leave me too. That's why we have to save him. Then everything can go back to how it was."

Back to how it was. Wild Boy didn't know if that was possible, but he realized something just then. He'd been wrong. He would never leave Clarissa, no matter what. They were together through everything. Without that, there was nothing.

Clarissa crouched beside Marcus. She wiped her eyes, sniffed back tears. "He always told us to clear our heads and think. That's what you got to do now, Wild Boy. Think like you ain't never done before. The killer's got all the black diamonds. That means he thinks his demon is strong again, right? Now he's gonna spread that poisonous smoke all over London. So how can he do that?"

"It ain't that simple, Clarissa. It's… It's…"

And then it happened. The magic returned. Wild Boy stared at Clarissa as a sharp thrill ran up the hair on his back. It *was* that simple. So many puzzles and clues had crowded his mind. He'd not been able to see through them to see the important question.

How would the killer do it?

There was only one way.

He rushed to the window, rubbed mist from the glass and looked out to the palace forecourt. Dark flakes swirled among the white storm. Polluted flakes.

How would the killer spread poisonous smoke over London?

"A factory," Wild Boy said. "He'd use a factory chimney."

But that wasn't enough. There were hundreds of factories along the river, and no time to search them all.

"What else, Wild Boy?" Clarissa urged. "Keep thinking."

"Well, whatever the killer burns to make the black smoke, he's gonna need a lot of it to poison all of London. He must've been planning it for a while, been in and out of the factory, taking supplies, setting it up. That means the place is probably shut down, where no one would see him come and go."

"So we look for a shut-down factory?"

"Yeah, but there must be a dozen. There's gotta be something else, something I'm missing. Of course! Feathers!"

"Eh?"

"The bloomin' feathers!"

He rushed to the killer's cloak and examined the white feathers stuck to its coarse black fabric. "Feathers," he repeated.

He threw open the doors, strode down the corridor and burst into the library.

Lucien was stoking the fire as the physicians laid the Queen on a couch. Ignoring them all, Wild Boy marched across the room. His eyes roved around stacks of books that filled the walls.

He pulled one of the books out and dumped it on a table. Dragging a lamp closer, he leafed through the pages. It was a book of birds – alphabetically listed descriptions of species, with sketches of beaks, feathers, claws. Wild Boy turned the pages, searching for a particular entry.

"D … D… Here: ducks."

"Wild Boy?" Lucien said. "Care to share your thoughts?"

Wild Boy whirled around. His eyes were wide and gleaming. "The killer's cloak. The feathers on it are duck feathers. Only they're from two different types of ducks; see, here." He jabbed drawings in the book. "Neither of them live in London."

"So?"

"So what are they doing on the killer's cloak?"

"You mean, where are they from?"

"Exactly."

"A pond?" one of the doctors suggested.

"An abattoir?" Lucien said.

"Yeah," Clarissa agreed. "Somewhere they pluck birds."

"No," Wild Boy said. "The slaughterhouses are all out east, Smithfield way. We're after something near the factories on the river."

"If you know, Wild Boy, just tell us."

Wild Boy didn't know, but he had an idea. "How about a pillow storehouse?" he said. "Duck feathers are used in posh pillows that get loaded into warehouses by the docks. I used to see it from my window, back in the workhouse. Some pillows snag and tear open, spilling out feathers. If we find one of them warehouses near a factory that's shut down … I bet *that* factory is the killer's hideout."

He slammed the book shut so hard that everyone jumped. A wedge of paper fell from Lucien's coat – the artist's ink sketches of Gideon and Dr Carew. Lucien picked them up and dropped them on the fire.

"Well," he said. "How should we go about the search?"

Wild Boy didn't hear. He stared into the fire, and the drawings going up in smoke. Suddenly his world was just those drawings and that fire. He felt as if the flames were inside him; a glow of satisfaction unlike any he'd known. Right then the last piece of the jigsaw fell into place, and the whole picture became clear. The feathers, the drawings, the ash rising up the chimney...

He flicked the book's pages until he found a picture of a crow, and with a finger traced over the bird's smooth, hunched shape. Thanks to those drawings and that fire, he knew everything now. Not just where the killer was, but *who* he was.

And he was gonna get him.

PART III

...the BLACKEST Memories of all THINGS PAST

❧ ·35· ❧

Once, at a fairground in Stepney, Wild Boy heard a priest describe the city of London as a spreading stain of sin.

The man, perched on a soapbox and bellowing through a speaking-trumpet, claimed that London was a godless place, where minds were as polluted as the factory-smogged air and almost everyone was guilty of one vice or another.

The priest's rantings gathered a crowd; mostly drunk and, not being from London, they roared with approval and damned the eyes of everyone who was. Only a few objected, hurling oaths, "God-save-the-Queen"s and rotten vegetables, until the priest slipped from his soapbox and tumbled with a cry to the mud.

Hiding under a caravan, Wild Boy had been thrilled.

London.

He should have hated the place. It was, after all, the city where he'd been abandoned as a baby and then locked up in a workhouse. But he couldn't. Each time he returned, hidden in the back of Finch's caravan, he'd watched the streets through cracks in the walls, wide-eyed with wonder. So much to see. So many people to spy on.

London.

It had come to mean so much to him. And now it was under threat from the same person who had tried to take Marcus from him. The killer planned to act out Lord Dahlquist's curse, spreading his terror across the city. Wild Boy couldn't imagine it. A million screaming souls.

He wouldn't let it happen. He, Clarissa and Lucien were in Lucien's carriage heading to the demon's lair.

The carriage jolted. Wind slammed against the walls as if an army was taking cannon shots at the cabin.

Outside, vagrants huddled under gaslights in a desperate attempt to glean warmth from their glow. Others sheltered in shop doorways. Wind swished the snowflakes so violently, it seemed impossible that any might settle. They *had* settled though, and so thick that the driver had to steer along tracks carved by other vehicles, turning only to dodge a night mail coach that had skidded across the street.

Their pace was maddeningly slow. Turning onto Westminster Bridge they waited for what seemed like an eternity for the toll man to open the gate. Factory chimneys rose from the opposite bank, dark giants belching fumes.

Lucien sat in silence across the cabin. His face, usually saggy and grey, had hardened into a lump of granite. He turned his pistol over in his hands, staring at the weapon as if the solution to all of his problems might be scratched on its barrel.

As if they'd fit.

Wild Boy remembered what Lucien said at Buckingham Palace about giving his whole life to the Gentlemen. And what had it come to? He'd failed in the worst possible way: the Queen had fallen victim to the terror. Surely no one was more determined than Lucien to catch the killer and get the cure.

The carriage jolted again.

Clarissa's jaw clenched so tightly that her teeth ground together. The terror was still in her mind, but she didn't fight it. Rather, she clamped her eyes shut, inviting more nightmares into the darkness. She was using the terror to fuel her rage, to give her courage to face the killer.

Wild Boy touched her arm. "Clarissa…"

She turned to the window. Her quick breaths steamed the glass.

They rode from the bridge into a warren of lanes that twisted among the riverside factories – the glassworks and soapworks, the brewers and candle makers. High walls blocked whatever moonlight might have reached the lanes, giving the area an eerie, nightmarish feel. Factory workers struggled through the snow, hauling barrels and boxes from dray carts. Coal barges dumped dusty cargoes at jetties along the riverbank. Snow fell through smoke and steam. The sulphurous smell of coal gas seeped into the carriage.

"Look," Clarissa said.

The snowflakes against the window turned fatter and whiter, as if they had been scrubbed clean of the pollution from the chimneys.

No, not snowflakes. They were duck feathers.

Outside a factory storehouse, stacks of pillows were piled on a cart, to be transported. Several had been torn open, shedding duck feathers into the wind.

The carriage stopped. The driver banged on the roof.

"We're here," Clarissa said. She flung the door open and jumped out. "Come on."

Wild Boy started to go after her, but Lucien grabbed his arm.

"We are here to get the cure," Lucien said, tucking his pistol into his coat. "For that we need the killer's blood. We must catch him alive, you understand?"

"That's what I'm here for an' all," Wild Boy replied. He tore his arm free and leaped from the carriage.

"And Miss Everett?" Lucien called.

Wild Boy pretended not to hear and kept running. But he knew exactly what Lucien meant. That look on Clarissa's face. This was her revenge. Not just on the person who tried to take Marcus from them, but against everyone who had wronged her. This was her chance to act out her anger. To let the storm break.

The factory rose above Wild Boy, a monstrous block of brick and grime and broken windows. Black smoke drifted from the chimney, even though the factory was halfway through demolition. Wooden scaffolding climbed the bricks where workers had begun to knock down the walls. Barbed wire around the doors reminded Wild Boy of the snarling teeth of Malphas. He ran faster, fear prickling the hair on his neck.

He scrambled through one of the broken windows and into the factory. "Clarissa?" he whispered.

Snowflakes settled on his hair. He looked up, surprised to see the night sky high above, where part of the roof had been demolished. All of the floors had been stripped away too, exposing the factory's criss-crossing skeleton of iron girders. Chains and winches hung from the beams. Baskets of salvaged bricks sat in puddles of melted snow.

Somewhere across the darkness, a light glimmered.

"Over here," Clarissa hissed.

He followed her voice, weaving through dozens of wooden barrels that leaked a thick black substance, slow and sticky like wax. The barrels were clustered near the source of the light: a huge industrial furnace. One of them was raised on an iron bracket, tilted so that its contents slid along a pipe and into a vat above the furnace. Inside the vat, the fluid boiled and bubbled, sending black smoke gushing up the factory chimney.

Clarissa pulled Wild Boy away from the smoke. "What *are* these?"

"It's the poison," Wild Boy said. "That liquid is what the killer burns to make the smoke."

"But where's the killer?"

Wild Boy crouched, pressed a palm against a lantern on the floor. "Still warm," he said. "He was just here."

Clarissa screamed in frustration. She turned to kick one of the barrels, but stopped. There was something in the darkness beyond them. Something large. It was moving.

Wild Boy picked up the lantern and struck the flint. Its circle of light was weak and trembling as he stepped closer to the moving object.

"It's the demon," Clarissa said. "It's Malphas."

It *was* Malphas – a twelve-foot high statue built from factory salvage. The bulk of its body was a soot-blackened furnace. Chains hung around it, like a puppet's strings suspending the monster's limbs. Tarpaulin wings flapped from chains that rose to the girders of the missing first floor. Its clawed hands were shards of glass, its head was rusty machinery. The blade of a scythe swayed in front of its face; a curving beak that seemed as if it might strike at any moment.

Wild Boy reached for the door of the furnace: the demon's chest.

"What are you doing?" Clarissa said. "Don't *touch* it."

"Remember Oberstein's story about Lord Dahlquist? He had a statue of Malphas in his cave in that village in India."

"So?"

"That was where he kept the Black Terror."

He opened the furnace door.

Inside sat the four diamonds. Wild Boy didn't know what he had expected. Something dazzling, perhaps, an incredible treasure. But not this. All he saw were four stones sat on a wad of dirty rags. These jewels had caused so much misery, from that village in India to here in London. And yet suddenly they seemed so plain and pathetic.

He reached for them, when a groan echoed around the factory.

"It's the killer," Clarissa said.

Wild Boy raised the lantern, scanning the gloom. Nothing moved other than a rat scurrying between the barrels. Maybe the sound was the wind, or the factory's metal beams moaning in the cold. Or perhaps Clarissa was right; it was the killer. They had to search the factory, but not yet. First they had an even more important task.

"We gotta stop that poison getting over the city," he said.

"No!" Clarissa kicked another of the barrels. "We have to get the killer."

"Miss Everett."

Lucien strode closer, wheezing from the effort of catching up. "You are not thinking," he said. "The killer is trying to poison London. Once he sees that he has failed, he will return. We will be waiting. So let's get on with it."

They worked for several minutes, raising the barrel and disconnecting the pipe, careful to keep away from the smoke. Gradually the black fumes from the vat reduced to wisps. Then, just as the smoke disappeared altogether, they heard another groan. This time it was louder, all around them at once. It wasn't the wind or the beams.

"Someone else is here," Lucien said. He took his pistol from his coat. "Split up."

They each took a different path, weaving between the barrels. Wild Boy's feet slid through the sticky black liquid seeping from one of the caskets. He listened for any sound, but all he could hear was his own breathing growing deeper and faster with fear. He slid a hand into his pocket and flicked the cork from the syringe. His arm muscles were as tense as tightropes, ready to strike.

Then his feet crunched on something hard and he stepped back. It was stone. Green stone.

"Jade," he said.

Another groan, right in front of him. Wild Boy staggered back and slipped onto his backside. "Spencer!" he gasped.

Oberstein's bodyguard lay between the barrels. His chest rose and fell with deep moaning breaths as he woke from some sort of stupor. His jade mask had shattered and was scattered across the ground. A new disguise hid his face.

A crow's mask.

The killer's mask.

"Over here!" Clarissa called. "I got him."

"And here!" Lucien called.

Wild Boy slid back and scrambled up. Barging through the barrels, he rushed to Clarissa, then to Lucien. They had found the other suspects – Gideon and Dr Carew. Both men lay on the factory floor, unconscious. Both wore the same black mask as Spencer.

"So?" Clarissa said. "Which of them's the killer?"

Wild Boy watched the three men, hoping he'd got the answer right. He'd been so certain back at the palace, but suddenly he'd begun to question his own deductions. He had to check, had to be sure. And there was only one way to do that.

"Let's wake 'em up and find out," he said.

·36·

"I don't know what happened."

Gideon reached for someone to help him up, but the help didn't come. Wild Boy moved back a step, making it clear that he was not here to rescue anyone.

If Gideon noticed the snub, he didn't react. His bleary eyes rolled as he pulled off his crow mask. "We were in the wax works museum," he said. "Someone hit me."

"I think I need to visit the hospital," Dr Carew groaned.

Dr Carew seemed the worst affected by the killer's attack. His shattered spectacles kept slipping from his face as blood slid from the top of his head. He tried to stand, but an icicle fell from one of the girders and smashed beside his feet. He staggered back as if the sound was shotgun fire, and collapsed again to the floor.

Only Spencer remained silent, glaring at Wild Boy through his crow mask. Behind him, the statue of Malphas writhed and jangled as the wind blowing through the factory windows swayed its chains. Its metal eyes glared down at the suspects, and its glass-shard claws flexed in anticipation of violence.

One of these men had built that statue. That same person had struck the others in the wax works museum and brought them here. Then he'd struck himself when he heard Clarissa break in. He didn't expect anyone to know which of them was the killer.

He had underestimated Wild Boy.

Wild Boy watched the killer, searching for fresh clues to confirm his deductions. But the man gave nothing away.

"Are you certain that one of these men is involved?" Lucien said.

"They're all involved," Wild Boy replied. "But only one is the killer."

"Now is the time to explain."

"This is all about what happened in that village in India sixteen years back," Wild Boy said. "You remember that, don't you, Gideon?"

Gideon lit his pipe. He sucked on the end as if it contained all of the air left in the world, and breathed out a plume of smoke. "I told you, I got nothing to do with that place."

"No," Wild Boy said, "you *want* nothing to do with it. Back at the wax museum you said that village was in *south-east* India, remember?"

"So? I heard it off Oberstein."

"No, she said it was in *south-west* India. She got it wrong, and you were right. You knew where that village was. Because you've been there."

Gideon sneered. He was trying to act cool, but his hand shook so hard his pipe fell to the floor.

Wild Boy kept talking, refusing him a chance to respond. "That passage you circled in the Bible about sin and forgiving. How quickly you loaded that pistol at Oberstein's shop. That tattoo on your arm. You were in the army, weren't you, Gideon? And remember when Oberstein mentioned the smell in Dahlquist's cave? You said it was the hearts. That was no guess. You knew because you were there. You were one of the soldiers sent to fight Lord Dahlquist."

"You?" Clarissa said. "That means you helped burn them villagers' bodies."

"You made it like they never existed," Wild Boy said. "That's why you're so ashamed, reading about forgiving."

Dr Carew lunged at Gideon, grasped his arm. "Is this true? Dammit man, is this true?"

"Get your hands off me!"

Gideon shoved him back, causing the doctor to stumble into Spencer. He stood for a moment, wheezing. Then he untied his neckcloth and pulled it away. In the lamplight, a scar gleamed on his neck, a shiny ring around his throat that the cloth usually kept hidden. The scar of a man who had tried to hang himself.

Gideon wiped his eyes with the scarf. His face relaxed, all of its usual tension easing away. "Marcus knew what happened in that village. He knew what I'd done and how much it had messed me up. He came to see me, gave me a new life, a second chance. You know that, Mr Grant."

Lucien's grip tightened on the pistol. "Marcus was worried for all of those men. It was a lot to ask of a soldier. But he never told me you were one of them. I did not know."

"I didn't want anyone to know," Gideon said, his voice cracked and weak. "I wanted to forget it. But I never could. I knew it would find me again some day."

"This sounds like a motive for murder," Lucien said. "You are ruined by your past. You sought justice for those villagers, and revenge against those who profited from your misery. Is that right, Wild Boy?"

Justice for the villagers. That was that a good motive.

Wild Boy turned to Spencer. "What about you, masked man?"

Spencer continued to glare at Wild Boy from behind his mask. Muscles strained at his sleeves; the veins in his neck stood taut.

"One thing confused me about Oberstein's story," Wild Boy said. "How did she know so much about Dahlquist and the Black Terror?"

"You're right," Clarissa agreed. "She said that the soldiers hid the evidence, but she knew every little detail. Sounded like she got the story from someone who was there. Someone in the middle of all that horror."

Wild Boy knew they were getting to Spencer. He could hear it in his silence, see it in the heaving of his chest.

"How did you get them burns on your face?" he asked.

"Burns?" Clarissa said. "Wild Boy, Oberstein said Lord Dahlquist's body was burned, remember? But it disappeared. Spencer *is* Dahlquist!"

Wild Boy had considered that, but it didn't make sense. Why would Oberstein befriend that madman? She spoke of Dahlquist with revulsion, not respect. She saved the respect for someone else.

"That ain't who Spencer is," he said. "Oberstein told us that one villager, the man who found the Black Terror, was tortured by Dahlquist. That man got help, saved the villagers. But she never said what happened to him afterwards."

He stepped closer to the bodyguard, holding his glare. "Did she, Sameer?"

Spencer's chest heaved so heavily that the seams down the side of his coat burst. But when he finally moved, his action was soft and slow. He reached up and took off his mask. His face, from chin to hairline, was ridged with welts and burns. Some were still raw, oozing pus that glistened in the lamplight.

"It is true," he said. "I am Sameer. Oberstein found me. She gave me a new life. She tried to help me forget the past. But how can you forget something like that?"

"You can't," Gideon said. "You can't forget it."

"So that is the solution," Lucien said. "The killer is Spencer. He is Sameer, and he has killed all of the people involved with the Black Terror to seek justice for the villagers."

"No," Wild Boy said. "Not for the villagers. This ain't about them."

Clarissa kicked one of the barrels. "Well, who *is* the killer, Wild Boy? What about Dr Carew? He knows about poisons and he was in India. Maybe he was there in that village? He wants justice for them villagers an' all."

Dr Carew nudged his glasses up his nose. He looked around the group through cracked, blood-smeared lenses.

"No," Wild Boy said. "That ain't right neither."

"Dammit, Wild Boy," Lucien said. "Do you know who is behind this or not?"

Wild Boy was certain now. The puzzle hadn't been about who did it, but *how*. How did the killer poison Prendergast, Marcus and Lady Bentick, and then Oberstein in her own showroom?

"I only realized at Buckingham Palace," he said. "When Lucien threw those drawings on the fire."

"The artist's sketches? What have they got to do with anything?"

Nothing. And everything. "They were *ink* drawings."

"So?"

"Prendergast opened the Queen's parcel and threw the wrapping on the fire. Moments later he was screaming. That wrapping only had one thing on it – an address written in black ink.

"And then there's that other question: Why did the killer save Clarissa at Lady Bentick's house?" He looked at Clarissa. "Why did he slip you that note? I didn't know. I couldn't even study it."

"Cos I threw it on the fire, like it said."

"Exactly. You threw it on the fire, and a minute later Marcus and Lady Bentick got the terror. And in Oberstein's shop, the guard took that card from me, the card with Malphas written on it by the killer. The guard threw it on the fire, and then Oberstein got the terror too. That *card* had the poison on, just like the wrapping on the parcel and the note the killer gave you at Lady Bentick's house."

"It was the ink!" Clarissa said.

"The ink," Wild Boy said. "That was what burned. That was the poison that made the black smoke. That's what's in all these barrels."

He stepped closer to the suspects. He felt his heart racing, the pulse in his neck. "After I realized that, only one question mattered. Who had ink? Who, this whole time, carried a pot of it everywhere he went, saying he was writing notes?"

Dr Carew stepped back. Lamplight gleamed off his broken spectacles.

Wild Boy followed him, hoping he didn't look as scared as he felt. "Only, you was really covering them pages in poison, weren't you, doc? You threw them on Oberstein's furnace, causing that smoke to come after us in the tunnel."

Dr Carew moved away through the hanging chains.

"You were in India when all that evil happened," Wild Boy said. "Only, that was sixteen years ago. You're a young man, doc, maybe thirty? So you'd only have been fourteen back then. Oberstein said Lord Dahlquist was a family man. Had a wife. Ain't that so, doc? He had a wife and *son*."

Dr Carew backed up against the statue of Malphas. The demon's tarpaulin wings stretched and snapped. Its claws swung on their chains.

"You truly are a special mind," Dr Carew said. "You and Clarissa have solved everything."

"Except for *why*." Lucien's grip tightened around his pistol. "Why did you do it, Carew?"

"Why…" Dr Carew whispered.

He looked up at the demon statue. His face was

pale and twisted, as if being pulled from different directions. "Because I am a Dahlquist," he said. "I am my father's son."

"Your father was a killer," Gideon said.

"*You think I do not know that?*" he yelled, his voice suddenly so loud it shook the chains. "I saw! I saw, just like you. I saw everything my father did in that cave. He made me watch. He forced me to watch! I lived with that memory, suffered from it like a disease. He tarnished my name. My mother, my dear beloved mother who never harmed a soul, took her own life from shame. But I would not!"

Spencer moved closer, heavy steps shaking the barrels. He breathed so hard that his words came out in broken gasps. "If you hated your father," he said, "then why did you not become someone better?"

Dr Carew stared at Spencer's face: the glistening, unhealed evidence of his father's evil. "I tried," he said. "God knows I tried. I trained as a doctor. I wanted to help people, to make up for his cruelty. But I could never escape him. He was always there, haunting me. I wanted to know why he did those evil things. I had to understand. So I concocted a poison that would bring him back to me. A way to speak to him."

"The terror," Clarissa said.

"Yes, my terror. I controlled the dose so it would not consume me. Just enough to see my father and talk to him. But I could not stop it. He wouldn't go away."

Tears streaked down Dr Carew's cheeks, cleaning lines through blood and sweat. "I was always so scared of him. I could never fight back."

"He still talks to you, doesn't he?" Wild Boy said. "In the maze, that didn't sound like you. It was him, talking through you."

"Yes, those were his words. I could see him there, standing beside me. He made me collect the stones, to reunite the Black Terror and give his demon power. He made me act out his curse. He is always with me. There is nothing I can do, just as I could do nothing all those years ago in his cave. I am too weak. I am his Servant, as he is the demon's."

The man was crazy, destroyed by his own past and drugs. But there was anguish in his face, too. Something good remained in Dr Carew. A light flickered somewhere inside.

Wild Boy slid a hand in his pocket, felt the syringe. He remembered the royal physicians' advice. Aim for the neck, the big vein called the jugular.

"You can still help us stop this," he said.

The doctor's eyes widened. "Yes, my blood. A cure... It could work."

He turned and looked at something beyond the statue, something visible only to him. "Father?" he said. "What should I do?"

The answer, whatever it was, was short and decisive. When Dr Carew turned back, the light inside him had gone out. There was only darkness.

He reached into the furnace and brought out the four diamonds. The jewels trembled in his hands, catching the lantern light. Their reflection beamed blackness at his twisted, pale face.

When he spoke again his voice was soft and distant, carried away by the wind.

"I am a Dahlquist," he said. "It is in my blood."

He turned and fled.

·37·

"**C**larissa! Clarissa, wait."

Wild Boy thrashed his arms, pushing away the chains that swung from the factory girders. He heard Clarissa cry out in pain, and fear sucked the breath from his lungs.

Brushing back his hair, he looked up into the derelict building. Iron beams criss-crossed the dark, where the factory floors had been removed. He saw Dr Carew move across one, a tightrope walk with a deadly drop. Clarissa limped after him, chasing the killer to the narrow gantry fixed to the wall, then up a spiral staircase to the next floor of beams. It looked as if she'd sprained her ankle. Wild Boy called to her again, but if she heard she wasn't stopping.

Clarissa didn't have the syringe. If she caught the killer she couldn't get his blood for the cure. But something deeper than that scared Wild Boy. He feared what would happen if she *did* catch Dr Carew. Might Clarissa become a killer too?

He ran up the stairway to the gantry fixed to the first-floor wall. To follow Clarissa he had to cross one of the beams to the next staircase. They were all barely a foot wide and gleamed with frost.

He took a few steadying breaths and stepped onto one of the beams. His bare feet trembled as he began to shuffle across. It was a straight drop, thirty feet to the factory floor, where he could see Lucien and Gideon coming after him.

He had to move faster.

He charged along the beam and leaped to the gantry at the end. His jump was too short though, and his leg dug into the platform's metal edge. Pain shot up his thigh and a roar came from his mouth. It felt as if he'd been bitten by a wolf.

Gritting his teeth, he hauled himself onto the gantry. Blood gushed from a cut above his knee so deep he could see glistening grey bone. He rolled over and screamed into the darkness.

Get up. Keep moving.

He pressed a hand against the wound and rose to his knees. Clanging footsteps rang from above as Clarissa chased the killer higher into the factory. Wild Boy had to keep going, but the only way to the next flight of stairs was by crossing another beam. He'd never make it with his leg wound.

He tried to stand, but his injured leg buckled and

he collapsed again. A basket of bricks sat a few yards away, tied to a chain to be winched to the ground. He crawled to it and, leaned his back against its side. The basket scraped towards the edge of the platform. Wild Boy pushed harder, but the effort brought on another flash of terror. It was the poison, still affecting his mind.

He was under attack again. Crows swooped. Claws flashed. Augustus Finch came across one of the beams, gliding like a ghost and grinning hideously. The factory filled with the cruel laughter of the fairground crowds.

Wild Boy curled up beside the bricks. "No…" he said.

And then, "NO!"

His cry was so loud, it drove the visions back into the darkness. He wouldn't let them stop him. He had to fight.

He pressed harder against the bricks. They slipped over the edge of the gantry so suddenly that he almost fell with them. Recovering, he rolled over and grasped the chain rattling up on its winch.

As the chain rose it lifted him from the platform and up into the darkness. He clung on tight as he went through the cat's cradle of beams, bashing against one and then another on the next floor. Blood slid down his wounded leg and dripped from his foot.

He saw Clarissa hobbling up a corkscrew staircase. Dr Carew stumbled along the gantry above.

The doctor turned and hurled the black diamonds at Clarissa, slowing her down.

Below, the basket of bricks crashed against the factory floor. The chain jerked to a stop, almost throwing Wild Boy off. Pain rippled up his arm as he clung on, swinging in the dark. He was ten yards from one of the gantries. He kicked his good leg, swaying the chain. With his free hand, he pulled the syringe from his pocket.

He had one chance. *One chance.*

Dr Carew ran along the gantry.

Wild Boy swung the chain harder, carrying him closer.

He let go. Momentum threw him to the gantry, and he landed on Dr Carew. As the doctor fell back, his head cracked against the wall. His spectacles fell from his face, and blood spurted from a gash on his forehead. His eyes rolled as he slipped in and out of consciousness.

The pain in Wild Boy's leg was excruciating, as if a spear had been driven into his thigh. He wanted to curl up and scream, but he forced himself to keep moving. Gripping the syringe, he scrambled over the doctor. He tore away the man's necktie, but it was too dark to see his veins. He had to try and hope. He aimed the needle and thrust it into Dr Carew's neck.

He pulled the plunger but no blood came out. He cursed, jabbing the syringe again, harder.

The pain roused Dr Carew back to life. A ferocious animal roar came from his mouth, with a spray of spit and blood. He tried to slide away, but Wild Boy clung on tighter, refusing to let go. He had to hold on and wait for Clarissa.

Then the killer did something unexpected.

Launching forward, Dr Carew dived through one of the factory windows.

Two things flashed through Wild Boy's mind. The first was that he and Dr Carew were about to plummet to their death. The second was the hope that Gideon and Lucien would be able to distinguish between their blood and still save Marcus.

But instead of falling, he thumped onto the boards of the scaffolding that crawled over the outside of the factory. His wounded leg struck the wood. He let go of the killer.

Wind lashed the wooden beams, threatening to tear the scaffolding from the wall. The clouds had begun to part. The creaking structure gleamed with ice in the moonlight.

Dr Carew scrambled across the planks, the syringe jutting from his neck. He climbed the next ladder and looked back. "You! You, Wild Boy, should understand. You cannot escape your past."

Wild Boy didn't bother to reply. Even if there was something good left inside Dr Carew, he didn't care anymore. That chance was gone.

He went after him as fast as his injured leg would

allow. The tail of his coat snagged on one of the beams as he scaled the ladder. He tore the coat off, let it fall, pulled himself onto the next level of the scaffold. Reaching out, he grabbed Dr Carew's foot as the killer climbed the next ladder.

The doctor kicked wildly, but this time Wild Boy wasn't letting go. He wrapped his arms around Dr Carew's legs and dragged him down. As they tumbled to the boards, he pulled the plunger on the syringe and yanked it from the doctor's neck. At the same time, Dr Carew threw him back. One of the planks collapsed, and Wild Boy crashed through and slammed to the level below.

The doctor scrambled higher, but Wild Boy let him go. With a shaky hand he raised the syringe. Moonlight caught its glass vial. Its content was the colour of rubies.

The scaffold shuddered as Clarissa climbed from below. There was a fierce look in her eyes, like a tiger on a hunt. It changed to confusion as she saw Wild Boy lying on the planks, coatless and bleeding.

Wild Boy held up the syringe, managed a small smile.

"Easy," he gasped.

She stared at him, stunned. A smile began to form, but then she staggered back against the factory wall, clutching her face as if she'd been shot. It was the terror again.

Wild Boy tried to stand, but the pain in his leg grew worse, as if the spear now pinned him to the boards. He reached out, calling to her. "Clarissa, you gotta fight it."

"I can't…"

Though a tangle of wet hair, she watched Dr Carew scramble higher into the scaffold. He was heading for what was left of the factory roof.

"He's gonna get away," she said.

"Clarissa," Wild Boy said. "We got the cure."

"But we ain't got *him*."

Her eyes burned as fiercely as the factory furnace. Wild Boy had never felt so scared for her, or so desperate to make her stop.

"I'm sorry, Clarissa. I should've told the Queen no. I should've yelled at her like you did. We're partners and I swear I won't leave you, no matter what. You're all I got, you and Marcus. It don't matter what happened to us in the past, we gotta keep what we have now."

She looked down at him. "You're all I got too," she said. "And *he* tried to take that."

"But he didn't, Clarissa. We beat him. If you go after him, you'll kill him and there's no coming back from that. All them people that done bad things to you will have won. Your bad memories won't ever go away."

He gritted his teeth, crawled closer. "I need your help. I can't do it alone."

Tears flowed down her face. She took a small step towards him, and he was certain he saw the slightest smile crease her freckled cheeks. Then she turned and climbed the ladder.

Her dress fluttered in the moonlight as she moved along the planks, higher into the scaffolding.

Wild Boy lay on the swaying boards, calling her name. It was all he could do, so he kept doing it until his throat ran dry. Suddenly the syringe in his hand meant nothing to him. She was gone.

The ice groaned.

The timbers wailed.

Thump!

Clarissa swung down and landed beside him. She smiled and held out Wild Boy's coat. "You dropped this," she said. "You don't look right without it."

The smile was like a rising sun, filling Wild Boy with a glow of something as far from terror as anything he'd ever felt. He wanted to grab her and hug her and scream with delight. Instead he just shrugged.

"Coulda got it myself," he said.

"You can't even walk! How did you even get up here? I bet you cheated."

She wrapped the coat around him and helped him stand, gripping a beam for support. Bricks fell from above, smashing planks along the scaffold. They looked up and saw Dr Carew clamber onto the remains of the factory roof.

Wild Boy felt Clarissa tense, and then relax.

He let her carry him to the window. They clung onto each other as if they were on a ship about to be wrecked by a storm. He wanted to tell her that everything would be fine, although he knew it wouldn't be that easy. Nothing in their lives would ever be easy. This didn't feel like a victory, that was for sure. They would still have to hide, and he had no idea how long they could stay in the palace, even with Marcus's protection. But whatever happened, they would be all right. Because they had each other.

Something dropped from above and they staggered back. It wasn't bricks. It was a crow. The scruffy bird perched in the window, blocking their path. Its eyes gleamed darkly and it jabbed the air with its black dagger-beak. The beak opened and the bird was about to caw when Clarissa lashed out a foot and booted it back into the factory. It disappeared with puff of feathers and a startled squawk.

Clarissa grinned. "Let's go save Marcus," she said.

As she helped Wild Boy inside, something rattled in her dress pocket. It sounded like stones. Four stones.

She looked at him. Her smile grew wider and her eyes glinted in the moonlight. "We don't have to tell him *everything*, do we?" she said.

The End

ABOUT THE AUTHOR

Rob Lloyd Jones never wanted to be a writer when he grew up – he wanted to be Indiana Jones. So he studied Egyptology and archaeology and went on trips to faraway places. But all he found were interesting stories, so he decided to write them down. Following on from *Wild Boy*, *Wild Boy and the Black Terror* is Rob's second novel, although he has written more than thirty other books for children, including non-fiction and adaptations of such classics as *Jekyll and Hyde*.

About writing *Wild Boy and the Black Terror*, he says, "After I finished the first book, I felt bad. I knew the events of that adventure would have left Wild Boy and Clarissa with scars. I wanted them to have a chance to face those fears, to use their skills again to find out just how tough they really are."

Rob lives in Sussex with his wife and two young sons, who have big eyes like Wild Boy but are not as hairy.

Visit Rob at

WWW.ROBLLOYDJONES.COM/WILDBOY